John Thomson was brought up in Suffolk, and joined the Royal Navy at the age of seventeen, serving in the Mediterranean and Far East fleets as a Seaman Gunner. His service on destroyers saw activity in the Suez conflict and the Cod war with Iceland. After leaving the Royal Navy, he worked as a painter and decorator after a brief spell in the Merchant Navy. He still lives in Suffolk, with his partner, and enjoys travel, fishing and clay pigeon shooting. He has previously written articles for a shooting magazine, and this is his first novel.

ABSENT WITHOUT LEAVE

John Thomson

Absent
Without Leave

Vanguard Press

A CIP catalogue record for this title is
available from the British Library

ISBN 1 84386 113 5

*Vanguard Press is an imprint of
Pegasus Elliot MacKenzie Publishers Ltd.*
www.pegasuspublishers.com

First Published in 2004

**Vanguard Press
Sheraton House Castle Park
Cambridge England**

Printed & Bound in Great Britain

Dedication

With Thanks

To my long suffering partner, Rosemary,
without her hard work and dedication,
this book would never have been written.

Chapter 1
Barracks

The taxi came to a halt. With difficulty the two sailors disembarked; unsteady on their feet they fumbled for money to pay the fare. Kit bags, cases and hammocks had been dumped unceremoniously beside the taxi by an unhappy-looking driver. He was glad to be rid of the sailors, one of whom had thrown up out of the open window over the side of his cab. Pints of rough cider had reduced them both to legless grinning idiots and now between them they couldn't muster the taxi fare.

"That's all we have, mate," laughed Lofty.

"Bloody matelots," whined the irate driver, taking the money offered, and moments later he roared off.

Firm friends the two had been since joining the Navy five years ago, and now fresh from Gunnery School (Whale Island) they were due to join a destroyer lying in the Basin, where they were to be part of the Advance Party. Unfit to live on, the destroyer had been in mothballs for several years, so it was to be barracks for them from where each day they would be transported to work on her.

Chatham Barracks was situated close to the River Medway and the naval dockyard. Chatham the town itself held many delights for sailors. Cider houses, and ladies of doubtful virtue, oblivion from the cider, comfort from the ladies, what more could a sailor ask for?

At this moment their most urgent need was to get themselves and their gear past the barracks' Master of Arms and to report to Anson Block. With supreme effort, kit bag on one shoulder, hammock draped over the other, case entrapped under one arm, they somehow managed to stagger through the gates to be met by the Duty Master of Arms.

"Able-seaman Bancock reporting for duty, Petty Officer."

"Able-seaman Gibbons, Petty Officer. We are to report to Anson Block."

Small and squat was the Petty Officer, his uniform was immaculate, the white belt and gaiters sharply contrasting with the dark blue. He stared at them with unblinking eyes. As with most Naval Police, he was full of his own self-importance. Slowly he looked them up and down, he shook his head.

"You two," he roared, "look like a couple of fucking scram-bags, and I have a good mind to put you both on a charge."

"Bollocks," muttered Lofty.

"What was that, Able-seaman Bancock?" snarled the Petty Officer.

"Nothing, Petty Officer."

"Well, take that bloody smile off your face and report to Anson Block. I will be keeping an eye on you two."

Ahead of them the road was lined with trees. On the right stood huge blocks of accommodation which housed large numbers of sailors awaiting draft or doing various courses. To the left was the dreaded parade ground, where many a young sprog had been reduced to tears. It was here that Sunday Divisions were held; a ship's company 'crew' is divided into two parts, port and starboard which in turn is split again, First Port and Second Port, likewise starboard; hence it becomes four watches, and so one becomes duty-watch every fourth weekend. It is on that Sunday that you get mustered on the parade ground for divisions.

Marching around the parade ground being screamed at by some demented Petty Officer or Chief Petty Officer. "Eyes right" past some pompous officer taking the salute as each squad marched past. Squads were then halted, called to attention to be inspected by the Duty Officer, who then moved slowly down the ranks of apprehensive sailors. Each man was then subjected to his critical gaze, and in a much practised upper-class voice, curtly stated, "Dirty hat, get a haircut, shoes need a clean," etc.

The officer was followed by a troop of underlings, one of which would be the Duty Petty Officer, with notebook in hand. The unfortunate sailor had his name, rank and number taken. He would then be ordered to report to the main gate after divisions.

After reporting to the main gate, the outcome would be the indignity of the dreaded kit muster. Hammock spread on the ground with his kit laid out in perfect straight lines with name showing, blankets neatly folded, one fault and the whole procedure would then be re-enacted the next day, which meant kit would be stowed away only to be laid out again until the officer was satisfied. The situation was ironic, for in most cases the officer was totally unable to do anything for himself except drink pink gins, talk with an upper-crust accent and have enough money to pay the wardroom officers' mess bills.

Lofty barged open the doors of the entrance to Anson Block. The two sailors pushed their way through the open doors. Sweating profusely under a mass of kit they made their way to the desk to report.

Seated at a desk sat a writer (Naval Clerk), a young-looking pimply-faced bespectacled individual.

Gibbo handed the writer their orders. He, without a word, took them and checked their names against the list on his desk. Lofty edged round the side of the writer and peered over his shoulder.

"Do you mind?" The writer spoke for the first time.

"Come on mate, gis a quick look at your list, might be some of our mates on it." And as if he wasn't there the writer completely ignored Lofty.

Gone from the tall sailor's face was the good natured grin, which was quickly replaced by a scowl of anger. What right had this jumped-up little writer got to take this attitude?

A loud voice defused the situation.

"What ho, you two bastards. Hi ya Gibbo, hi ya Lofty."

They turned. It was Spike.

'Spike' A B Milligan was an old shipmate whom they hadn't seen since they paid off from the *Flintcastle*. What a run ashore, not that they could remember much about it. Vague recollections of this huge woman, half dragging Spike by his arm towards the bar door, and his cries of protest were to no avail as he was in no fit state to resist. "Never thought we'd see you again, mate," beamed Lofty.

"All right, all right you two."

"Cor she was a big un Spike, did yer get close enough to get yer end away, mate?"

"Can't remember, woke up in the morning with a terrible hangover and there was this mountain of flesh beside me. Every time she moved there was more movement from her than a ship in a force ten gale. I looked at her for a while, legs like tree trunks, tits like barrage balloons; it was frightening, so I was up and legged it. Anyhow, what are you two doing here?"

"Draft to the *Jutland*," Gibbo replied.

Spike grinned from ear to ear. "And me the very same mate, and guess who else is with us? Only six dicks Alby."

Able-seaman Albert Lacey had been one of the first in line when the male appendage was handed out.

"Not again!" Gibbo lifted his hand in mock horror.

"I'll have to check the washrooms now before I go in. He makes me feel inadequate."

"Have you lot quite finished?" The voice belonged to the writer. "Here are your bed numbers, meal tickets and rum cards."

"Thank you darling, now give us a kiss." Gibbo puckered his lips and closed his eyes.

Blushing bright red, the writer quickly turned away in acute embarrassment. The laughter of the three sailors rang in his ears as they left to find their bed spaces. Tonight would be an early night for them, lack of funds being the main factor.

Like some demented banshee, the shrill whistle of the bo's'n's pipe wailed out through the Tannoy system of Anson Block.

"Call the hands, call the hands, wakey wakey, rise and shine, the weather is bright, the day is fine."

Shortly, the dormitory was to become a bustle of activity with sailors dressing and making their way to the washrooms. The time was 6:30; breakfast began at 6:45, finishing at 7:45 with hands falling for duty at 8:15.

Now washed and dressed in their number 8s (working gear) which were blue shirts and dark blue cotton trousers, they made their way down the stairs through the main doors and across to the nest block which housed the large mess hall. At the front of this building was the foyer in which the daily rum ration was issued before midday meals.

Wafting into the foyer was the delicious aroma of cooked bacon.

"Hope it tastes as good as it smells," Gibbo said as he handed his meal ticket to the duty ticket-snipper who deftly punched a hole in the breakfast section. One clip and they were in, on routine the navy ran, no ticket no meal.

Breakfast was self-service. Soon their plates were heaped with eggs, bacon, beans and fried bread. A mug of steaming coffee completed it.

Gibbo jumped as a hand was laid on his shoulder.

"Saved you two places on our table, mate."

"Christ, Alby you scared the living shit out of me, I thought that a certain Petty Officer had caught up with me.

Thoughts had flooded back of his brief but torrid affair with this Petty Officer's wife Jane. Too late he had discovered she was married. He had only been saved by a timely draft to the *Flintcastle*; it would only have been a matter of time before the Petty Officer caught up with him, with dire results.

"Serves you right, you randy sod."

Alby and Spike had just about finished breakfast. Spike shovelled the last of his beans into his mouth, reached for his mug of coffee and washed them down.

"Give us a fag, Alby."

Spike took the offered cigarette. Lighting it, he inhaled deeply. He blew a stream of smoke into the air, and he watched the smoke for a moment.

"*Jutland*, she's battle class, ain't she?"

"So I'm told," replied Lofty. "Bet she's in a right old state."

"Bastard thing rolls like a cow."

"Can't roll no worse than the *Flintcastle*."

"Hands to fall in ten minutes."

"Hands to fall in ten minutes."

Spike pushed back his chair and stood up. "Well, we had better make a move, then." The three other sailors followed and made their way to the foyer through the open doors and on to the road.

"Out pipes. Hands to fall in. *Jutland's* working party to muster outside Anson Block."

"Petty Officer Wilson to muster outside Anson Block." The Tannoy clicked off.

"No surely not, can't be." A look of anguish spread over Lofty's face.

Petty Officer Wilson was a Gunnery Instructor at Whale Island. He was a stickler for discipline, and everything was done by the book. "Right you lot, fall in, jump to it."

Lofty's worst fears were realised. It was him.

Petty Officer Wilson was tall and heavily built. He had joined the navy as a boy straight from an orphanage. Now in his mid-forties, he had spent nearly thirty years in service.

During the Second World War he had been gun's crew on a destroyer. The gun had received a direct hit with most of the gun's crew killed and himself badly wounded; he had continued to load and engage the enemy single handed, for this he was awarded the Military Medal.

"Form two ranks! Come on, move your horrible bodies."

Petty Officer Wilson surveyed the now formed two ranks of sailors.

"You lot are working on the *Jutland*, and I am Petty Officer Wilson, who has the dubious honour of being in charge of you revolting lot. Now listen for your names to be called. When your name is called, shout out loud and clear, then board the bus."

Petty Officer Wilson then proceeded to go through the names on his list.

On reaching Lofty's and Gibbo's he paused and looked up.

"Able-seaman Gibbons and Able-seaman Bancock. Fall out to one side I will be with you in a minute."

On completing the roll call he strode over.

Now look lads, we are no longer at Gunnery School, and I, I am not your instructor." He gestured towards the bus. "Most of them are bloody national servicemen who can't tell right from left."

With a jolt the bus moved forward.

On reaching the Wrens Quarters they turned left; ahead of them the huge sprawling naval dockyard. A naval policeman suddenly appeared as they neared the dock gates. Recognising the driver, he waved the bus on.

The bus gathered speed as they moved along the main dock road past massive cranes that reached majestically skyward. Untidy heaps of tangled metal and machinery littered both sides of the road. Large machine shops, bright blue flashes from the welders.

Slowing, the bus turned off the main road towards the River Medway. In view came the superstructures of destroyers, frigates and sweepers. Now alongside the jetty the bus bumped along the uneven road and came to a shuddering halt.

Tied up alongside the jetty was a destroyer. The destroyer instantly gave you a picture of grace and power, her high bows, the sleek lines running down to her low stern, two twin 4.7 turrets forward, a single 40mm bofor next to the bridge, amidships a single 4.7, and her after-decks housed four twin 40mm bofors, in her waist five torpedo tubes.

After being laid up for several years her sides were

streaked with rust as was the superstructure. No flags flew from her mast-head. Her decks were festooned with air hoses and electronic cables. An army of dockyard workers swarmed over her like ants.

At the top of the gangway an officer was watching as the sailors alighted from the bus.

"Working party fall in."

Petty Officer Wilson called the working party to attention, who turned to face the officer who by this time had descended down the gangway.

"Working party ready for duty, Sir."

"Very good, Petty Officer; I would like you to deploy half the working party below decks, remainder upper deck, ratings with a trade to work with dock personal."

"Aye aye, Sir, one problem, Sir, most of the ratings are national servicemen straight from basic training."

"Dammit, still carry on Petty Officer, and do the best you can. Incidentally, my name is Jenks-Powell and I will be the First Lieutenant on board." (Second in Command)

Petty Officer Wilson smartly saluted the First Lieutenant and turned to face the working party.

"Now then you lot sort yourselves out. Gunnery rating, T.A.S. (Torpedo Anti Submarine) Bunting tossers, (Signalmen) in respective groups, national servicemen over there."

Twenty six the working party numbered. Spike stood on his own, the only T.A.S. rating. Two bunting tossers and five gunnery ratings, left were eighteen sprogs.

"Able-seaman Milligan, take three of the national servicemen and start work on the torpedo tubes. You two bunting tossers, you will find the dockyard workers in the signal room. See if you can be of any help to them. Gunnery ratings can start stripping down the breeches of the 4.7's, the rest of you follow me."

Quickly the Petty Officer made his way up the gangway; and he walked along the starboard side of the destroyer stopping at a locker.

"Right you lot, inside this locker are brooms, buckets and scrubbing brushes, grab them; I am about to turn you into housewives."

"Shiner is the name and this 'ere is me mate Jeff."

"Pleased to meet yer both." Lofty grinned, "This is Gibbo, Alby and I'm Lofty."

Introductions over, Able-seaman Wright and Able-seaman Pringle joined the three friends as they gingerly picked their way forward towards 'A' turret. The decks were littered with rubbish left by the dockyard workers. Shiner tripped and stumbled as his foot became ensnared with one of the many cables that criss-crossed the upper deck.

"Lazy bastards these dockyard workers. All they ever do is make a mess and drink tea."

Reaching 'A' turret, Alby unclipped the turret door. Tobacco smoke flooded out in a blue haze. Inside half a dozen dockyard workers sat around smoking, drinking tea and reading papers.

Shiner stuck his head in the doorway. "See what I mean. It's like a fucking Chinese knocking shop in there."

"What you want?"

The voice belonged to a sullen-looking, short, overweight man in a pair of overalls two sizes too big for him.

"Sorry mate, orders to strip down the breeches."

Shiner again stuck his head in the doorway. "Don't be so bloody polite to them, Alby. Out you lot, we've work to do."

Meekly, to their utter surprise, the inhabitants of the turret, filed out muttering and carrying their tea-making

20

paraphernalia with them. As the last one departed, Shiner shouted after them. "And don't you fuckers move into 'B' turret either."

Inside the turret, the deck (floor) was covered in cigarette ends. The trays that swung over to load shells and cordite charges were full of old newspapers and milk bottles; the turret reeked of tobacco smoke and stale body odour.

"Bloody mess, I'm off to get a broom to clear up a bit."

"Good idea, Lofty, we'll make a start."

"How's it going, lads?" Petty Officer Wilson's cheerful voice interrupted them.

"Fine," Lofty replied. "We've one breech stripped."

"How's it look?"

"Now the grease is off, it shines like a new pin."

"Good. Does the name Jenks-Powell ring a bell with any of you?"

All morning the name had been on the Petty Officer's mind. Try as he might, he just couldn't place it.

Jeff broke the silence. "Heard that name before. Something to do with the *Apollo*, I think."

"That's it, that's it." The Petty Officer cried jubilantly. "Just couldn't place it, been driving me crazy all morning. That bastard near caused a mutiny on the *Apollo*. By all accounts they shipped him off. He treated the hands like dirt, all in all, a right pig; they say he was weaned on the navy news and standing orders."

Shiner pulled a face; he could foresee an encounter with the First Lieutenant in the very near future due to his volatile disposition.

"Petty Officer, what is this rumour about us going to the Middle East?"

"You lot know as much as I do," replied the Petty

Officer. "What I have heard," he continued. "Is that we are to be commissioned and join the *Trafalgar*, *Dunkirk* and *Agincourt*."

"Me and Gibbo just got back from there," groaned Lofty.

"Anyhow we're just working party."

"No, our orders said advance party," Gibbo corrected him.

Jeff so far had taken little part in the conversation.

"It's that bloody Nasser," he said. "Getting all het up over the Suez Canal, reckons to take over. He can have it. Egypt's a rotten hole, all camel shit and flies."

Chapter 2
Sea Trials

Almost six weeks had passed since work had started on *Jutland*.

Work had progressed at an amazing rate. Gone were the rust streaked sides and superstructure, her fresh paint gleamed. Her gun turrets mowed smoothly from port to starboard, while her 40mm mountings chased make-believe targets in the sky.

From her mast-head the white ensign fluttered proudly. Living accommodation was now nearly up to standard and the working party now lived on board.

A steady influx of crew had arrived; soon they would be up to full strength.

As of yet, they had no skipper on board. How strange to be going to sea without a Captain. It just increased the speculation and rumour of the urgent need to get *Jutland* ready for sea.

"Let go forward.

"Let go aft."

Orders came through clear and precise from the ship's Tannoy system.

On the bridge, the First Lieutenant watched as the berthing wires were released from the jetty bollards, he bent over the wheel-house voice pipe.

"Wheel-house, this is bridge, port engine slow ahead, starboard engine slow astern."

Jutland shuddered as her screws turned. Her bows slowly turned towards the river.

"Both ahead slow, starboard twenty."

The destroyer moved towards the centre of the river and the deep water channel. Her bows gently lifted in slight swell. Ahead of them, port and starboard buoys winked their red and green lights marking the deep water channel. Now clear of the breakwater at the mouth of the river her bows lifted but this time dipped into white capped waves, stinging salt spray swept the foc'sle as they stowed berthing wires and ropes for sea.

"Sea-duty men to close up.

"Hand to breakfast."

"Some bloody hope," moaned Spike as he wiped the salt water from his eyes with a grubby handkerchief. "Where the hell are Lofty and Gibbo?"

"Cooks of mess," Alby replied.

"Should have bloody well guessed, crafty bastards," moaned Spike. "Them two drinking tea in the mess and us mothering this friggin' lot."

A sorry lot the national servicemen did indeed look, wet, cold and bewildered.

Alby, Spike and Shiner had sworn at, pushed and bullied them. Somehow, they managed to secure the anchor cables and stow wire ropes on their appropriate reels; it would take time but learn they would.

Alby was the first to descend the ladder into the mess-deck. "Thanks, you two. It's not bloody funny leaving us with that lot, they haven't got a clue."

"Tea, mate?"

Lofty pushed a steaming mug of tea across the table. Gibbo had fetched breakfast from the galley, large tin trays of scrambled eggs, bacon and fried bread. Breakfast now well under way, the talk once again turned to the Middle East, what role would they play, if any. Rumour after rumour had swept the ship for days.

"Hey, Peanuts!" Shiner growled at the little radio operator who was billeted with the seaman until a full ship's company was on board. Then with the other radio operators and signal-men, they would have their own mess.

"What's the latest news?"

"Don't know, mate, we don't get any signals."

"You lying little bastard," snarled Shiner.

"Honest, Shiner," protested Peanuts. "The First Lieutenant picks up the signals from the main signal office ashore."

Further talk was cut short as the ship's Tannoy clicked on.

"Hands to fall in on the quarterdeck."

Pulling on oilskins, the sailors made their way to the upper-deck. By now, the destroyer had increased speed to twenty knots. Dark clouds moved rapidly across the sky chased by a strong North West wind. The seas were rising and *Jutland* began to pitch and roll heavily. Reaching the quarterdeck they found Petty Officer Wilson already there, as was the First Lieutenant.

"Move, you lot, get yourselves fell in, hands attention." He turned to face the First Lieutenant.

"Hands fell in, Sir."

"Thank you, Petty Officer, stand them at ease."

"Aye, aye, Sir. Hands at ease."

"Can everyone hear me? I have called you together to dispel any rumours. Before we sailed, I was called to the Admiralty. We are to be part of the 7th Destroyer Squadron; we are to join *Trafalgar*, *Dunkirk* and *Agincourt*. We have one week to complete sea trials, gunnery and weapon training. We return to harbour at 17:00 hours today. Tomorrow afternoon the rest of the ship's company will be joining us. The following day we take on stores and provisions, on completion, we sail and anchor in the Sound to take on munitions. "Captain R. Warrington has been appointed to *Jutland* and he will be on board tomorrow. Now are there any questions?"

"Sir, is there any truth about us going to the Middle East?"

"As far as I know, Milligan, no!

Lacey, your question?"

"Sir, I was drafted as advance party; I thought that meant till trials were completed."

"I should think, Able-Seaman Lacey, you will be with us a while yet, probably eighteen months," the First Lieutenant smiled broadly.

Alby failed to see the funny side of it.

"Any more questions? No. Carry on Petty Officer."

"Hands attention." The Petty Officer saluted the First Lieutenant who returned his salute. Grinning, he quickly made his way forward.

"Don't believe a word of it, mate." Jeff looked at Shiner.

"Yeah, Jeff's right," Shiner said. "A mate of ours on the *Ocean*, she was due to start her home cruise, one run ashore at Weymouth then back to Malta."

In a group, the national servicemen stood talking, excited at the prospect of service abroad; to them the Mediterranean seemed like some far-off exotic place. To the old hands it was one of the worst drafts. Now the Far East, that was a different story. Great drunken runs ashore, Tiger beer, all nights in with those sexy Orient women, a far cry from the Mediterranean.

By now the seas had become much rougher. The destroyer was shipping water amidships, waves washed inboard along her port side, the bows lifted high before plunging down into the trough of the next wave. Her screws raced as her stern cleared the water, and she shuddered as her bows ploughed through the waves.

Petty Officer Wilson shouted above the wind, "Right lads, back to the mess, stand easy (Tea Break).

Able-Seamen Lacey and Wright, look after O'Brady, the rest of you national servicemen make your way forward. Not by the weather-decks you bloody idiots, you will be swept over the side, go via the gun-decks."

With that, the Petty Officer climbed the vertical ladder onto the gun-decks, and was gone.

Ordinary-seaman O'Brady lay draped over the top guard rail, his face ashen; he had thrown-up into the wind, the remains of his breakfast festooned over his face and shirt.

Shiner looked at the young seaman and felt for him, well he could remember his first time at sea; God, he wished he could have died, but the tough sailor would show no sympathy to O'Brady.

"Alby, if Nasser could see him now, he would take over. Come on, O'Brady on yer feet, get forward and get yer head down." (Sleep)

The young sailor looked up and, without a word, unsteady on his feet tottered to the ladder. With difficulty he began to climb. Shiner and Alby followed behind keeping a respectable distance. O'Brady had somehow managed to negotiate the steep ladder. Making his way along the catwalk he began to retch, again he was sick, and he dropped to his knees retching violently, stomach empty he continued to retch.

"Come on, mate." Alby spoke softly, concern showed on his face. "Let's get you to the mess. Have something to drink and get some dry bread down yer. It won't make you feel any better but you'll have something to bring up."

Upon reaching the mess-deck, several of the national

servicemen looked desperately unwell; any thoughts of service in the Mediterranean had long gone.

"Up spirits, leading hands of mess to draw rum."

Spike was already on his way to draw the mess rum ration before the Tannoy clicked off. Each sailor on reaching the age of twenty was entitled to draw his tot. If one declined to draw, he would then receive the princely sum of 4d a day. The tot was made up of two parts water to one part rum, approximately half a pint. Chief Petty Officers and Petty Officers drew theirs, neat.

The rating that collected the rum was called 'The rum bo's'n.' With the job went the perks of sippers and spillers, each time he handed the measured tot to an eager sailor, he took a small sip (sippers.). Spillers occurred in the transfer of the tot to the glass, any rum that failed to make it into the glass went back into the rum container (spillers.).

Two of the national servicemen were eligible to draw their tot, but of them there was no sign. The smell of the rum, combined with the heavy rolling of the destroyer, required a strong stomach.

"Seaton, Clarke, where are yer, me little mates?"

"Won't hear you, Spike, both of them are in the heads (toilets) with their heads down the pan."

Gibbo gulped the rest of his tot down. He winked at Alby. "Reckon we ought to do them a favour and share theirs out."

"Not you, Spike," snarled Shiner. "You've got more spillers than tots left."

"Rum bo's'n's perks, mate."

"Greedy bastard," Shiner whined.

"Take no notice of him, mate." Jeff knew Shiner only too well; drink and trouble went hand in hand with him, sober, easy going, drunk, dangerous and unpredictable, as the First Lieutenant was to find out to his cost at a later date.

"Cooks to messes, hands to dinner."

Tension evaporated as the sailors prepared for dinner. Soon they would return to harbour. On the morrow they would have a full ship's company. The prospect of weekend leave and a run ashore up in the Smoke (London) *was* most appealing.

Jutland had returned to harbour and was tied up at the jetty. Her crew had turned in early, they were about to be rudely awakened. The bo's'n pipe wailed out through the Tannoy followed by the toneless. "Call the hands. Call the hands. Rise and shine, cooks to the galley."

"Bloody hell; put a pillow over that friggin' Tannoy." Peanuts pulled his blanket over his head.

Spike's head appeared over the side of his hammock.

"Who's duty-cooks of mess?"

"I am," came the reply from Ordinary-seaman Seaton. "Me and Nobby Clarke."

"Well, off you go and wet some tea."

Pulling on his trousers he grabbed the large teapot and headed towards the galley.

Legs appeared out of hammocks as sailors swung down from hammock rails.

Petty Officer Wilson could be heard shouting in the after-seamen's mess-deck. As he made his way forward, his boots clicked on the steel decks as he entered the seamen's mess. He moved between the hammocks. "Come on you lot, up you get, hands off cocks, on socks. I will be back in five minutes; any man left in his wanking pit will be on a charge."

"Gormless bastard," muttered Peanuts as he swung down from his hammock. "I'll be glad when I move to the signal mess."

Gibbo smiled as he looked at the little radio operator, "Never mind, Peanuts, full ship's company today so you won't have to rough it with us much longer."

Hammocks were lashed and stowed, that is rolled into a sausage shape, the whole length tied with half hitches and stowed in the hammock rack.

Comfortably the two mess tables seated the eleven sailors. All this would soon change with the influx of a full crew; the mess numbers would swell to thirty. Living together in such a confined space would require a great deal of tolerance, but, there would be problems. Paramount was the importance of cleanliness. Any man who failed to maintain a high standard of hygiene would be stripped naked, hauled by force to the bathroom where he would be held down and scrubbed with a hard scrubbing brush. Harsh as this treatment might seem, it never failed to have the desired effect.

Washing of kit was carried out in a bucket. Repairs of kit and ironing was down to the individual. The navy in its infinite wisdom even supplied a 'housewife,' that is, a packet of needles, black and white cotton, also a thimble for the use of.

"Hands to fall in on the fo'c's'le. Cooks of mess stand fast."

"Put that cigarette out, Milligan," barked Petty Officer Wilson. Spike nonchalantly flicked his cigarette over the side. He watched as it spiralled down into the water.

Captain Warrington strode along the port-side onto the fo'c's'le; he was closely followed by Lieutenant Commander Jenks-Powell.

Hands called to attention, the Petty Officer turned, faced the captain. "Hands mustered and correct Sir."

"Very well, thank you."

Captain Warrington returned his salute. He was short

and stocky with greying hair. He had been on board a matter of hours. Peanuts had served with him on the *Decoy*.

"Can you all see me? Please shout out if you cannot hear. First I would like to take this opportunity to thank all of you for the excellent work you have done these past weeks, and also to introduce myself to you. As you are aware we will have a full ship's company today. Shortly we will be embarking provisions, later today hands will be paid and leave will be granted at the First Lieutenant's discretion. Any rating that has served with me in the past will know that I am a firm believer that a happy ship is an efficient ship, and that means discipline. There will be no ship's commission ceremony; the object is to get fully operational as soon as possible. Doubtless with the situation in the Middle East, there has been speculation on what our role will be. As soon as I have any information you will be informed, thank you, that is all, carry on Petty Officer."

Captain Warrington turned and caught a glimpse of Peanuts.

"Nice to see you again, Turner."

"Thank you, Sir." Peanuts squirmed in embarrassment at the unwelcome attention.

Smiling broadly, the First Lieutenant departed the fo'c's'le in the wake of the Captain.

Alby watched him go. "Wonder what's amusing that bastard?"

"Who gives a frig?" Shiner was in a good mood. "Pay day today," he grinned.

Three blue naval buses pulled up along the destroyer; her crew had arrived. Spilling off the buses they struggled, pushed and cursed their way up the gangway under a mountain of kit, to be met by the proverbial writer. Armed with the tools of his trade, a list of names and a pen, he allotted each man to his respective mess.

Lofty and Gibbo surveyed the scene below from 'B' gun-deck.

Eventually the jetty cleared save for three hammocks and kit-bags.

One bus remained; the driver shouting and thumping on the rear window of his bus. They watched with mounting amusement as three sailors somehow managed to negotiate the one step down from the bus, in full uniform. One had lost his cap. The other two, with arms draped around each other, staggered towards the gangway, tripping over a hammock, they lay where they fell, laughing uncontrollably.

Lieutenant Commander Jenks-Powell stood at the top of the gangway, a scowl on his face he switched on the Tannoy.

"Duty Petty Officer report to the bridge, at the double. Petty Officer Stannard appeared, adjusting his cap as he hurried towards the First Lieutenant, then came to attention.

"Duty Petty Officer, Sir."

"Petty Officer, I want those ratings charged." He waved his hand with vigour towards the jetty.

"Aye aye Sir, what charge?"

"Out of the dress of day, drunk and disorderly, failing to report for duty; I will not tolerate this drunken behaviour. Put them on my report."

Able-seamen Gordon, Heron and Stringer were soon to have their first encounter with the First Lieutenant. Captain Warrington's hopes of a happy and efficient ship would depend to a greater degree on the First Lieutenant. Although a brilliant seaman whose ship's handling could never be called into question, his ability to understand and administer discipline to the lower ranks left a great deal to be desired. Petty misdemeanours would incur harsh punishment far beyond what was called for.

Endless lorries for the stores had arrived. A human chain from lorry to ships hold, case after case of tinned food passed hand to hand. A dirty-looking oil tanker was discharging fuel oil into the destroyer's tanks.

Naval store-men (Jack Dusties) organised the various stores to the appropriate places. Hour after hour the labour continued. The flood of lorries slowed to a trickle. At long last the final one was being unloaded with great enthusiasm.

Shiner passed the last case of beans on to Lofty.

"Cor, thank fuck for that," he groaned. Sweat ran down his face, his blue shirt stained dark with sweat.

"Never mind, mate, down the N A A F I tonight."

"Why the N A A F I ?" Shiner looked at Alby.

"Haven't you heard? Dance down there tonight, the new intake of jenny wrens will be there."

"Prissy little cows," retorted Shiner. "All talk and no go."

Shiner didn't have a lot of time for the Wrens. He had never forgotten the time he was perimeter sentry round the Wren's block. The half open window, curtains drawn back with the lights on, the large window at ground level afforded an excellent view of the inside of the room.

Two Wrens frolicked about in a near state of undress. Every time he passed by an item of clothing had been removed. He had stopped to light a cigarette. One Wren, by now down to her bra and pants, the other removed her bra with a flourish, and she ran her hands over her ample breasts. Shiner couldn't believe his luck as they beckoned him in, he was through the window like a rat up a drain. Once inside he was confronted by two screaming Wrens.

In a blind panic he tried to scramble out. Halfway out of the window his legs were held in a vice-like grip by a big buxom Petty Officer wren. Shiner had been arrested by grinning naval police, while the big Petty Officer Wren still clung on to his legs. Shiner had been fortunate to get away with fourteen days stoppage of leave and pay.

"Hands to stand easy, no smoking on upper-deck, hands will muster for payment at 14:00 hours."

Utter confusion greeted them as they entered the mess-deck, kit-bags strewn around, and partly unpacked cases as the new arrivals stowed kit into lockers. In the corner near the hammock rack, lay the three drunken sailors still in uniform, fast asleep. And oblivious to the pandemonium around them.

"Martin's the name, lads." The leading hand made his way over as the friends found a place to sit.

"What a friggin' shambles. We didn't have time to get sorted out before the stores came. Nice to see some older hands, most of these are sprogs."

"Call me Pincher, I'm to be the leading hand of the mess."

"Hey you!" Pincher addressed a slightly built ordinary seaman. "Grab that teapot, up to the galley and make some tea."

"But leading hand."

"No buts, off you go," interrupted Spike. "Hard job to get staff," he smiled.

Pincher produced a packet of blue liners and offered them around.

Peanuts poked his head in the doorway. "Have you lot seen the daily orders?"

"What yer on about, are yer gonna tell us? If not, then fuck off to yer own mess." The little radio operator ignored the comments.

"There's no weekend leave, only till 23:00 hours each night, so you girls won't be going to London."

Alby pulled a face. "It's that bastard First Lieutenant, the N A A F I dance finishes at midnight, fat chance of a pull now."

"Peanuts, if you're lying ..."

"Honestly Shiner, go look for yourself; by the way, a signal arrived for the skipper from the Commander in Chief about how they are going to monitor the gunnery trials. I took the message to the old man, the First Lieutenant was with him, and he said to the skipper it was imperative that we put up a good show against *Trafalgar*, *Dunkirk* and *Agincourt*."

Alby looked at Jeff. "So that's his game, the bastard is stopping weekend leave in the hope we don't get hungover and perform better on Monday."

Jeff's mouth twitched into a half smile. "Well, we'll see."

"Peanuts, come round at tot time for gulpers."

'Gulpers' was a sailor's way of saying thank you for a big favour; small favours earned 'sippers.'

"Out pipes, hands to carry on work, gunnery ratings muster on the quarter-deck."

"Come on lads, off you go."

Pincher stubbed out his blue liner and rose from his seat.

"A couple of you ordinary-seaman stand fast and tidy the mess up."

Petty Officer Wilson was deeply engrossed in conversation with a Chief Petty Officer. In small groups the gunnery ratings stood talking. Hardly noticed, the tall slim Lieutenant walked onto the quarter-deck. On seeing him, the chief came to attention and saluted.

"Gunnery ratings mustered, Sir."

"Thank you ,chief," he replied quietly. "My name is Anderson, I am the Gunnery Officer."

"Pleased to meet you, Sir. My name is Brown and this is Petty Officer Wilson."

"Right, gather round. Our programme for Monday: we will be testing the main armament, the target for the 4.7s will be a towed splash target. *Trafalgar* and *Dunkirk* will also take part, *Agincourt* is still in dock and will be joining the squadron at a later date. Also, the close-range weapons will carry out a shoot against a drone. Aimers, needless to say, watch out for the tow aircraft. Dockyard armourers are to fit four 20mm Oerlikons to increase our air defence capability, but I do not visualise them being fitted in time. One more thing; the First Lieutenant is most anxious that we perform well. He conveyed this to me in no uncertain terms, but, as the Gunnery Officer I am far more concerned that we work as a team and everything functions. Any questions?"

"Why ain't we being granted weekend leave?" The question came from a stocky seaman from the after-seamen's mess; his muscular arms were covered in tattoos.

"I am sorry but that is out of my jurisdiction, which is the First Lieutenant's department. Chief, is there anything else?"

"Yes, Sir, Defence and Action Stations will be posted on the notice board."

"Thank you, chief, please carry on."

Disaster was the only way to describe the N A A F I run.

Shiner, drunk, sullen and aggressive, spent the evening taunting a group of soldiers; and he was goaded on by the two jocks, Heron and Gordon, who had served with him on the *HMS Manxman*. Confrontation was only avoided by Alby and Lofty who calmed the situation down. The fact the two sailors had to be back by 2300 hours was the factor that prevented a full scale brawl, and as they left the laughter of the soldiers followed them, then shouts of "Shall we tuck you up in your hammocks sailor boys?" At this point Shiner had to be restrained.

"Pongo bastards, they don't know how close they came to visiting hospital," growled Spike. The soldiers would have been no match for the tough sailors, veterans of many bar-room brawls.

With a clatter, the anchor cable bounced and jumped over the foc'sle as it disappeared down to the cable locker. With a loud bang the anchor slotted into the hawse pipe.

Slowly the destroyer moved away from the ammunition lighters. Now loaded with munitions, her magazines housed the 60lb shells, also the cordite in brass cases needed to propel them.

Countless boxes of 40mm ammunition, four rounds to a clip, four clips to a box; the heavy boxes were being manhandled and distributed to the ready used lockers on the gun-decks. Oerlikon magazines and thousands of 20mm shells for the heavy machine guns, boxes of rifles and Bren guns completed the ordnance.

Dockyard armourers had arrived with the lighters. Four oerlikons had been hoisted inboard. With a methodical skill they progressively assembled the guns; the mountings had been welded to the steel decks.

Shiner watched with interest as the armourer tightened the bolts that held the gun to the swivel. "Yer missed yer boat home, mate?"

"Yeah, big flap on, orders are stay on board till fitted and tested. Still, it's a quiet number. I was in the navy till a couple of years ago, got a job in the dockyard. As an armourer in the navy, it was easy; most of the dockyard workers are sharing one brain cell between them anyhow."

Shiner smiled as he nodded in agreement. "Let the cooks in the galley know you and your mates can eat with us in the forward seamen's mess."

"Will do, mate. See you later."

Chapter 3

Gunnery Trials

On the distant horizon an Aldis lamp blinked out its message. They had made contact with *Trafalgar* and *Dunkirk*.

"Main armament crews to close up. Clear the upperdeck."

Orders came over the Tannoy clear and precise; it was only an exercise but it never failed to send a shiver of anticipation through the gun crews.

Trafalgar took up position, the splash target some 12,000 yards to starboard. The guns would be under director control. The director, high above the bridge would adjust range. Once in director control the guns would automatically traverse and fire from the director. All the turret's crew would be required to do was to load the guns. In the event of a hit on the director, gun captains could switch the two switches over to turret control and turret fire, then each turret was independently controlled from the turret. Inside the turrets the shells and cordite came direct from the magazines by hoist. Heavy 60lb shells were manhandled into the loading tray, over went the loading tray in line with the breech; the shell was then rammed home under power. Seconds later, followed the cordite. This procedure would be duplicated the other side of the gun, fire gong would sound, an ear shattering crack, the gun recoiled viciously, two empty brass cordite cases would be ejected. Breeches open, the gun would return to the loading position.

Trafalgar had started her firing run. Through the gun-layers gun sights Gibbo watched as a puff of smoke drifted away from *Trafalgar*.

"She's fired her first ranging shot," shouted Gibbo. Moments later a towering column of water rose to partly obscure the target.

"Spot on," called the young gun-layer. "She's got the range already; her second shell was slightly long."

Salvo after salvo followed. The target was straddled again and again.

Lofty grinned, "Bet the First Lieutenant is pissed off."

Dunkirk moved into line, but no way could she match the awesome gunnery of *Trafalgar*.

Now it was *Jutland's* turn, turrets swung to starboard.

"Q gun load, Q gun load, Q gun to be ranging gun."

Shiner grunted as he slammed the heavy 60lb shell on the loading tray, in a flash he hit the load button. The tray swung over, the ram came forward the shell was loaded. Able-seaman Stringer (String) had the cordite charge in the tray almost before the tray had returned to the load position, Shiner hit the button again, and, cordite loaded, the breech snapped shut.

"Q gun ready to fire," bellowed Shiner.

Pincher sat in the layers seat watching the target, on hearing Shiner he spoke through his headphones.

"Director, Q gun ready to fire."

Jeff looked down from his position in the director high above the bridge, below him, the Captain and the First Lieutenant stared at the target through binoculars a smile flitted across his face as he turned back to watch his radar plot screen.

"Q gun one round open fire."

Lieutenant Anderson quietly gave the order. The fire

gong blared out in Q gun.

Shiner half-closed his eyes as he winced in anticipation of the ear-shattering crack as he reached towards the hoist for another shell to reload.

His face contorted in anger, the First Lieutenant screamed into the Tannoy.

"Q gun fire, fire."

Back came the reply.

"Q gun misfire, Q gun misfire."

Jeff from the director, watched as the fuming First Lieutenant vented his anger on the Gunnery Officer. Lieutenant Anderson ignored the ranting and ravings coming over the director's communications with the bridge. He spoke quietly and calmly. "A gun load one round."

"Stand by." The fire gong sounded again and the order was greeted by the same response.

"A gun misfire, A gun misfire."

Jeff peered from the director, the First Lieutenant was beside himself with anger. His eyes bulged. A torrent of abuse followed Lieutenant Anderson, who unperturbed, spoke in his quiet manner, "Gun-layers switch turrets to local fire control. Stand by A and Q guns."

A and Q guns fired simultaneously, the twin columns of water erupted a full 100 yards astern of the target. From *Trafalgar* the Aldis winked out its message. A grinning Peanuts scribbled the message on his pad. He saluted Captain Warrington as he handed him the signal. Captain Warrington smiled slightly as he read the signal. He handed it to the First Lieutenant, the signal read.

"Would you like the name of my optician?"

"Any reply Sir?" grinned the signal-man.

"No," snarled the First Lieutenant. "Don't be so impertinent Turner."

In the director, Jeff watched as Q gun fired. "Long Sir," he called out as he plotted the fall of the shot. "Approximately 300 yards."

"Very well, chief, decrease range 400 yards."

"Aye, aye, Sir." Once again Q gun fired. "Short Sir, about 50 yards."

"Very good chief, adjust range."

Lieutenant Anderson spoke into the turret communications. "Stand by to engage target."

Five shells hissed their way towards the target as the fire gong sounded.

"Straddle Sir."

Even as Jeff spoke, the next salvo was on the way as the highly trained gun-crews engaged the target.

The reputation of the English gun-crews went back to Nelson's days, when they completely devastated both the French and Spanish fleets. Their high rate of fire and efficiency was twice that of the French and Spanish gunners.

Salvo after salvo crashed out to straddle the target.

"Cease fire, cease fire. Turrets train fore and aft. Gun-crews to fall out. Close range weapons to close up."

Lieutenant Anderson smiled broadly; he was well pleased, after a disastrous start things had gone well.

"Well done, chief, well done, everyone. Let's hope we perform as well with the anti aircraft shoot."

"Sure we will, Sir. Petty Officer Wilson was saying at gunnery school two of the best gunners were Able seamen Heron and Lacey."

In line ahead the destroyers steamed, as they waited for the planes towing the drone targets.

Alby lowered the twin barrels of the Bofors gun, "Take the muzzle covers off, mate."

Ordinary seaman Seaton unlaced the canvas covers.

Covers off, Alby."

"Right you two stewards, start opening the ammunition boxes, and filling the ready use racks on the guns. Come on, move yourselves, you Jim, Rob up on the loading platforms and stand by to load."

With twenty clips in the ready use racks, the two stewards stood talking.

Alby glared at them.

"Come here you two wankers. Just what the fuck are you doing? Get opening them boxes, I want you to pile the clips of ammo on top of the lockers ready to use. Twenty clips, 80 rounds you stupid bastards. Do you realise that each barrel fires 100 rounds a minute between forty and fifty clips. Once we engage, one of you keep the ready use racks full, the other keep the clips coming."

"Close range weapons load. Stand by to engage."

The two loaders grabbed a clip of shells, clicking and the clips made their way down the guides.

Alby pulled the cocking levers back. A shell dropped into the breeches pushing it forward. The twin 40mm was ready, another clip of shells followed down the guides. Alby glanced up at the ready use racks; he was relieved to see the four clips had been replaced.

Ahead of them *Trafalgar* was first to engage, tracers filled the sky, shells burst all around the drone. *Dunkirk* now added her firepower, Alby watched as the canvas drone came towards them.

Jutland's four twin 40mm Bofors and two single mountings tracked the target as did the four 20mm Oerlikons awaiting the order to fire.

Blizzards of shells swept skywards as the order was given. The incessant banging of the 40mm guns punctuated by the frenzied chatter of the Oerlikons.

Alby grinned as he watched his tracers rip into the

ragged drone.

Cheers came from the gun-crews as the canvas drone spiralled seawards. Part of the tow rope hung from it as sporadic fire chased it.

"Lieutenant Commander Jenks-Powell beamed as he watched the drone splash into the sea.

"Damned good show, Sir."

"Yes, Number One, it was," he agreed, "but I feel I must have a word with you about your intolerance towards Lieutenant Anderson. I have never witnessed such a display from an officer towards a subordinate, in future while on my bridge you will act like an officer and a gentleman, is that fully understood?"

"But Sir ..." the smile had vanished from his face.

"Shut up," snapped Captain Warrington, "you will learn to control yourself, is that fully understood?"

"Yes Sir," the First Lieutenant replied meekly.

"Carry on." The captain dismissed him curtly and turned away.

"Gun-crews to muster on the quarterdeck."

Lieutenant Anderson watched as the gun-crews mustered. He stood there for what seemed an eternity just shaking his head. "What the bloody hell is going on?" he demanded. "I tested the circuits with Leading Seaman Martin; needless to say they were fine. What imbecile changed the circuit indicators round? The indicator said director fire when in fact they were on local."

The Gunnery Officer glanced over the assembled sailors. His gaze stopped on Jeff.

"Able-seaman Pringle, why did you not report the circuit indicator light was not on?"

"Just thought the bulb had gone Sir."

"That is bloody negligence; have you anything else to say, Pringle?"

"No, Sir."

"Right, First Lieutenant's report. You can explain to him. I want you all to understand I am not going to get my balls chewed off so you lot can annoy the First Lieutenant.

"To end on a brighter note, I would like to congratulate the guns-crew on their performance. Thank you that is all."

"She seemed a bit upset." Shiner pulled a face as the Gunnery Officer hurried away.

"Bloody bastard put me on report," moaned Jeff. "The First Lieutenant will crucify me."

"Anyhow, who did change the indicators?"

Jeff looked at Jock, "It was me."

Shiner tapped his head with a finger, "Mate, yer want to use this a bit more." He again tapped his head.

With two strides the big sailor reached the fire hydrant, bent down and picked the hose out of the rack. With slow deliberate steps he walked to the ship's side, holding the heavy hose over the side, 'oops butterfingers,' with a splash the hose disappeared into the sea.

Alby watched in amazement, he shook his head, "Shiner what the fuck did you do that for?"

"Haven't you girls worked it out yet? Jenks-Powell signed for all the upper-deck gear, can you imagine the red tape and bollikings. Dockyard stores ain't going to replace anything without a chit."

"Shiner, me ole mate, you're a genius, one hose down five to go. Come round for a gulpers of me tot."

"With pleasure, mate."

Chapter 4

Passage to Malta

Trials now complete, they had been joined at sea by *Agincourt*. Rumours about where they were heading were still rife, but the general consensus was the Middle East.

At one time Peanuts had confused the issue. He said he had seen charts and maps of Singapore in the chart room on the navigating officer's desk.

President Abdel Nasser, strongly nationalistic, decided to nationalise the Suez Canal, although both Britain and France retained a large share in the company that ran the Suez Canal.

France was in favour of military action. A joint Anglo-French naval supported landing seemed a distinct possibility to protect both countries' interests.

"First Lieutenant's defaulters to fall in after the Captain's address to the ship's company."

The mess-deck fell silent.

"This is the Captain speaking, I would like to take this opportunity to put you all in the picture as to what is going on. We are at this moment proceeding to Malta. I know there has been a great deal of speculation due to the situation in the Middle East. I have orders to rendezvous with the French battleship *Shaun Bart* and two destroyers.

"Jutland, Trafalgar, Dunkirk and *Agincourt* will accompany them to Malta. Ship's company will be called to Action Stations and Defence Stations, and we will be subject to mock air attacks by Sea Hawks from the aircraft

carrier *HMS Eagle*, that is all."

Lofty looked glum, "I knew it. Fuck Nasser, let him have the Canal."

His remark fell on deaf ears as a babble of excitement ran through the mess.

"Gis a fag, Gibbo." Taking the offered cigarette he drew deeply at the spluttering flame deep in thought.

"First Lieutenant's defaulters to fall in."

"Away you go, Jeff."

"Doesn't he look nice in his uniform?"

"Give the First Lieutenant a kiss for me."

Jeff ignored all the comments as he made his way up the ladder towards his encounter with the First Lieutenant.

This encounter of course would be totally uneven, the First Lieutenant's job was to administer fair punishment for minor offences, more serious offences would be dealt with by the Captain.

Punishment the First Lieutenant awarded the ratings was harsh, he seemed to delight in their misfortune, but in Jeff, as in the older sailors they had an inborn toughness and would not appease in the hope of getting a lighter sentence. The favourite punishment was 10A; for each day awarded the sailor lost his rum ration, shore leave and four hours extra work a day.

Loss of rum was not a problem as each man on the mess gave part of his tot to the man under punishment.

For being drunk, the two Jocks and Able-seaman Stringer had all received ten days 10A, by the time they reached Malta their punishment would be completed, the Jocks now harboured a bitter resentment of the First Lieutenant. They had expected three days.

Standing in the port passage-way, Jeff waited to be called into the First Lieutenant's office. The door opened, Petty Officer Wilson, the duty Petty Officer, appeared with a wink at the Able-seaman.

"Able-seaman Pringle quick march off cap."

Quickly the seaman marched to the First Lieutenant's desk. His hand went up to his cap. In one movement he removed his cap and returned cap and hand to his side.

"What is the charge, Petty Officer?"

"Able-seaman Pringle is charged with failing to carry out his duty, namely Sir, not reporting the circuit light between the director and turrets was out."

"Thank you, Petty Officer, and what have you to say Pringle?"

Jeff looked long and hard at the First Lieutenant, his eyes never left his.

"Well, Pringle, speak up man."

"Well, Sir, I was distracted by all the noise on the Bridge."

Colour drained from the First Lieutenant's face, his piggy little eyes narrowed. A smile of utter contempt - appeared on the sailor's face.

"So you think it's funny Pringle? You can reflect on it while doing 21 days 10A."

"Thank you, Sir." The smile broadened.

Passing Gibraltar on their starboard side, the four destroyers entered the Mediterranean Sea, away to port was North Africa. At twenty-five knots the sharp bow cleaved through the calm sea creating a large bow wave. A school of dolphins frolicked and gambolled in the frothing bow wave. Soon they would be making contact with the French Warships.

It was a beautiful day. The sun shone from a cloudless blue sky, sun glinted off the destroyers as they steamed in formation, and this idyllic scene was rudely interrupted by the harsh orders which blared from the Tannoy.

"Hands to Action Stations."

"Aircraft warning red."

Men appeared as if by magic, pouring from doorways and hatchways. Running feet pounded the decks, covers hastily thrown off anti-aircraft weapons, gun-crews reported to director as they closed up.

Alby, manning the M1 twin swore loudly. "Where the fuck did they come from? Seaton, did you switch on communications between us and Radar Plot?"

Ordinary-seaman Seaton looked completely bemused. Alby realised the unhappy looking Seaton hadn't a clue what he was talking about.

"You see that small Tannoy?"

Seaton's eyes followed Alby's pointing finger, he nodded.

"Put the two switches down beside it."

What a start. Alby's 40mm twin had been trained starboard with every other gun pointing astern. The fire gong had sounded with Alby searching for the target blind. Unlike the shoot at the towed drone, the aircraft came in at random, bearings requiring constant update at their approach.

Communications now established, the voice of the radar operator came through the Tannoy.

"Aircraft, aircraft, off the starboard bow closing, close range weapons engage, this includes M1."

"Bollocks," cursed Alby as the mounting rapidly slewed round to meet the mock attack, the dot in his giro-scope rapidly transformed into a Sea Hawk as he locked on. The Sea Hawk came in at sea level, it lifted and rolled just clear of the mast, jet engines screaming it was gone.

For the next half hour, the Sea Hawks carried out mock attacks on the destroyers. The skill of the naval pilots was impressive.

"Gun-crews to stand down, action stations to secure."

Alby eased himself out of the aimer's seat.

"Ordinary-Seaman Seaton, I will leave you in charge. O'Brady, Clarke and you two others, put the gun-covers on secure and switch off."

"Sorry, Alby ..." Seaton began.

Alby waved a hand, "Forget it, mate, you'll know next time."

Leaving them he made his way forward.

"Able-seaman Lacey."

Petty Officer Wilson stood by the doorway leading to the mess-deck. "I would like a word with you."

Alby held his hands up, "Guilty, Petty Officer, my fault."

"Not good enough, that friggin' First Lieutenant chewed out Anderson, who in turn put my arse in a sling, anyhow what happened?"

Alby was reluctant to blame Seaton.

"Speak up," the Petty Officer was losing patience.

"I failed to tell my number-two to switch on communications."

"But you, as Captain of the gun, should have checked."

"I can't do everything," protested Alby, "all the gun-crews are National Servicemen, they don't have a clue."

Petty Officer Wilson was a fair man. He thought for a moment before nodding his head in agreement.

"Yes, perhaps you're right, but what I heard, they will soon be in at the deep end. Don't ask me anymore you will find out soon enough."

"You can tell me, Petty Officer."

"Tell you. Come off it, Lacey, it would be all over the ship like a dose of crabs. Now get back to your National

Servicemen. Your merry men will have gun drill, which I will take, so next time there will be no cock-ups. Carry on."

Alby entered the mess-deck.

"Cup of tea, mate?"

Lofty poured the strong tea into the mug and pushed it across the table towards Alby.

Sugar, milk in, Alby slowly stirred, "What's the latest buzz," he directed the question at Shiner.

"Ain't heard a thing. That Peanuts don't know nothing. If he does, he ain't saying."

"Well ..." Alby began, "Petty Officer Wilson reckons we'll be in at the deep end soon."

"He could well be right," Pincher said.

"Just think, what the hell is that frog battle wagon doing heading for Malta?"

"What about *Eagle*? She has just finished nine months in the Med."

"Got a mate on her." Jeff pulled a face, "Won't be seeing him ashore. Fuck the First Lieutenant, I'll still be under punishment."

Further conversation was interrupted by the Tannoy.

"Hands to carry on working ship. Ordinary-seamen O'Brady, Seaton, Mills and Merton report to M1 gun-deck."

Chapter 5

Malta

Malta: a small Island, 122 square miles in area, taken by Norman Sicily in 1090, and then given to Knights Hospitallers in 1530. It was annexed by the British in 1814, and now a major naval base for the Mediterranean fleet. The large naval dock-yard provided the main source of income for the people of the island.

Jutland waited her turn to enter Silema harbour. *Trafalgar, Dunkirk* and *Agincourt* were already riding at anchor.

"Hands to stations for entering harbour."

"Sea duty men to close up."

"Anchor party muster on the fo'c's'le."

Jutland moved slowly past the breakwater into the harbour.

Incredible was the sight that greeted them, the whole harbour was full of destroyers and frigates both French and British. The huge French battleship had left her escort of destroyers and was heading for Valletta harbour, but most ominous was the vast numbers of tank and troop-landing craft.

Gibbo pushed his hat back, looking at Lofty who was staring in disbelief at the scene before them.

"Bloody hell, mate. I wonder what's at Valletta harbour?"

Valletta was the deep-water harbour where the larger warships anchored.

The Petty Officer's voice boomed out, "Come on you two, cut out the cackle. Able-seaman Bancock, man the telephone."

Lofty unhooked the phone and smartly wound the handle beside the phone clockwise which in turn rang the phone on the bridge.

"Bridge this is the Fo'c's'le, anchor on slip."

"Very well stand by."

Minutes later the order, "Let go anchor."

"Petty Officer from the bridge let go anchor."

Petty Officer Wilson nodded to Pincher who raised the sledge-hammer. With one deft blow he removed the slip shackle which held the anchor cable. The anchor hit the water sending a shower of salt water over the Fo'c's'le. The heavy iron shackles of cable banged and clattered their way up from the cable locker, over the steel deck through the hawse pipe to follow the anchor to the seabed. The destroyer shuddered as the anchor took hold to arrest her movement.

"I will leave you in charge, Leading-seaman Martin. Take up the slack on the cable and secure bottle screws."

"Duty Petty Officer to report amidships."

"Out boat booms."

"That's me," Petty Officer Wilson hurried away.

Again the Tannoy barked out orders.

"Duty-watch to muster."

"Starboard watch will be granted leave from 18:30 till 07:00 hours."

"Cooks to messes, hands to supper."

Lofty and Gibbo leaned on the guard-rails looking towards Silema front. Pop music could be heard blaring out from the many bars. Enterprising Maltese catered well for the sailors, big eats and booze. It was after all the best way to transfer the free spending sailor's money to better use.

In Valletta, the capital, the Straight Street, better known as 'The Gut,' notorious for its bars, loud music, mind-blowing cheap wine, flop houses and loose women.

They began to reminisce, was it nearly five years since their first run ashore down The Gut?

A big grin contorted Lofty's face, "Mate, was we green."

Gibbo laughed, "You remember that, Anna? All night you lashed her up with drinks. Wait for me outside sailor, she purred, we will be closed soon. There was you waiting out the front and she legs it home from the back."

Lofty grinned, "Yeah, she should have been in the bloody Olympics."

"What about them bottles of blue (local brewed beer)? They both burst out laughing; well they could remember pushing their way through the swing doors of the 'Big Ben' trying hard to look like seasoned sailors. Lofty had tossed his money on the bar counter, "Gis us two blues," he ordered.

Taking his money, the old crone had pushed two opened bottles of blue towards them.

Leaning on the bar, the two sailors drank from the bottles.

Smiles from the watching sailors in the bar had erupted into hilarious laughter. The two friends had looked at each other in total bemusement, with each swig the laughter increased into a crescendo, and in acute embarrassment they fled the bar.

"What the fuck was that about?"

Gibbo peered over the top of the swing doors.

"Hey Lofty, no wonder them bastards were laughing."

In disbelief they watched as the grey haired wrinkled old crone with much encouragement from the sailors decapped a bottle. Placing it on a low stool she lifted her skirt and backed over the bottle. Taking careful aim she lowered herself, the grey haired mott engulfed it. She arose like a star to the cheers of the sailors, a huge toothless grin on her face; she placed it beside another already on the bar to await the arrival of two more unfortunate 'sprogs'.

Well they remembered the feeling of nausea; beer would now be drunk from a glass. Now they could laugh about it. As Lofty would say, it was oral sex by proxy.

Cooks of mess struggled to dish up supper.

Sailors draped in towels returned from showers, others changing into uniform eager to get ashore. With visions of exotic adventure ashore, most of the National Servicemen were already in uniform.

"Look at them bloody sprogs," Shiner grinned as he shovelled food into his mouth.

"Like lambs to the slaughter. First time away from mummy. Anyhow me an' the two Jocks are down the Gut later, you lot coming?"

Lofty shook his head at Gibbo, "Might see you down there later, mate. Thought we'd have a look at Valletta's harbour see what's in."

Jeff was still under punishment. The calming effect he had on his mate would not be there. Shiner ashore with the two Jocks, it would be interesting.

Jock Heron was short and stocky with a mop of black curly hair; his body was covered in tattoos. He had joined the navy as a boy after being disenchanted with the crofter's life in West Scotland.

Jock Gordon was slim, tall and fair, he had also joined as a boy, a tough upbringing in a children's home. Drink had played a large part in their many encounters with naval discipline. The tall Scot was easy going, but Jock Heron, like Shiner was volatile and unpredictable when drunk.

"Well," Shiner said pushing his empty plate away. "I'm off to get me bits washed."

Petty Officer Wilson watched as the sailors filed down the gangway into the waiting shore-boat.

"Remember, you lot," he shouted, "your leave finishes at 07:00 hours tomorrow morning, last boat back tonight is 23:59, miss it and you wait till the morning."

Rapidly the boat made its way to Sliema jetty; alongside, she disgorged her cargo of white clad uniformed sailors, and then sped off back to the *Jutland*.

Shiner and the two Jocks were first off, crossing the road they disappeared into the first bar.

It was early evening, the sun still hot as it shone from a cloudless sky. Sounds of the latest pop songs blared out from the many bars,

"Catch a bus to Valletta shall we?" Spike stopped at the bus-stop.

Battered and looking much the worse for wear, the bus screeched to a halt. The sign on the front indicated its destination was Valletta. Boarding, the four sailors sat down. A young Maltese boy looking no more than about ten took their fares, with a cheery grin he shouted, "Hold tight!"

Narrow pot-holed roads, donkeys and carts, it made no difference as they headed for Valletta at breakneck speed. Horn honking loudly the driver sped on like a man possessed, slowing down only to deliver a torrent of oaths through his open window to anyone who dared impede his progress. The bus came to a jolting halt, Valletta.

"Never again," moaned Alby.

Spike picked up his hat which had fallen off during their mad dash; he had been too busy hanging on to bother about it while the bus was in motion.

"Stirling Moss," he muttered. "These fucking Malt drivers."

Crunch went the gears as the bus departed in a cloud of smoke and dust on its return journey.

What they saw before them confirmed what they already knew, an armada of British and French warships, heavy cruisers. Planes lined the decks of aircraft carriers, overshadowing these, the huge French battleship, with her huge 21inch guns able to propel her one ton shells over twenty miles.

Shore-boats were busy ferrying French and British sailors ashore from the anchored warships.

Groups of French sailors stood about talking, not quite knowing where to go. It would be a safe bet that most of them would end up down the Gut.

"Well, lads," Gibbo looked impatient, "what's it to be, the Barbary Coast, or the Gut?"

"What say you, Spike?"

"Easy mate, whatever."

"Come on, let's get a beer."

Alby made his way to the nearest bar, and walked through the open doors.

"Four blues, John, cold ones."

"Six shillings please."

"How much?!" demanded Alby, "you robbing fucker."

"Special price for you, four shillings."

"Normal price you mean."

Alby handed the barman a ten shilling note. The price of beer fluctuated in relation to how many ships were in. More ships, higher prices.

Typical was the bar, wooden tables and chairs, tiled floor. The centre piece, was the large bar with its many shelves displaying every kind of spirits in abundance.

Notices advertised the various, so called, cocktails, with names such as 'Depth Charges'; 'Atom Bombs'; and 'Earthquakes.' Woe betide any young sprog tempted to drink any of these, he would soon be reduced to a free-spending moron.

Despite the frequent brawls, and the profane language often directed at them, the Maltese people had a great affection for the Royal Navy.

"Hey, John, four more blues here."

Spike stared at the barman as he hurried over with the beers; the threat in his eyes dared him to overcharge. Five French sailors walked into the bar, spotting them the barman scurried back behind his bar. The leading Frenchman nodded politely and smiled as he passed the four seated friends.

Holding up his hand to the barman he indicated he wanted five beers.

With diligence the barman uncapped the bottles.

"Ten shillings."

Smiling to themselves they finished their beers.

Steep and narrow was the winding road that led up from the harbour to Valletta's main street. Twenty-five minutes later at the top, they looked down on the harbour, and in the fading light, numerous lights twinkled and reflected in the sea from the many anchored warships.

Main street Valletta, white uniformed sailors both French and English mingled with the local shoppers. Some already unsteady on their feet, old men sat around the main square drinking coffee, smoking and talking.

Sounds of loud music ahead, they were approaching the Gut.

"Could be an interesting night."

Lofty nodded. "Well, Alby, one thing's for sure, want

to give Shiner and the two Jocks a wide berth."

"Fat chance of that, mate, once trouble starts everyone's involved, like it or not."

At the entrance to the Gut stood a massive Maltese Policeman, close by, were six Naval Military Police.

"Hey, Tiny."

The big policeman turned in surprise. "You back again? Not long you go home."

Tiny shook his head. "Not good tonight, too many sailors, much trouble later, better you go Sliema, much better."

"Let's be having you, let's go." Spike was eager to get a drink.

"See you, Tiny, take it easy, mate."

It seemed like the entire French Navy was crowded into the narrow street. Pushing and shoving they managed to enter the Big Ben. Inside, the air was thick with tobacco smoke, music from the juke box blared out.

Girls were draped over sailors, swearing undying love, with promises of an erotic night of love. The conversation always ended with, "Buy me a drink, sailor?"

Two shillings for a shot of coloured water, for which she would receive half. Her undying love would end abruptly when the drinks stopped coming.

On one side of the bar sat the French sailors, the other the English.

Sitting at one table a pair of familiar faces, Pincher and Peanuts.

"Your round, Spike."

Alby pulled out a chair and slumped into it.

"What's the latest, Peanuts?"

"Not good mate, lots of signals regarding troop movements to Cyprus?"

Peanuts stopped as if he had said too much, the little

signalman continued.

"Don't let this go any further, but they're flying in Paras to Cyprus."

"Come on, it won't come to nothing, them sand-hoppers are only good for selling dirty postcards and dodgy watches."

Gibbo swallowed his beer. "Drink up, my round."

A crash of chairs signalled a fight between two French sailors over one of the girls.

"Stupid bastards," growled Spike. "She only wants their loot."

She completely ignored the fighting sailors and moved to another lap.

"See what I mean, fickle cow."

"Bloody hell look who's here?"

Alby held his hands up in mock horror.

Shiner had pushed open the bar doors, in his wake the two Jocks.

He stood there swaying slightly; he glared round the bar as if to defy anyone to challenge him.

"Maybe he won't see us."

"Some hope, here he comes."

The two Jocks seated themselves on the two remaining chairs leaving Shiner standing.

"Where's me fucking chair?" he demanded.

Without a word he strode over to a table at which four French sailors were seated, grabbed a chair and made his way back.

"Got me a chair," he announced with a big grin.

With a tray of drinks in his hand, the big French sailor returned to his table. Where his chair had been, was an empty space.

Lofty watched as the sailors shipmates with much hand waving and pointing towards Shiner explained what had happened.

With a determined look on his face, he made his way over to confront Shiner.

Shiner watched the approach of the Frenchman with complete indifference.

"Right, that's it Shiner, give the Frog his fucking chair back."

"Fuck off, Pincher, nothing to do with you," snarled Shiner.

"Here, mate, have this one."

Peanuts appeared holding a chair.

With a polite nod, the Frenchman accepted the chair and rejoined his countrymen.

"Och mon, yea are no mair tha a big lassie."

Jock Heron directed his remark at Peanuts, like Shiner, he was spoiling for a fight.

"Well lads, I think I'm going to Sliema, have a few drinks and catch the boat back at midnight."

Pincher stood up.

"Anyone coming?"

Lofty shrugged, "Yeah, might as well, think we'll join you for a drink."

Shiner gulped down his beer and waved a hand.

"Well, fog off then ladies, me and the Jocks are staying."

Sliema's front had more than its fair share of bars, but unlike the Gut with its bars both sides of the street; it did not attract the mass of sailors or the drunken brawling.

Back in Sliema, they sat drinking in the Lord Nelson. After several drinks the conversation once again turned to Nasser.

"Reckon we'll be homeward bound soon."

Peanuts frowned and shook his head. "I doubt it Pincher, you saw the landing crafts, hundreds of them."

"Yeah, reckon you're right Peanuts."

"Well," Lofty pushed his empty glass towards Spike. "Your round ain't it Spike?"

With a crash the swing doors flew open, in staggered Ordinary-seaman Clarke close behind O'Brady.

Obviously the worse for drink, he swayed, a stupid grin on his face.

"Hey yer, me ole mates, me and Jim just come from the Gut. Utter chaos, Naval Police everywhere, the place is a shambles, bars wrecked. Someone said it had started in the Big Ben. The Frogs are getting the worst of it."

Pincher yawned, "Sounds like Agincourt. What's the time Lofty?"

"Ten to twelve."

"Right that's me lot, gonna get the boat back."

Chapter 6

Passage to Cyprus

Hammocks stowed away, breakfast was being dished up by the duty cooks.

"Pass the slide."

Alby spread butter thickly on his bread. "Thought it was quiet, no Shiner or Jocks, reckon they're being entertained by the Naval Police ashore."

The bos'n's pipe wailed through the Tannoy.

"Sea-duty men to close up at 08:00 hours. Attention all hands, the First Lieutenant will address the ships company."

"This is the First Lieutenant speaking. We are to proceed to sea at 08:15 hours, once at sea the Captain will address the ship's company. It has come to my notice that members of this crew were involved in the disgraceful scenes ashore last night. Bars have been damaged and a number of French sailors have been admitted to hospital. Seven members of this ship's company were detained by Naval Police; they are being escorted back and will shortly be back on board. I intend to make an example of them. That is all."

"Hands to stations for leaving harbour. Special sea duty-men to close up."

Petty Officer Wilson looked over to Spike.

"Able-seaman Milligan, stand by capstan ready to take in cable."

"Aye, aye, Petty Officer."

"Able-seaman Bancock, report to bridge ready to hoist anchor."

"Bridge, this is Fo'c's'le, ready to hoist anchor."

"Thank you, Fo'c's'le, carry on, hoist anchor."

Orders through the Tannoy came in quick succession, "Stand by amidships to hoist motor-cutter.

"Away scrambling ladders to embark hands from Naval Police launch.

"Close water-tight doors.

"Duty Petty Officer amidships."

Petty Officer Wilson looked up. "That's me."

"Leading-seaman Martin will leave you in charge. Secure for sea."

"Will do, Petty Officer."

Lofty grunted as he took another turn on the bottle screw that secured the anchor-cable.

"Should do it, Pincher."

Pincher nodded, "You can guess why Petty Officer Wilson is away amidships."

"Yeah, Shiner's contribution to Anglo-French relationships."

Petty Officer Wilson saluted the First Lieutenant.

"Duty Petty Officer Sir."

"Thank you Petty Officer. I want these ratings charged and put on my report."

"Aye, aye, Sir, what are the charges Sir?"

Lieutenant Commander Jenks-Powell handed the Petty Officer a folder.

"Charges are detailed in the Naval Police report."

"Very well, Sir."

Abruptly he turned to face the accused ratings. Reading from the charge sheet he began.

"Engine room artificers Brown, Barker, Jones and Harper, you are all charged with taking part in an affray, consequently you are on the First Lieutenant's report.

"Right turn, quick march, get changed and report for work.

"Now we come to you three clowns. Able-seamen Wright, Gordon and Heron, my, my, you have been busy."

Petty Officer Wilson tried hard not to grin, his eyes twinkled in merriment. He surveyed them for a moment, Shiners white uniform stained and filthy, the jacket ripped, no hat, a large swelling under his eye. The two Jocks were in no better state.

"You three are charged with:

1. Causing an affray.

2. Conduct prejudicial to naval discipline.

3. Able-seaman Wright, striking a Naval Patrolman.

4. Also you did urinate over a statue of the Virgin Mary."

"Not true," protested Shiner. "Me and me mates were set upon by these Frog sailors."

"You don't have to explain to me, you will have your say to the First Lieutenant. You are all on report. Get changed and turn to."

Malta was fast becoming a speck on the horizon as the destroyer cut through the calm waters of the Mediterranean at 25 knots. Ahead of them numerous ships as far as the eye could see; the huge convoy of slow moving troop-ships, landing craft and support vessels flanked by cruisers and destroyers. *Jutland* took up station to the rear of this vast amphibious force; soon she was joined by *Dunkirk, Trafalgar* and *Agincourt.*

Aldis lamps constantly winked as messages went back and forth between the destroyers.

Lofty stared at the incredible sight before him, thus engrossed he failed to hear the click of the Petty Officer's steel-capped boots as he made his way across the gun-deck towards him.

"Some sight, eh?!"

Lofty turned with a start.

"Christ, Petty Officer, you made me jump. Was miles away."

"Never seen so many ships."

"What's the latest, Petty Officer?"

"Don't really know anymore than you. The Frog battleship and *Eagle* put to sea early this morning, that's all I know."

Lofty nodded, "Shiners back on board then?"

"He is," confirmed the Petty Officer. "And his two mates, the First Lieutenant will throw the book at them."

Further talk was cut short by the shrill wail of the bos'n's pipe through the Tannoy.

"Attention all hands, the Captain will address the Ship's Company."

"Good morning, this is the Captain.

"We are at the moment on passage to Cyprus, and shortly in company with *Trafalgar*, *Dunkirk* and *Agincourt* we will be leaving the convoy. Our task will be to escort troop and landing craft in a joint Anglo-French landing in Egypt. We pick up our charges at Limassol Bay, Cyprus. Ours will be the initial attack to secure a bridgehead for the main landing which is this convoy. We will have air support from the *Eagle* and two French aircraft-carriers, also from our bases in Cyprus. We will be required to carry out a close support bombardment prior to the landing and during the attack by '42' and '40' commando. French and British paratroopers will be dropped to secure key positions. Egypt has a modern well-equipped air force, in fact she has Russian MIG fighters and bombers, but a pre-emptive strike should neutralise her air force. We will be going to Defence Stations as we near Cyprus. That is all."

"Well, well, all the rumours have been true," Lofty muttered to himself.

Rapidly the four destroyers increased speed.

Now at 34 knots the destroyers quickly overhauled the slow-moving convoy. An air of anticipation swept over the ship. Groups of sailors stood around discussing the forthcoming action.

Alby climbed the rungs of the ladder to the gun-deck two at a time.

He waved cheerfully, "Hi Petty Officer, hi Lofty."

Lofty nodded an acknowledgement, "Why so cheerful? Could get yer arse shot off soon."

"No way mate, them sand-hoppers will be off."

Petty Officer Wilson adjusted his cap, he looked very thoughtful.

"You could well be right," he said, "a lot will depend on the Russian advisors who are training them. What bothers me is the MIG fighters, if they were to be flown by Russian pilots."

"How long before we get to Cyprus, Petty Officer?"

"We should be there about six tomorrow morning."

Lofty considered this for a while. "Reckon we'll be going in the day after tomorrow."

"How'd you work that out?"

"Easy Alby, it's all a matter of timing. We arrive about six, the main force will be twelve hours behind us, by the time they near Cyprus we will be on our way. I reckon by the time we get ourselves sorted they will be close behind."

"Elementary my dear Doctor Lofty," grinned Alby.

Lofty laughed, "Don't take the piss, get fogged."

"Well you two, this won't do, I had better get on," the Petty Officer made to leave. "Oh, before I forget, check the aft 40mm, hydraulic oil everywhere, main pipe coupling possibly loose, get Ordinary-seamen Seaton or O'Brady to clear the oil up. By the way, have either of you two seen Wright, Heron or Gordon?"

"Yeah, Shiner and both the Jocks are crashed out in the messdeck, sleeping like babies."

"Stupid bastards," growled the Petty Officer. "Ain't they in enough trouble already without the First Lieutenant catching them asleep?"

Morning quickly merged into afternoon as the destroyers relentlessly shortened the distance to Cyprus.

In the hot afternoon sun, sailors sweated and cursed as they manhandled the heavy aluminium boxes of 40mm ammunition from the magazines to the guns, clips of shells removed from boxes were placed in the racks, 20mm magazines were being filled.

"Hands to tea."

"First dog watchmen to muster."

Alby hacked at the loaf of bread.

"Now what delights have we got for me sarnie? Don't tell me it's jam or spam."

A groan came from the hammock storage, Shiner had stirred.

"Lazy bastards," Spike complained. "We've worked our balls off today. Pincher, get them fuckers up, middle watchmen will want their hammocks to turn in soon."

Pincher, as a leadinghand was responsible for the running of the mess and discipline on the messdeck, it was a difficult tightrope to walk, unlike the next rank up of Petty Officer, and they had a mess of their own. Pincher realised that he now had to be a leadinghand, and he walked over to the hammock racks.

"Shiner," he shouted. "Up you get." He leant over and

shook the nearest Jock hard.

"What yer want?" demanded Shiner.

"I want you up now."

"Fuck off, Pincher, I've got a headache."

"Able-seamen Wright, Heron and Gordon, up now and that is an order."

Shiner lurched to his feet sullen and angry. "No need to pull rank on me, Pincher."

"Anyhow, the three of you, get those uniforms off, change into working gear; you are all on first watch in three hours."

Captain Warrington yawned; it had been a long night on the bridge. Dawn was breaking; soon they would anchor in Limassol Bay, Cyprus, and then a chance to sleep.

"Bridge messenger."

Ordinary-seaman Seaton came to attention. "Yes, Sir?"

"Could you chase up the duty steward, coffee and sandwiches for Lieutenant Anderson and me? Thank you. Also ask the steward to give the First Lieutenant a shake."

"Aye, aye, Sir."

Captain Warrington turned and lifted the cover off the voice-pipe to the wheelhouse.

"Wheelhouse this is bridge, decrease revolutions to one, zero, zero."

"Aye, aye, Sir, revolutions one, zero, zero on Sir."

"Very well, thank you."

Alby felt the warmth of the early morning sun on his back. Through his binoculars a French cruiser appeared briefly in the sea mist to disappear again. The sun rapidly burning off the mist, the cruiser again appeared and beyond her more ships appeared.

"Contacts, Sir on the starboard bow."

"Very well look-out," Lieutenant Anderson replied.

Even at their considerable distance, Alby could make out the silhouette of three big aircraft-carriers ringed by destroyers; of the French battleship there was no sign.

Sounds of footsteps from the officer's stairway leading to the bridge; involuntarily, Alby glanced over his shoulder as the First Lieutenant came on the bridge.

"Good morning, Sir, good morning Anderson."

Curtly, Captain Warrington replied, "Good morning Number One."

Hard as he had tried to conceal his dislike for the man, it was difficult. His attitude towards his subordinates was abysmal. Putting his feelings aside Captain Warrington addressed the First Lieutenant.

"Number One, I have given the matter of going to Defence Stations some considerable thought," he paused for a moment. "I have decided to close up just one guns-crew while anchored at Cyprus. Once we get under way for Egypt we will go to full Defence Stations. Of course, as we near our objective the ship will go to Action Stations. Any questions?"

"None Sir," Lieutenant Anderson nodded.

"You Number One?"

"Your decision, Sir," he replied. It was abundantly clear the First Lieutenant did not approve.

"Yes, Number One it is," the captain said quietly.

"Lieutenant Anderson, I want you to rotate the gun-crews every two hours. I would like the men to get as much rest as possible."

"Will do, Sir."

Captain Warrington watched as the destroyer slowly edged her way into Limassol harbour.

"Wheelhouse this is bridge."

"Pipe cable and anchor party to muster on the fo'c's'le."

"M1 guns-crew to close-up."

"Hands to breakfast."

Before them a profusion of tank landing and troop landing craft. Lighters were moored beside supply vessels off-loading stores. Troops were being ferried from shore to troop ships.

Lieutenant Anderson reached for the bridge telephone as its harsh screech demanded for it to be answered.

"Fo'c's'le, Sir, anchor and cable party closed up ready to slip anchor."

"Very well, Lieutenant, let go anchor, look-outs and bridge messenger, fall out."

Alby made his way down the bridge ladder followed by Ordinary-seaman Seaton.

"How are yer, mate?" Lofty greeted him.

"Bloody fed up, just spent two hours on the bridge, friggin' look-out. I take it this is breakfast?"

Alby pulled a face as he spooned two rubbery looking eggs onto his plate, curled up bacon followed.

"Look at that bacon," moaned Alby. "Looks like it's had a bloody perm." A slice of fried bread completed his breakfast which made a distinct clunk as it hit the plate. "Any tea left?" Alby asked hopefully.

"Just brewed a fresh pot, mate."

Spike poured a mug full of steaming hot black looking tea.

The shrill sound of the bo's'n's pipe came through the Tannoy.

"Forenoon watch to muster amidships port-side."

"Uncover close-range weapons.

"Hands will not be required to work ship.

"Special sea-duty men will fall-in at 16:00 hours when the ship will proceed to sea. Hands will then go to Defence Stations."

"Well, mate, I think I'll sling me wanking sack and have a kip."

Alby made his way over to the hammock rack for his hammock.

Chapter 7

Suez

"Special sea-duty men close-up.

"First dog watchmen to muster."

Leading-seaman Martin watched as the heavy anchor cleared the water.

"Easy on the capstan," he shouted. "Up slow, Gibbo give the bridge a ring, report anchor clear of water."

With a dull thump the anchor slotted into the anchor housing.

"That will do."

Sounds of cheering as a troop ship passed them on the portside, the upperdecks crowded with waving soldiers; troop and tank landing craft were under way.

"Soldier boys are in good voice," observed Lofty. "Won't be cheering tomorrow, poor sods."

"Poor sods," retorted Alby. "What about us, we'll be close inshore."

Lofty put his arm round Alby's shoulder. "Never mind, mate, I'll look after you."

Cyprus was now well astern as the destroyer increased speed to take up position on the flank of the convoy; abeam of them on the portside, heavy cruisers with both the ensign and the French tricolours fluttering from the mast-heads. Beyond them, the aircraft carriers with the massive battleship, French and British destroyers fussed around them like terriers.

"Hands to Defence Stations."

"Hands to Defence Stations."

"Close-range weapons load."

Alby was first to reach the twin 40mm. He eased himself into the aimer's seat and depressed the barrels as Ordinary-seaman Seaton rushed on to the gun-deck. Already he began to remove the muzzle covers.

"Well done, mate. O'Brady, switch on communications, right lads load."

Alby pulled the breech levers back as the first two clips of shells dropped down the guides, lever forward the first two shells were loaded. Standing on the loading platform, the two National Servicemen, O'Brady and Seaton, quickly loaded another three clips for each barrel from the ready-use racks on the mounting.

Sitting on the ammunition locker the two stewards were engrossed in conversation, with flamboyant gestures. They were oblivious to what was going on around them.

Alby stared at them in disbelief. "Ordinary-seaman Seaton report to director Ml closed up and cleared away for action."

Alby with an effort extracted himself from the cramped aimer's seat; and he walked over to the two stewards.

"Excuse me, I do hope I am not interrupting you, do you remember our little talk the other day?"

"Yes, Able-seaman," the steward smiled.

Alby's big hands shot out; roughly he grabbed the steward by his shirt. He whimpered in terror as Alby lifted him bodily off the locker. "Then what the fuck are you two fairies doing? Get them boxes open and replace the clips in the racks."

"Ammunition, supply them two," he groaned at Ordinary-seaman Seaton. "Would be better suited in a handbag shop."

In the western sky, a dull red glow replaced the sun as it dipped beyond the horizon; in the fading light the ghostly shapes of numerous ships. The heat of the day soon gave way to the chill of the night. A full moon bathed the ship in bright moonlight, phosphorus danced and glowed luminous in the ships wake. Fitfully gun-crews tried to sleep.

Hot soup and rolls were being ferried round to gun-crews.

Jock Heron swore profusely and loudly as awaking with a start. Cracking his head on the protruding giro-sight, he stretched noisily as he disentangled himself from the aimer's seat. "Where's me soup?" he asked brusquely rubbing his head with diligence.

Jock Gordon ladled the steaming hot soup into a mug.

"Here yea are, mate, noe bad, at least it's hot."

Jock Heron nodded his thanks; he gulped at the soup, in between gulps he looked up. "Hey Jacko, get Stormy to spell yea on the headphones."

Able-seaman Jackson raised a hand in acknowledgment; gently he shook Stormy who awoke with a start.

"Sorry, mate, your turn on communications."

Half asleep, Stormy donned the headphones. Ordinary-seaman Hook had acquired the nickname of Stormy by his frequent and much contorted tales of adventure and rough seas, told only to National Servicemen. During one of his tall tales to an engrossed sprog Shiner had overheard.

With his usual finesse Shiner had ridiculed him without mercy, calling him Stormy weather, the only sailor in the British Navy to spend a week on the same wave.

Acutely embarrassed at first by Shiner's constant

barracking, he now revelled in his nickname of Stormy.

Jacko sat on the ammunition locker. He fumbled in his shirt pocket for his cigarettes, involuntarily he shivered, and it was as much with anticipation of the coming dawn as to the chill of the night.

Stormy's eyes had closed, and he jumped as a message came over the headphones.

"Hi, Jock," he called. "Message from bridge, captain of guns detail one rating to make tea."

"Cheers, Stormy. Nobby go brew up, mate."

Ordinary-seaman Clarke made to comply but was stopped by Jacko.

"As you were Nobby I'll go."

Jock called after him, "Bring us me jumper, Jacko, bloody frozen I am."

Lieutenant Norton, the Navigation Officer intently pored over his charts. So engrossed was he, that he failed to hear the footsteps of Captain Warrington entering the chart room.

"How's it going, Lieutenant?" he smiled benevolently.

Taken aback for a brief moment the Navigation Officer replied, "Just fine, Sir."

"At our present course and speed, Lieutenant, when will we be in visual contact with our objective?"

Lieutenant Norton made some hurried calculations.

"Sir, approximate reckoning about three hours ten minutes would put us ten miles off the coast."

"Thank you. One more thing, how much water is there four thousand yards off shore?"

"Not a lot, Sir, it varies from six fathoms down to three."

Captain Warrington frowned. "Dammit, doesn't give us much sea room to manoeuvre."

"No, Sir, it does not."

Captain Warrington liked the young Lieutenant, as the Navigation Officer he was excellent, more so, he felt completely at ease with him.

"Well, thank you, Lieutenant, I must get back to the bridge."

Thoughts flooded through his mind as he ascended the few steps from the chart house to the bridge. Fully, he was aware of the catastrophe that would engulf them if the Egyptians and their Russian advisers were dug in and waiting for them.

"Sir, permission to go to Action Stations," the First Lieutenant spoke excitedly.

"Yes, Number One, carry on."

Hurriedly the First Lieutenant, his voice rising rapidly spoke down the voice-pipe.

"Wheelhouse, this is bridge."

"Pipe hands to Action Stations."

In the director, Lieutenant Anderson quietly acknowledged as the gun-crews reported ready for action.

"Able-seaman Pringle."

"Yes, Sir."

"Report to the bridge, all guns closed up."

"Aye, aye, Sir."

Jeff replaced the phone.

"Sir, from the bridge, could you report to the Captain?"

Lieutenant Anderson came to attention and saluted. "You wanted to see me, Sir?"

"Yes, guns, as you are aware we are to provide fire in direct support of the landing force. Our main armament will be director controlled, all 40mm weapons to engage independently, it is imperative to suppress all defences before the troops land."

"I understand, Sir, how is the opposition, Sir?"

"That, Lieutenant, is the big question, there is unconfirmed reports of a tank brigade guarding the canal; brief all gun-crews to put them in the picture."

"Aye, aye, Sir."

Saluting, the gunnery officer turned and hurried off to the director.

Peanuts wrote on his signal pad as the Morse telegraph tapped out its message.

"Oh, Petty Officer." He waved his pad. "A message from *Trafalgar*, it reads, '*Jutland* from *Trafalgar*, increase speed to 220 revs and follow mothers stern.'"

Petty Officer Barber grinned.

"Better get this to the old man right away."

Captain Warrington read the signal.

"Thank you, Petty Officer, make to *Trafalgar* lead on mother."

Alby felt the throb of the engines increase as the destroyer picked up speed. Astern of them the dark shape of *Dunkirk*.

Overhead the sound of jet aircraft.

Jacko stared skywards. "Sounds like the birdie boys are on their way to give ole Nasser's air force an early morning shake."

The first streaks of dawn appeared in the eastern sky; the land mass of Egypt on the portside, dark and foreboding, and joining the four destroyers in line ahead, *HMS Diamond* and *Duchess*, two modern 'D' class destroyers.

"A.B.Q turrets load."

"Stand,by to engage."

Shell trays swung over as the 60lb 4.7 high explosive shells were rammed home.

Lieutenant Anderson answered, "Very well," as each turret reported ready.

"Bridge, this is director, all guns ready to engage, Sir."

"Thank you director, we will commence fire in two minutes."

Alby slewed the mounting to port. Through the giro-sight he could make out the shoreline dark against the beach.

"Open fire."

Simultaneously the five 4.7 guns fired. The destroyers were briefly illuminated by their gun flashes in the half light. Tracers arced shoreward as the 40mm guns racked the shoreline with a murderous fire. Seconds later a welter of flaming eruptions as the 4.7 shells slammed into the shore.

Rocket firing naval Seahawks, like big birds of prey swooped down, sending streams of flaming rockets to burst in spectacular blasts against Nasser's defences.

Troop landing craft made their way painfully slowly shoreward. Aboard, the first wave of landing craft 40-42 commandos.

Dawn was breaking as the assault neared the beach; plumes of water thrown up by near misses obscured the leading landing craft.

Jock Heron shifted targets as muzzel flashes faintly blinked from shore. The twin 40mm poured a stream of shells towards the danger.

"Stormy, fur fuck's sake, mair ammo." Jock Gordon yelled over the vicious crack of the 4.7s.

Stormy cursed loudly as he kicked empty shell cases which littered the gun-deck, out of his way. Sweat poured from him as he passed clip after clip of 40mm ammunition to the loader. His counterpart Nobby grinned as he tossed clips of shells to Jacko, who deftly caught them to feed the other barrel of the twin, the hungry quick firing twin devoured them ravenously.

Captain Warrington lowered his binoculars; he winced slightly as A.B.Q. turrets fired. He moved closer to the First Lieutenant shouting to make himself heard above the incessant banging of the 40mms.

"There seems to be very little incoming fire now, Number One."

"No, Sir, looks like they have pulled back," confirmed the First Lieutenant.

As the landing craft hit the beach, naval Seahawks flying at wave-top level pounded the beach and shore ahead of them.

Drifting over Port Said a huge dense pall of black smoke from a burning oil tank.

"Cease fire, all guns cease fire."

40-42 commandos stormed ashore as the naval barrage lifted. Sporadic machinegun fire greeted them as the few remaining Egyptian troops retreated in disorder.

Captain Warrington unhooked the speaker on the Tannoy.

"Attention, this is the Captain speaking. Well done is the message I have received from Captain D. The Commando's are now ashore, they have secured a bridgehead. At this moment the Royal Berkshire Regiment are landing with Centurion tanks. 45 Commando are being flown in by helicopter to reinforce 40 and 42 Commando. The British 3rd Para Brigade has taken Gamil airport, while Port Fouad is in the hands of French Paras. On the down side, un-confirmed reports that a British frigate has been attacked by MIG fighters, the ship will remain at action stations, air-raid warning red. Captain of guns detail one man to fetch soup from the galley, thank you that is all."

"Ta, skips," grinned Alby, he looked across at the two stewards. "Which one of you girls are going for the soup?"

"Why us?" retorted one of the stewards.

"Because I say so," Alby fumed. "Now you fuck off and get the soup."

"Can't we both go?" the steward said hopefully.

"You taking the piss?" Alby glared at him. "Why do you want to go hand in hand? No, I've told you once, off you go." Alby pointed to the nearest steward, "And you start picking up these empty shell cases and stow them in the used ammo boxes."

"You big brute," the steward muttered as he made his way down the gun-deck ladder.

Alby glared at the two laughing young seamen, O'Brady and Seaton.

"Just what do you find so bloody funny? When I joined up sailors went ashore with a packet of three, now look at 'em. It's friggin' matching handbags."

Lieutenant Anderson watched intently as the two blips on the radar screen approached from the starboard beam, constant update of speed and bearing came from the Radar Plot room.

"Sir," Jeff interrupted the gunnery officer. "From Radar Plot, if unidentified aircraft maintain present course and speed they will be in range in four minutes."

"Very good, thank you."

"Bridge, this is Director, Sir, the two unidentified aircraft are closing fast."

"Thank you, Lieutenant. Stand by to engage."

A head appeared as the steward struggled up the ladder with soup, rolls and mugs.

"Give him an' hand," Alby screamed. Through his

headphones came the bearing of the aircraft, the 40mm mounting rapidly swung to starboard.

"Close-range weapons hold your fire."

The harsh sound of the fire-gong sounded, followed by the sharp crack of the 4.7s as they engaged the distant aircraft.

Moments later, puffs of smoke, from the bursting shells, hung like balls of cotton wool low in the sky 10,000 yards away.

Through the gun-sights Alby watched as the aircraft came on, 4.7 shells burst all around them.

"Close-range weapons commence firing."

Streams of tracer criss-crossed low over the sea as the 40mm guns opened fire, above their constant banging the chatter of the 20mm Oerlikons.

A bright orange flash and a cloud of black smoke as one aircraft disappeared; the other turned and rapidly began to climb.

Relentlessly the tracer pursued the remaining aircraft. Smoke billowed from it as it spiralled down to cascade into the sea amid a cloud of spray and smoke.

"Poor bastards, that's the end of their potential distinguished flying careers. Still, it was them or us."

Alby made the statement with a solemn face.

Petty Officer Wilson made his way along the gun-decks, stopping for a few moments to speak to each guns crew; he stepped onto M1 gundeck.

"Hey lads, everything alright, any problems?"

"Bloody soups cold," grinned Alby. "Bar that, no problems. Heard anything more about that Frigate that was hit?"

"Yeah, was the *Aine*, she was attacked off the coast near Rashid, several killed and injured. She's making her way back to Malta under escort. Seems like the Israelis have joined in, reports coming in confirm that Israeli armoured units are advancing through the Sinai Peninsula towards Port Suez."

"Sounds like it could be all over in a few days."

"You could well be right," agreed the Petty Officer.

The midday sun was pitiless as it beat down on the guns crews now stripped to the waist.

Profound boredom now replaced the adrenalin rush of the early morning action. Tired men dozed at their positions. The destroyer now cruised well offshore.

The fact that they had now been closed up for twenty hours was all too apparent.

On the bridge, Captain Warrington was all too aware of his tired crew. He himself was exhausted. He, unlike the guns crews had been unable to snatch brief periods of sleep.

"Number One, I am going to fall-out half the guns crews for dinner. We will then revert back to sea-watches, but keep half of the armament closed up, the men need to get some rest and so must I. Could you get Lieutenant Anderson to report to me in my sea-cabin. Number One, I will leave you the bridge; get the steward to wake me in three hours."

"Aye aye, Sir, will do."

Shiner swore with venom as he tried to get comfortable.

"Me back is friggin' killing me," he moaned. "Wished I hadn't joined up, bloody stuck out here."

"Well mate, at least you have one consolation," Pincher chuckled.

"Yer, what's that?" Shiner demanded.

"You haven't been up before the First Lieutenant for

defaulters yet."

Shiner pulled a face. "I hadn't forgotten, anyhow me an the two Jocks are innocent."

"Come off it, Shiner, it's me, Pincher yer talking to, not some stupid officer."

"More bad luck than anything, I called this frog a big French fairy, he turned round and said, 'Monsieur are you talking to me? Can't take a joke them frogs.'"

"One minute, mate." Pincher listened intently on his headphones; he nodded to himself as he removed the headphones and switched off the communications.

"We are to stand down, gonna keep just two twin 40mm closed up."

Shiner opened the turret door. "That's me off to get me tot and nosh."

"Cheers, mate." Shiner waited impatiently as Pincher measured out his tot and took sippers.

Shiner reached for his tot. "Looks a drop of good," he smiled as he gulped back half with a satisfied smack of his lips.

"Where's the two haggis eaters?"

"On their way," Jacko replied. "Stopped off at the galley to pick up the mess meal."

"Good oh, I'm famished, come on, Nobby get the plates and irons out. Who's duty cooks?"

"Me and Alby," Jacko acknowledged. "Alby's still closed up on M1."

"Dinner is served." The voice at the top of the ladder announced the arrival of the two Jocks.

With trays placed on the mess table, the two Jocks lost no time in collecting their tots.

"Well?" Shiner inquired. "What's for dinner?"

Jock Heron sat down beside Shiner. "Well mate, in them trays is a culinary delight, cookie has surpassed hissel."

"Don't fuck about, Jock, what have we got?"

"Bangers, beans, eggs and mash."

"Yeah, that sounds about right, what's for afters?"

"Rabbit turds in the snow."

"Bloody hell, not rice and friggin' currants again."

Petty Officer removed his hat as he entered the seaman's mess.

"Listen-up lads, as you know we still have two guns crew closed up. You have an hour for dinner, and then Able-seaman Heron, you and your crew will relieve Able-seaman Lacey on M1. Shiner, you take Able-seaman Stringer and three Ordinary-seaman and do the same on M3."

"But …" Shiner began to protest.

"No, why me?" interrupted the Petty Officer. He tapped the crossed anchors on his sleeve that signified his rank.

Shiner grinned but refrained from any comment.

"Just as a matter of interest, it looks like the Egyptians are negotiating for a cease-fire; message came through from *HMS Tyne*."

"Surprise surprise," said Lofty.

"Yeah," Shiner growled with contempt. "Nasser is on his camel and away, them boot-necks (Royal Marines) and Paras will kick his arse if they catch him."

"Petty Officer, before you go …" Jacko asked, "What's the drill after dinner?"

"Going back to normal sea-watches but keeping two 40mms closed up. Enjoy your dinner, lads, I am off to get mine."

With diligence Jacko dished up dinner.

"Don't forget Alby and the rest of them that's still closed up."

"Got it sorted, Pincher," Jacko replied. "Hey, Nobby, run these dinners up to Cookies oven."

"Everyone had their tot?" Pincher glanced around the mess.

"Yeah, reckon so."

"Hang about Shiner, Alby and Jeff to come, looks like two tots over."

"Good on yer mate gulpers all round," beamed Shiner. He watched as the first tot was passed around, by the time it reached him very little remained in the glass. He looked at it with disgust. "Ain't no sippers left yer greedy bastards."

"Before you get out of your pram." Pincher handed Shiner the second tot.

"Didn't say anything mate." Shiner smiled as he took a large gulp.

Reverting back to normal sea-watches, the destroyer's crew relaxed and caught up on much needed sleep. The original cease-fire had broken down, but now three days onward a firm cease-fire now held.

Captain Warrington had informed the Ship's Company that 3 Commando Brigades and the 16th Parachute Regiment Regiment were being embarked on *HMS Empire Fowly* enroute to Malta; they had been detailed to escort them back.

42 commando were to remain in Port Said to prevent looting. Already LCT *Reggio* and *Bastion* were making their ponderously slow way back to Cyprus loaded with tanks.

Daily broadcasts from the BBC coming over the ships broadcast system did nothing to boost morale. The Americans had threatened economic sanctions against Britain unless an immediate withdrawal was put into effect; the outcry in opposition to the landings was such that broadcasts were turned off.

"What's it all about, mate?"

Spike shook his head. "You tell me, Alby, just a waste of friggin' time."

With the cease-fire holding, *Jutland* was now anchored.

Pincher leaned against the guardrails. He gestured shore-wards. Equipment and troops were being ferried from shore to waiting troop ships and landing craft.

"Bloody Yanks want to mind their own business, they done the same with the Panama Canal."

"Never mind," Jeff said. "We could be home by Christmas."

"Do yer reckon? That bloody Nasser sunk all those block ships in the canal. No ship can navigate it now. Chances are the navy will have to clear them."

With a click the Tannoy came on.

"Hands to supper. Cooks to the galley."

"Right, mate, let's get supper."

As the two sailors entered the mess, supper was being served up as cooks of mess busied themselves serving out meals.

Lofty paused as he reached for the teapot.

"Yer up before the First Lieutenant tomorrow morning ain't yer, Shiner, and the two Jocks?"

"Yeah, I ain't likely to forget am I? Everyone keeps reminding me."

"Why don't you plead guilty but insane?" quipped Jeff.

"And why don't you go frig yourself cos it ain't funny mate. Anyhow, Lieutenant Allan the divisional officer had a word with me. He's going to put forward mitigating circumstances." Loud laughter greeted Shiner's statement.

"What mitigating circumstances?" laughed Lofty.

"Well I told him I had a Dear John letter and was upset, he understood, he said I committed the offences under emotional duress."

"What a plonker! But it's good, Shiner, very good, the only trouble is, mate, the First Lieutenant will think you're taking the piss."

"We will see," Shiner said with an air of confidence.

"Anyone for a game of uckers?" Spike asked.

It had been an early night for the sailors. Breakfast now finished, they sat around the mess talking, waiting to turn to.

"Hands to fall in work ship."

"Cooks of mess to stand fast."

"First Lieutenant's Defaulters fall in."

"Off you go, lads turn to." Pincher nodded to Shiner and the two Jocks. "Good luck, you three."

"In the bag," grinned Shiner. The two Jocks didn't share his confidence.

Alby grunted as he forced the mop up one barrel of the twin. "Depress a bit, Lofty, that will do, mate."

With a scrubbing movement he worked the mop back and forth, and then finally pulled it clear wiping his oily hands on his overalls. He joined Lofty leaning on the guardrails.

"Won't be long now before we sail for Malta." Talking to Peanuts he said, "the *Empire Fowley* should be ready to proceed late forenoon."

"Good, Alby, the sooner we get away from this bloody shambles the better."

"Well, look who's here!" grinned Lofty.

Below them Shiner walked slowly along the weatherdeck. He seemed deep in thought.

"Hi ya, mate, how did yer get on?"

Shiner looked up and frowned. "Don't ask. That bastard, I'll have 'im. Fourteen days stoppage of pay, fourteen days stoppage of leave and fourteen days 10A."

"What happened to the mitigating circumstances mate?" Shiner's mouth twitched into a half smile but he ignored the question.

"He had a look at me comic cuts (Service Records).

"-Able-seaman Wright,-" he mimicked the First Lieutenant.

"-Your record is absolutely abominable.-"

"Stupid bastard," snarled Shiner. "Anyhow, I have now taken on the job of postman."

"Postman," Lofty looked at Shiner in amusement.

"Yeah, gonna post all these fire-hoses to Davy Jones's locker."

Shiner glanced around. Nobody in sight. He strode purposely over to the fire hose, lifted it out of the rack and nonchalantly tossed it over the side.

"Two down four to go," Shiner grinned.

Foghorn blaring, *Jutland* signalled her departure as she turned westward towards Malta, nine hundred miles away. On her port-side *HMT Empire Fowley* was underway.

Ahead of them a cluster of LCT's with two French destroyer escorts.

Cheering waving troops lined the upper-decks of the troop-ship *Empire Fowey* as *Jutland* passed her to take-up station ahead. Flying fish launched themselves from the bow wave to skim across the calm sea on large wing-like pectoral fins.

At ten knots it would take four days to reach Malta. The ship was in routine sea-watches which would allow the sailors to catch up on dhobing (clothes washing) and ironing and to play 'Uckers', a form of Ludo which was taken very seriously. Mixed blobs knocked off the board would result in tempers being frayed. Inter-mess competitions were popular.

With a cry of "Uckers yer fuckers" the competition would commence. With each throw of the dice the counters would be moved with cheers and moans from the opposing sides. Tension would increase as one competitor would land against a mixed blob and attempted to throw the appropriate number of sixes to knock it off. Gulpers would be wagered on the outcome of matches.

Time had passed quickly. *Jutland* entered Sliema Harbour, and now released from her charges who had safely anchored in Grand Harbour.

"Hands to stations for entering harbour."

"Special sea duty-men close up."

"Attention to port."

The shrill call of the bos'n's pipe called the hands working on the upper-deck to attention as they faced to port.

HMS Aine rode at anchor, her ensign proudly fluttering at half-mast. Jagged blackened holes in her side, bridge badly damaged, her two aft 40mm mountings a twisted mass of distorted steel.

"Bloody politicians," Spike spoke quietly. "They should be made to see the results of this fiasco."

Gibbo nodded. "Yeah, mate, but it won't do them poor sods any good."

"Right lads, stand by to drop anchor," Petty Officer Wilson said sombrely.

Once again they were anchored in Sliema, but this time no rumours of impeding action. Just one question remained: How long would it be before they sailed for home?

Back in England the argument rumbled on in Parliament about the abortive attempt to seize the Suez Canal. Eventually resulting in the resignation of the Prime Minister, these events needless to say held no interest for the sailors.

Chapter 8

Courtesy Visit

Days merged into weeks as they awaited orders. By now the rest of the 7th Destroyer Squadron had joined *Jutland* and was now anchored in Sliema.

Shiner brooded as he served out his punishment. With just a few days to go he was anxious to be going ashore. The two Jocks had received a lesser sentence of ten days 10A and were about to go ashore.

"Never yea mind, mate," Jock Heron put a consoling hand on Shiner's shoulder. "Only three days left."

"Yeah, I know Jock, but, mate, yer forgetting I got stoppage of pay. It will be a northeaster (not entitled) for me this pay-day."

"Dinna yer worry, mate, us Jocks will sub yea, do yea ken?"

"Cheers, Jock," Shiner answered but with little enthusiasm.

"Liberty men to fall-in abreast starboard gangway.

"Men under punishment fall-in on the quarter-deck.

"Away motor boats crew."

Shiner grimaced and stuck two fingers up at the Tannoy.

"Seems I am being paged, off you go, girls, don't miss the shore-boat."

From the quarter-deck, Shiner watched as the Liberty boat made its way shore-ward.

"Wotcher, mate, how's it going?"

Able-seaman Smith (Muffer) and Able-seaman Wilson (Tug) from the after-seamen's mess joined Shiner.

"Hi yer, Muffer, you under punishment?"

"Yeah, five days 10A," Muffer replied. "That bastard of a First Lieutenant. Me an' Tug just missed the morning boat by minutes; we got a Maltese boat-man to row us back, got back as the Liberty boat was pulling away from the gangway. The duty Petty Officer went to give us our cards back! Charge them Petty Officer, the bastard said."

Shiner nodded in sympathy.

"Right you three desperadoes," duty Petty Officer Stannard addressed the trio. "The First Lieutenant would like you to sweep and hose down the upper-decks, any questions?"

"None, Petty Officer," beamed Shiner.

"Any problems, you will find me in the Petty Officers' mess."

"Well, mates," Shiner volunteered. "I'll fetch two stiff brooms while you two hook up the hose." A buoyant Shiner made his way amidships to the broom locker, returning a few minutes later to be confronted by a grinning Muffer and Tug.

"No hoses, mate, any up forward?"

"Dunno," Shiner shrugged innocently. "One of us had better inform Petty Officer Stannard."

"What do you mean no hoses?" the Petty Officer demanded.

"Ain't our fault," protested Tug. "We looked but there ain't none."

Angrily the Petty Officer disappeared back to his mess to reappear with hat and jacket on.

"Wilson, if you and your cronies are having me on, you will be for the high jump."

With Tug close behind, the Petty Officer hurried

along the upper-deck. Glancing momentarily at the two empty hose-racks amidships, he frowned and shook his head.

"Just my luck," whinged the Petty Officer. "So much for my quiet duty-watch. You three had better make yourselves useful, start sweeping down the decks; I will report this to the First Lieutenant."

Shiner grinned with delight; the thought of Jenks-Powell put into a compromising position filled him with rapture. He swept the decks with gusto as he awaited the arrival of Jenks-Powell. His hatred for the man was now an obsession which would reach a climax at a later date.

Petty Officer Stannard stood looking at the empty hose-racks amidships. With him the First Lieutenant, his high-pitched near hysterical voice could be plainly heard.

Shiner smiled to himself as the two approached.

"You two, over here," the Petty Officer called out to Muffer and Tug. "The First Lieutenant would like a word with you."

The First Lieutenant glared at them. "Where are the damned hoses?" he shouted.

"I dunno, Sir," Muffer replied.

"What about you, Wright, what's so funny? Take that grin off your face, you bloody imbecile," he screamed in rage.

Shiner's eyes narrowed. Deliberately and quietly he said, "I know nothing about the hoses, and, Sir, with respect, you have no right to talk to me like that."

"You impertinent bastard," shrieked the First Lieutenant.

"Sir, I think Able-Seaman Wright has a point."

The Petty Officer came to attention and looked straight at the officer.

His face red and contorted in rage, the officer turned

and hurried away.

"Thank you, Petty Officer," Shiner grinned his appreciation.

"No need for thanks, lad, he may be an officer but certainly the man is no gentleman. My advice to you is tread wary or he will have your arse in a sling, now carry on, get these decks swept."

Shiner's encounter with the First Lieutenant had been the talking point on board; with Shiner revelling in the limelight the story earned him countless gulpers.

But talk was now centred on the courtesy visit to Civitavechia, western Italy, a port just 30 miles from Rome. After a five day visit the 7th Destroyer Squadron was to escort the French battleship, *Sharn Bart,* back to her home port of Toulon, and then home to Chatham.

"Hands to muster for payment, muster outside the purser's office.

"Duty watch the First of Port.

"Leave will commence at 17:00 hours until 07:00 tomorrow morning."

A disgruntled Shiner joined the queue for payment.

"Now why the fuck should I have to wait here like a big girl's blouse to be told I ain't entitled to any pay?" he moaned.

"It's all part of the master plan, mate," grinned Jeff.

"Just to remind yer that you've been a naughty boy."

"Able-seaman Wright." Shiner stepped forward with cap extended. The Petty Officer paymaster looked up over his spectacles. "Not entitled, carry on."

Pincher banged loudly on the mess table.

"Listen up, lads, we're taking a collection for Shiner, if we all contribute half a crown each the old bastard will have enough for a couple of rums ashore now he's off punishment. Pass the hat round."

Shiner was visually moved for a brief moment, he was lost for words as he accepted the money offered. A broad smile spread over his face.

"Cheers lads. Who's for a run ashore down the Gut?"

"Count me an' Lofty in," affirmed Gibbo. "But mind yer, Shiner, no more rucks."

"No way, mate, just big eats, a few beers and a leg over for Jock, ain't that right, Jock?"

Jock Heron grinned and stuck two fingers up. "Aye, but yea didna hae to tell everyone."

"Take no notice of him Jock, I might come with yer to see yer pull, might pick up a few pointers."

"Oh, he'll pull all right Spike," Shiner laughed. "You see, mate, he has this system, the crafty bastard picks the most ugly woman in the bar. She's so grateful she can't wait to get her knickers down. As Jock will tell you, you don't look at the chimney when you poke the fire."

Pincher winked at Jock.

"Shiner, are yer sleeping ashore tonight?"

"Dunno mate, see how it goes. Why do yer ask?"

"Just wondered if yer was planning to kip at Snowy's dosshouse."

"Very funny, Pincher, very funny. Yer dicks not yer own in there."

"Yer seem to know a lot about it," chuckled Spike.

"Come off it, Spike, everyone knows that Snowy's is the stomping ground of the Phantom Gobbler. Funny thing is nobody knows who he is, he always strikes in the dark, he only ever speaks three words, 'it is I?' Anyhow, yer piss takers, I ain't kipping at Gobblers Gulch. Now I might get a quick hand job under the table from Marie, she's got a muscle in her right arm like a weight lifter."

"Now, now, Shiner," Spike feigned mock concern.

"What sort of influence are you having on these young National Servicemen?"

Shiner grinned broadly. "All part of life's rich tapestry ain't it, mate? Take young James here, he indicated to Ordinary-seaman Ashton, he's shy and well brought up. Two years with us and who knows, he could turn into a drunken minge muncher."

Ordinary-seaman Ashton blushed uncontrollably. "You're disgusting," he blurted out.

"That's my middle name," Shiner said unperturbed. "Anyhow, come on, ladies, are we going ashore or not?"

Now ashore, the sailors strolled leisurely down Main Street in Valletta. Young Maltese girls in groups giggled their way past them as the local dandies strutted and preened themselves like so many displaying peacocks.

"Can't understand these Maltese lads. Why don't they get stuck in and chat the girls up."

"It don't work like that here, Shiner," Alby replied. "Gibbo, you remember Shady Lane don't yer?"

"Yeah mate, poor old Shady, he was courting this Malt girl, she was some looker. He met her at some big eats joint where she was a waitress, Shady was smitten. He asked her out but her old man said no. Old Shady wasn't put off, in fact, it made him more determined. Every time he went ashore he was straight round for big eats. After about three months the old man relented, by this time Shady was as fat as a hog. Shady planned his first date with military precision, a day trip to remote Gozo Island. He arranged to meet her at Valletta Harbour. A quick dash to the sick bay for a packet of three and he was off. On reaching the harbour, he noticed a crowd waiting for the boat, the object of his affections was waiting with her mother, three sisters and two aunts. Needless to say, Shady was right pissed off. After several dates with half of Malta acting as chaperones Shady decided the financial burden was such it would be cheaper to get married. So away he goes and puts a request in to see the skipper to get married. Within a week the navy had shipped him home. Shady was heart broken."

"Typical bloody navy," Alby said. "What happened to Shady?"

"We saw him at Chatham Barracks six months later; he was engaged to a Wren."

At the entrance to the Gut stood two naval policemen. One of them eyed Shiner nervously, the big sailor glared at him. "I remember you, yer entertained me an' my two mates last time we were ashore. Hey, Jock, look who's here."

"Aye, Shiner," Jock Heron grinned at the policeman. "Dae yer nae ken me?"

"Come on you two, knock it off." Spike stepped in front of Shiner.

"Lay off, Spike, this here is the joker who took a swing at me while his mates held me. Just wondered if he fancied a return match."

"Much more of this and you'll end up in the brig again." The naval policeman didn't sound over-confident.

Shiner smiled, he glared at the naval policeman. Quietly, he said, "In the words of Vera Lynn, 'we'll meet again'."

He laughed loudly as he turned and strode off down the Gut with Jock Heron in his wake.

Relief showed on the military policeman's face as he recovered his composure. He assumed an air of authority. "You," he looked at Alby, "keep them two out of trouble."

"I ain't their friggin' keeper, mate," Alby said. "One

word of warning. If them two get half pissed you would do well to keep out of their way."

"I didn't ask for your advice," the reply came with sarcasm.

"Please yourself," Alby called over his shoulder as he hurried to catch up with his shipmates.

"Six blues." Shiner beckoned the barman over.

As the barman scurried over with their drinks on a tray he eyed Shiner with apprehension.

"What's up, Mario?" Shiner asked as he reached for a beer.

"Boss man he says you big trouble, no serve if drunk."

"Cor, talk about giving a dog a bad name," retorted Shiner. "Girl Guide I ain't, but, Mario me old mate, this is me first beer and I'm as dry as an Arab's underpants. Anyhow, who's the new girl with Marie?"

"Her name is Velda, she start work here last night."

"Not bad, does she jig a jig?" Shiner grinned.

"Why you ask me, how I know?" an embarrassed Mario beat a hasty retreat back to his bar.

Maria pouted provocatively as she seated herself down and beckoned Velda over.

"Who's going to buy us a drink then?" she smiled sweetly.

"Aye, I will but nae yer coloured water, a proper drink, what will yea hae?"

Velda gave Jock a look of bewilderment.

"Velda!" Lofty caught her attention, "I translate for Jock, what he said was, do you and Maria want a drink?"

"Yes please," she smiled at Jock. "I will have an Anisette."

"There yer are Jock, do yer want me to negotiate a bunk-up for yer?"

"Awa yea go an' frig yersel bloody Sassenach," Jock

replied good-humouredly.

Marie toyed with her drink; with little enthusiasm she took a sip.

"What's up, Marie?" Shiner asked. "You don't look very happy."

"Place empty, earn no money."

"Yeah, we leave for Italy tomorrow. Anyhow, it won't be long before the fleet will be back from Egypt. Well you can take me home tonight."

Marie shook her head. "All the time you say that to me, you know I have husband at home."

"What about Velda, has she husband?"

"Yes, but he no good, he leave her with small daughter. She has flat in Sliema, but no money so she work. Velda, she nice girl."

"Seems so," agreed Shiner, "she's far better than Jocks normal chat-ups; look at him, can't keep his eyes off her. Hey, Jock yer randy Scotch git, looks like yer in love. Come on, whose round is it?"

"Mario," Lofty waved a hand, "same again and two drinks for the ladies."

"Might as well have stayed on board," Alby said, "it's like a bloody morgue here. How about going back to Sliema for big eats at the Lord Nelson?"

"Yeah," Spike nodded in agreement.

"Suits us," Lofty replied for Gibbo, "how about you Shiner?"

"See yer later, mate."

"Well lads, are yer ready?" Spike finished his beer and stood up, "you take it easy, Shiner. See yer, Jock hope your torpedo runs deep and true."

"Awa yea go," grinned Jock, "see ya in the morning."

Main Street was deserted bar for a few locals. It seemed strangely quiet without the throngs of rumbustious sailors.

"Let's get a taxi."

Spike banged on the window of the battered looking taxi. The driver woke with a start.

"How much to Sliema, the Lord Nelson?"

"Two pounds, special price for you very cheap."

"Mate, we want to hire this wreck not buy the fucker. What time's the next bus?"

"All right, John, just for you, one pound ten shilling."

"How about fifteen shilling and a five shilling tip?"

"Ok," the taxi driver shrugged, "hop in."

Moments later they came to an abrupt halt outside the Lord Nelson.

After paying the driver, Spike pushed open the swing doors. Inside, two sailors from the *Dunkirk* sat eating.

"What's the nosh like, mate?" Spike drooled at the sight of the huge steaks that covered their plates, chips piled high on side plates.

"Choice mate, first class," the sailor replied in between mouthfuls of steak.

"Cheers, mate I think I'll have some of that."

A bored looking waiter made his way over to their table.

"Four blues, my good man," smiled Spike, "and four steak and chips. Hey, Lofty, stick some money into the old jukebox, might as well have us some music, any of you lot been to Rome?"

"Been to Naples," said Lofty with a wry grin, "don't ask me what it was like, me an' Gibbo got legless on Chianti."

"Typical matelot," Spike shook his head, "been all over the world but what have they seen, the nearest bar or knocking shop. Tomorrow we sail to Italy, how many of us will see the great Roman architectural achievements, the Colosseum or the Pantheon?"

"Bloody hell, Spike, didn't know yer was into that."

"Ain't mate, read it on the ship's notice board of places to visit. Can yer see Shiner and the Jocks clutching their cameras asking their way to the Pantheon?"

"Talk of the Devil," Alby looked up as Shiner walked in. "Hi yer, mate, didn't expect to see you."

Shiner pulled a face and sat down. "Scotch git," he growled. "All he was interested in was getting his bloody end away, felt like a spare dick at a wedding; he was all over that Velda like a rash."

"Now, now, Shiner you're jealous mate. Poor old Jock, got to keep the rust off it, ain't he? Ah, here comes my man." Spike rubbed his hands as the waiter hurried in carrying two plates of steak.

"I get other steaks," he beamed, "then I bring chips." Moments later, two more steaks appeared with plates of chips.

Shiner eyed the steaks with relish. "Hey John," he addressed the waiter, "chuck another steak on, mate."

The waiter shook his head. "You catch last boat back to ship?"

"Yeah, so what?"

"No time to cook steak, must be cooked slowly, soon your boat she come, no time."

"For fucks sake, I'm bloody famished. Do yer know what? I couldn't get a bunk up in a brothel tonight with a pocket full of money."

"What's yer steak like, Alby?" Lofty tried hard not to grin.

"Delicious, mate, dunno if I'll be able to manage it all."

"You two, very funny! Hey, John, five blues and bring us a plate, knife and fork, me mates are going to contribute a bit of steak, a few chips, and Shiner has his supper."

Spike pushed his plate away and looked at his watch. "Time to go lads, boat will be here in a couple of minutes."

Out of a cloudless sky the full moon cast its silvery light on the glass like sea as the sailors waited for *Jutland's* boat. The faint throb of the liberty boat's engine announced it was on its way shore-ward. Moments later it was alongside the jetty.

Jeff cut the engine as the bow-man tied up the boat.

"On yer get, lads, good run ashore?"

"Bloody dead, mate," complained Shiner. "I ain't even got a gibber on, had about six blues."

"Just as well," Jeff said. "That First Lieutenant has been poncing about the gang-way half the night. He's had a good look at the cards to see who went ashore. Reckon he's waiting to see if you come back pissed, Shiner."

"Well the fat bastard's gonna be sadly disappointed, ain't he?"

"Right, bow-man cast-off."

Jeff started the engine, and rapidly they pulled away from the jetty. Effortlessly, the liberty boat's sharp bows cleaved through the calm sea. Moments later they were alongside the gangway.

Petty Officer Stannard stood at the top of the gangway, to one side of him the First Lieutenant stared intently down the gangway.

Spike put his hand on Shiner's shoulder. "Yer old mates up there, Shiner."

"Yeah, seen him."

"Don't forget to salute as you go on board."

Shiner smartly snapped to attention at the top of the gangway, he took his watch card from the Petty Officer. "Thank you, Petty Officer." He turned to face the First

Lieutenant. "Good evening, Sir, a nice night, is it not?" His voice was heavy with sarcasm.

For a moment the officer's face contorted in anger. His eyes narrowed to a slit as he stared at the grinning sailor, he turned and walked away.

"Now look what yer done, yer gone and upset him," said Alby with a smile.

Petty Officer Stannard leaned over the gangway.

"Motor boat crew, tie up and secure. You will not be required any more tonight, and you four jokers go get your heads down and no noise."

Able-seaman Jackson stretched and yawned, it had been a long night on the gangway. As quartermaster he had the responsibility of ensuring no unauthorised person boarded the warship. He was assisted by a bos'n's mate.

Jacko glanced at the gangway clock. "Stormy," he called to his bo's'n's mate. "Better call the hands and pipe away the motorboat's crew."

"Will do, mate, then I'll make us a couple of mugs of rosy lee."

"Cheers, Stormy."

Petty Officer Stannard adjusted his tie as he strode towards the gangway.

"Good morning, how's it going, Quartermaster?"

"Just fine, Petty Officer."

"How many still ashore?"

"Only six."

"Well, I'm off forward to make sure the hands are up. If the First Lieutenant comes poking about I will be in my mess, send the bos'n's mate to let me know."

"Aye aye, Petty Officer."

Jacko sipped his tea as he watched Jeff bring the motorboat alongside the gangway.

"Look at Jock," grinned Stormy. "Cor, don't he look

rough?"

"Yeah," agreed Jacko. "The dirty bleeder has had an all night in."

Jock somehow managed to stumble up to the top of the gangway more asleep than awake. Automatically he stuck his hand out for his card.

"Here yer are, Jock; hey, Stormy look at his eyes; they're like piss holes in the snow."

"Why don't yea go shag yersel?" yawned Jock.

"Only trying to help, mate. One day yer dicks gonna drop off then you'll have to transfer to the wrens."

Jock ignored the comment; he yawned again and made his way forward.

"Better pipe cooks to the galley." Jacko switched on the Tannoy. "Be glad when our watch is over, Stormy, can't wait to get me head down."

"Look up, Jacko, here comes the First Lieutenant."

"Bloody hell, just what we need, nip down and warn Petty Officer Stannard."

"Quartermaster?"

"Yes, Sir."

"Have all the ratings reported back from shore leave?"

"Yes, Sir, all on board."

"Where is the duty Petty Officer?" he demanded with a superior air.

"Gone forward, Sir, to check the hands are up."

"They damn well should be. Call the hands went twenty minutes ago," he snorted. "Out of my way, Quartermaster, I need to address the Ship's Company."

Jacko moved aside as the First Lieutenant pushed past him and switched on the Tannoy.

"Attention, attention, this is the First Lieutenant speaking, the ship will proceed to sea at 08:30 hours, special sea-duty men will close up at 08:15. Duty watch will be required at 08:00 hours to hoist motor cutter and to bring the gangway inboard. The ship will arrive at Civitavecchia tomorrow morning at 09:00 hours. The pay Office will be open between 16:00 hours till 18:00 hours to exchange Maltese pounds into lira; any rating requiring advance payment of wages will be paid in Lira, that is all."

Pincher stuffed the last of his bacon sandwich in his mouth, washing it down with a gulp of tea.

"Did yer hear that, Shiner? Yer can get a sub."

"Yeah, mate, good ain't it; reckon it could be a good run."

"Means you could miss going ashore in Toulon then," Jeff said.

"How'd yer make that out?" demanded Shiner.

"Come on, mate, your idea of a good run is to get pissed up and end up in a brawl; those eye'tie police will have you in the brig and chuck away the key."

"Yer make me sound like a real desperado," complained Shiner. "Tell yer what, mate, why don't we all go ashore together and yer can take me under yer wing?"

"Like the time in that London club, you mean?" Jeff's eyes twinkled.

"You go fuck yerself," Shiner growled. "You know I was pissed."

"Yeah I know."

"Get on with it," Spike eagerly looked at Jeff. "What happened?"

Shiner pulled a face. "Yer might as well tell 'em, yer seem to have got their attention. Anyhow, I don't give a frig."

"Well," Jeff began. "We had this run up the smoke, both of us half pissed and near out of loot. We spotted a nightclub up this side street. The place was full of benders. Anyhow, we made our way to the bar followed by an

106

entourage of limp hands. "Hello sailors can I buy you a drink", they chorused. As soon as we drunk one drink, two more appeared on the counter. Shiner was throwing them down his neck as hard as they came. After a while this tall blond bit came over, she draped herself over Shiner. "You want to come home with me sailor?" she purred.

"Thought you'd never ask," Shiner said, as his hand slipped down for a quick crotch hold.

"You dirty bleeder." Alby looked at Shiner.

"I was pissed," Shiner said. "Out of my head."

"Have you two finished, shall I go on?"

"Well, a look of horror appeared on Shiner's face, his hand shot out from under the blond bits skirt, "she's got a friggen' toggle and two", he blurted out."

The mess erupted in laughter.

"Go on yer fuckers have a good laugh, it wasn't funny at the time." Shiner managed a wry grin. "Anyhow, toggle and two didn't think it very funny after I drew him one off. I ain't no turd burglar."

More laughter was interrupted by the Tannoy.

"Duty watch to muster amidships. Hoist motor cutter."

Pincher grinned widely and shook his head.

"Come on, lads, let's get the mess cleared up, duty watch away you go."

Captain Warrington peered into the chart room as he made his way up to the bridge.

"Good morning, Lieutenant Norton," he addressed the navigating officer.

"Good morning, Sir."

"How is the weather forecast, Lieutenant?"

"Very good, Sir, it should be a pleasant passage."

"Thank you, Lieutenant, if you need me I will be on

the bridge."

Captain Warrington surveyed the empty bridge; soon it would be transformed into a hive of activity. He would be glad when once again they would be at sea. He felt a sudden surge of pride at the way the ship and crew had performed. It was a good and efficient ship with an excellent crew, and his one concern was the effect the First Lieutenant was having on the morale of the lower deck ratings. He had learned with dismay of the punishments awarded for the most trivial offences, he knew full well Rome, with its many clubs, cheap wine and bright lights, would result in drunkenness and the subsequent brawling. The high spirits of the sailors and the temperament of the Italian males would be a volatile mix. He must have a word with the First Lieutenant on the way he administered discipline. "Damn the man", he thought angrily.

"Special sea-duty men to close up. Hands to stations for leaving harbour. Cooks of mess to stand fast."

Lieutenant Anderson saluted as he came on the bridge.

"Good morning, Sir, Duty Officer of the watch reporting, Sir."

"Very good, Lieutenant Anderson, are you looking forward to Rome?"

"Yes, Sir, very much so, will be nice to take in the sights."

"Bridge, this is wheel-house, coxswain closed up, telegraph men closed up."

Captain Warrington bent over the voice pipe.

"Very well, coxswain, thank you."

Lieutenant Anderson reached over to answer the bridge telephone.

"Sir, the fo'c's'le closed up and ready to slip."

"Very well, tell the fo'c's'le to let go."

"Aye aye, Sir."

"Wheel-house, this is bridge, both engines slow ahead."

Once again the bridge phone wailed.

"Sir, from the First Lieutenant, all secure ready for sea."

"Very well, thank you, could you ask the First Lieutenant to report to me in my cabin in 15 minutes."

"Aye aye, Sir."

Captain Warrington sat down. He stared at the half written letter on his desk to his wife, 'Must get that finished before we get to Italy,' he muttered to himself. Further thoughts were rudely interrupted by a sharp knock on the cabin door.

"Come in."

"You wanted to see me, Sir?" The First Lieutenant removed his hat as he entered.

"Yes, Number One, just a little chat, please take a seat. Now this is entirely off the record, there seems to be a great deal of animosity towards you from the lower deck."

"But, Sir, officers are never popular with the ratings."

"Please, Number One, let me finish. I do take on board what you say, but I cannot fail to notice, Lieutenant Anderson, Allen and Norton seem to have a good rapport with the ratings. The point I must make is about attitude."

"Attitude, Sir, I don't understand."

"No, Number One, it's painfully obvious you don't, which brings me to my other concern, that is, punishment. The amount awarded for minor offences I feel has been to excess."

"But, Sir, we must have discipline."

"Yes, yes, Number One, I am quite aware of that, but tempered with a little commonsense," exploded Captain Warrington.

"I examined the punishment book. How can you possibly justify awarding Able-seamen Wilson and Smith five days 10A for being two minutes late on board, damn it man a sharp rebuke would have been appropriate."

"Yes, Sir," a subdued First Lieutenant mumbled.

Peanuts strained to hear through the cabin door, the signal from *Trafalgar* in his hand forgotten.

"That will be all, Number One." Curtly the captain dismissed the officer.

Peanuts jumped aside as the First Lieutenant opened the door and stormed out.

"Out of my way, Turner," he glared at the signalman as he pushed past.

Peanuts stepped through the open door and saluted.

"Message just came through from *Trafalgar,* Sir."

"Thank you, signal-man."

Captain Warrington nodded as he read the message.

"No reply, thank you."

Peanuts hurried back to the signal office, he couldn't wait to spread the word that the First Lieutenant had just received a bollocking from the skipper.

By the time Jacko got the news it had been embroidered tenfold. He related the story as he had heard it to a jubilant seamen's mess.

"Yeah," Jacko said. "The old man gave him a right bollocking, told him to go easy on us poor sailors, he called him a jumped up turd."

"Where'd yer get this from?" asked Spike.

"Peanuts, he heard it all, and then the old man told Jenks-Powell to fuck off out of his sight."

"Nice one," beamed Shiner, "about time that ugly

bastard had a frig stuck in him."

The short passage to Civitavecchia passed quickly. Now slowly, the destroyer edged its way towards the jetty. Heaving lines snaked out from the destroyer to be caught by the Italian berthing party who heaved the heavy wire hawsers attached towards the bollards.

Petty Officer Wilson watched as the berthing party dropped the eyes of the hawsers over the bollard.

"Take a couple of turns on the capstan," he shouted. "Stand clear of the hawser, heave in slowly." The powerful capstan took up the slack. "Avast heaving, secure the hawser, well done, lads that's it. Able-seaman Lacy, give the bridge a ring, report all secure forward."

With its high pitched wail the bos'n's pipe screeched out from the Tannoy.

"Duty watch the first part of port. Duty watch to muster starboard side amidships. Erect awnings, out gangway. Leave will be granted from 12:00 hours until 23:59 hours."

Spike rubbed his hands. "That's what we wanted to hear. Rome here we come."

"Me old locker is full of Lira; I feel like a baron," laughed Shiner.

"You'd better enjoy the feeling, mate, it won't last, tonight you'll be legless and skint."

"Yeah, Lofty, after that disaster of a run ashore in Malta yer could well be right."

Crowds of sightseers gathered on the jetty, young women waved with enthusiasm and shouted greetings.

"Cor, look at that one in white, what a pair of lungs."

"Forget it, Alby, once yer get ashore mate they won't want anything to do with yer. Go get yourself a double bromide. Well, ladies, I ain't got time to stand here all day gawping at the crumpet. Got me white front to iron and me hat to blanco, then a quick shower and powder me bits."

"Hang on to the iron for me, Shiner."

"Can't Alby go and borrow Pincher's. Them National Servicemen will be poncing about on the mess iron all day. They ain't got a clue."

"Liberty men to muster. Muster port-side amidships. Duty Petty Officer and officer of watch muster at the gangway."

"Right you lot, cut the cackle and get fell in. And you, Wright, put that bloody fag out. Come on, come on form two ranks, do you want to go ashore or not? You're like a flock of bloody Wrens."

"Liberty men attention."

Petty Officer Wilson turned about and saluted Lieutenant Anderson.

"Liberty men mustered ready for your inspection, Sir."

"Very well, Petty Officer, thank you."

Lieutenant Anderson moved slowly along the ranks of sailors, briefly scrutinising them as he walked by, he nodded his approval.

"Carry on, Petty Officer."

"Aye aye, Sir."

"Liberty men stand at ease. Before you lot inflict yourselves on Rome a word of advice, go steady on the Chianti, or better still drink beer. Don't provoke the Italians remember they can't talk to you without waving their arms around like windmills. Lastly, do not miss the last train back from Rome. Remember your leave expires at 23:59 hours. Stay out of trouble."

Civitavecchia was a vibrant and busy town with its

port and tourist industry. The main street bustled with throngs of shoppers. Bars and cafes abounded on both sides of the street.

"Well, shall we get a quick drink?" Spike waved his hand towards the nearest bar.

Shiner was the first through the open door; a large Italian woman smiled a greeting.

"Buongiorno, signor."

"Three bottles of Chianti, mama." Shiner held up three fingers and made the shape of a bottle and eight glasses.

"Si si, signor!" The woman nodded and smiled broadly.

"Inglese, si?"

"Yeah, mama, English, how mucha lira you wanta?"

Shiner pulled out a wad of notes; she deftly plucked two, one thousand lira notes from his wad.

"Grazie, grazie," she said.

Spike poured himself a glass of Chianti.

"What's it like, Alby?"

"It's bloody terrible, mate, like drinking friggin' vinegar."

"Trouble with you peasants is, yer ain't got a delicate palate like me."

Shiner drank his Chianti down with one gulp. "Chianti is what yer might call an acquired taste, the more yer have the better it tastes, anyhow just over a quid for three bottles, what yer want, champagne?"

"Come on then, drink up." Pincher rose from his chair. "Gotta find out where this train station is; hey Shiner, you seem to have a flair with the lingo, ask mama."

"Just one of me many talents." Shiner waved an arm towards mama. "Hey mama."

"Si, signor?"

"Choo choo, chuff chuff." Much to the amusement of the other sailors Shiner moved around the bar imitating a train, the choo choos were punctuated frequently with the word, Rome.

"Steady on, Shiner, yer getting up a rum head of steam."

"Always the bloody comedian ain't yer, Spike?"

"Dunno about that, mate, but yer made her laugh." He gestured towards mama who was leaning against the bar convulsed with spasms of laughter, controlling herself she grinned her way towards the bar entrance beckoning Shiner as she did so.

"Signor, treno treno, Roma Roma." She indicated up the street, "No choo choo," she smiled. "Electrico." She pointed up at the electric light.

"Grazie, mama."

Shiner playfully patted her ample rump.

"Signor …" She waved a chubby finger at Shiner as she reproached the big sailor with good humour.

"Right you ladies, are you ready?"

The sailors blinked in the bright sunshine after the comparative gloom of the bar.

Groups of white uniformed sailors mingled with the many shoppers; others drinking alfresco, seated at tables outside the many cafes. One such group from *Trafalgar,* their table overflowing with empty wine bottles. As they passed, a booming voice rang out. "What ho, Shiner, yer old bastard, hi yer, Jeff."

A short, stocky, bearded sailor stood up and strolled over grinning broadly. The three sailors embraced warmly slapping each other on the back.

"Long time no see, Dinke, how yer been, mate?"

"Fine, mate, bit pissed off about being shipped to

Trafalgar. I was on leave just got back from the Far East. You lot off to Rome?"

"Yeah, we're now off to catch a train, you coming?"

"Better stick with the lads," Dinke replied. "Tell yer what, why don't you and Jeff come on board tomorrow night, have a few beers and catch up on old times?"

"Sounds good," Jeff nodded. "Anyhow, the chances are we could stagger into you in Rome."

'Treno per Roma' the large sign read. An arrow indicated left.

Inside the station, bright sunshine streamed through the glass roof.

Long queues waited patiently as they slowly shuffled their way forward towards the ticket kiosks.

Alby lifted his arms in despair. "Bloody hell," he moaned, "be here all day."

"Hang about," Spike pointed towards the front of the queue. "Ain't that Peanuts?"

"Yer know, Spike, you're right, little ole bunting tosser, he can get our tickets."

"Hello, Peanuts, me ole mate."

Peanuts looked at Shiner with suspicion. "What yer want? You ain't normally this friendly."

"Just a favour, mate, can yer get our tickets to Rome?"

"Say pretty please, then."

Peanuts realised as he spoke it would have been better unsaid.

"What you say? Yer cheeky little fucker, yer heading for a knuckle sarnie."

"Stow it, Shiner, Peanuts is only winding you up. Let's be having yer money lads, two thousand each. Pincher held his hand out to Shiner who gave a wry grin as he handed his money over; he had no wish for a confrontation with Pincher.

Tickets obtained, the sailors followed the Roma signs to the platform. Waiting, a train with its doors open, carriages were full with standing room only in gangways; doors slammed shut, slowly the train moved from the platform, rapidly gathering speed. Small farms, woodland and villages flashed past as they sped through the rural Italian countryside.

Pincher lit a cigarette. "Anyone want a fag?"

"Cheers." Spike reached over and took the offered cigarette. "What we gonna do then," he said. "Be in Rome soon, how about we have a kitty?"

"Yeah, who's gonna be banker?"

"Reckon Pincher's the man. How about it Pincher?"

"All right by me, three thousand each should be enough for a start, just a thousand from you Shiner as you bought the first round."

Alby handed Pincher his money. "How about we have a look round before we go on the booze?"

Jeff nodded in agreement.

"Bloody big girl's blouse," muttered Shiner. "Yer'll have me visiting the Pope next."

Rural landscape gave way to the sprawling suburbs of Rome. The train decreased speed as it approached the station.

Carriage doors opened, passengers poured out into the narrow gangway pushing and jostling for position near the exit doors.

"Dae yer nae mind?" Jock Gordon snarled at the short swarthy Italian who roughly barged into him.

"Inglese." The Italian spat the word out with contempt.

"Leave it, Jock," Pincher said firmly. "Let it be,

mate."

Jock glared intently at the Italian for a moment, then with a shrug of his shoulders turned away.

Outside the station, the wide roads were full of traffic, cars, buses and taxis drove at hectic speed, horns honking loudly.

With a screech of brakes a taxi came to a halt beside them, a smiling driver leaned out of his window.

"Hey Inglese, you want taxi? Very nice club, pretty girls, jig a jig."

"Now that sounds more like it, better than looking at heaps of rubble."

Pincher waved the taxi away. "Don't worry, Shiner, yer got plenty of time to make an idiot of yerself."

"Charming," grinned the big sailor.

Peanuts pointed. "It's right here." The sign said Colosseum one kilometre.

"Fuck you lot," moaned Shiner. "If I wanted to do all this tramping about I would have joined the friggin' army. Let's stop at the next bar and get a drink." Shiner briskly strode ahead of the group without a backward glance.

"So now we know," Pincher said.

"Well, mate, yer ain't gonna keep Shiner out of a bar for very long, are yer?"

"Yeah I know, Alby but it's a bit early to get pissed up."

Shiner pushed open the bar door and strode in, close behind the two Jocks.

"What we gonna do, go for a drink or leave 'em to it?"

Alby waved his hand in resignation. "We came ashore together; might as well stick together."

Pincher shook his head as he made his way to the bar. He shot a glance at Shiner. "Yer happy now; whadda want?"

"Chianti, mate, don't be like that Pincher. All I want is a drink."

"Fair enough, just the one, what's it to be lads, Chianti all round?"

"Not for me, mate." Alby pulled a face. "I'll have a beer."

"So will I," Peanuts added.

Two elderly Italian men sat playing dominoes; one of them briefly glanced up as the sailors sat down. A young woman hurried through the open door behind the bar; long dark hair cascaded over her shoulders, and a low cut blouse vainly tried to cover her bouncing bosom. "Si signor."

"Er …" stammered Pincher as he with difficulty averted his gaze. "Three bottles of Chianti and two bottles of beer."

"Si signor, you sit I bring," she smiled.

"Cor, I reckon I could give that one," remarked Pincher as he sat down.

"Dear o dear, you lot, a flash of tit an you've all got yer hands in yer pockets playing with yer brains."

"Don't reckon she's got a toggle and two, Shiner?"

"You little runt," snarled Shiner. "Don't push yer luck." It was an episode that caused the big sailor acute embarrassment.

With a pronounced wiggle of her hips the young woman flounced her way over to the seated sailors. Her short skirt exposed ample thigh, slowly she leaned over the table and placed the tray of drinks upon it. Her breasts hung down, the top button of her blouse strained to contain them.

Shiner reached for a bottle and poured himself a glass of Chianti. "You lot can put yer eyes back now, yer got no chance of getting yer leg over with that, but if you Casanovas fancy yer chances we could have another round."

"Yer right, mate," Alby agreed. "She's just a dick teaser, let's drink up, have a gander at the Colosseum, get some nosh and hit the bars."

Shiner now walked on with a purpose. His mission was to reach the Colosseum as fast as possible. Ten minutes later the road veered to the left, before them the Colosseum.

"Bloody hell." Lofty stood and stared. "Rum building ain't it?"

They walked across the neat lawns to the base of the building, which towered above them.

"Must be two hundred feet high!" Pincher shielded his eyes from the sun as he looked upward.

"Must admit, it is impressive."

A large information board proclaimed the facts relating to the Colosseum in several languages. Taking ten years to build, the structure was the largest of its kind in the ancient world. It could seat up to 48,000 spectators who watched gladiators fight to the death, also chariot racing.

"Well, well if the devil could cast his net now."

Lieutenant Anderson's soft spoken voice made them turn towards the speaker; he was accompanied by Lieutenant Norton.

"Good afternoon, Sir." Pincher saluted the officers.

"Bit of a surprise to see you chaps here, thought you would have been in the Piazza Novona area."

"Not us, Sir, us lads we like a bit of culture."

Shiner grinned unconvincingly.

"Just as a matter of interest, what is this Piazza Novona?"

"Well, Wright, I don't think it would interest you as you're into culture; it's just a concentration of bars, clubs and restaurants."

"That'll do me, Sir," Shiner beamed. "I ain't really into this culture lark, more of a connoisseur of the local plonk. How far is this Piazza Novona?"

"Not far, just follow this road and it's first on the left, one word of caution there was a rumpus going on when we came through. Seems some of the *Dunkirk* crew had a run in with the local lads. It would be advisable to hang on a while before you arrive on the scene."

"Police everywhere," added Lieutenant Norton. "The last thing you chaps want is to get into trouble, the First Lieutenant is duty officer tonight."

Spike looked long at the officer, he at last spoke. "How the fuck did a bastard like him ever become an officer?"

Lieutenant Norton was taken aback by Spike's vehement tone. "I don't think I heard that, Milligan, and you well know it's not appropriate for me to comment on a fellow officer regardless of any personal feelings I may have."

Lieutenant Anderson felt uncomfortable. He felt a great camaraderie with the high spirited sailors. He had always treated them with respect and he knew in turn they respected him. His position as an officer compelled him to stay aloof from them, but his immediate thoughts was to extract himself and his fellow officer from a situation that could well lead to a breach of naval discipline.

"Well chaps, Lieutenant Norton and I are away, enjoy your run ashore."

Relief showed on Pincher's face as he saluted the officer. "Thank you, Sir, will do."

Returning the salute the two officers turned and

walked away.

Pincher looked at Spike, "You're a lucky fucker, mate, any other officers would've had yer on a charge."

Shiner put an arm round Spike. "Good on yer, Spike let's get a drink."

Police stood around in pairs as they entered the Piazza Novona. Music blared from the bars, Italian males stood around in groups talking excitedly arms flailing.

"Into the valley of death rode the six hundred."

"Shut up, Peanuts; don't be so bloody stupid," snapped Jeff.

Pincher gestured towards the nearest bar. "How about this one, it's as good as any."

As they walked across the road towards the bar, the nearest group of Italians moved towards them.

"Watch them fuckers," snarled Shiner as he pushed his way to the front. "Looks like the eye-tie spaghetti boys have come to play with Uncle Shiner."

The pace of the advancing Italians slowed as the sailors stood and waited for them. Confidence in numbers turned to apprehension, the sight of Shiner grinning and beckoning them on did nothing for their morale. Stopping a few feet away they shouted obscenities. One Italian, braver than the rest, darted forward. Jock Heron aimed a vicious kick at him. The blow caught him in the groin. He collapsed, moaning loudly.

"Nice footwork, Jock, yer should've been a footballer."

"Dunno about that, mate," Lofty said. "Whoever heard of a footballer kicking two balls at once. Hope ole matey wasn't on a promise tonight."

"His hard luck," grinned Alby. "But Jock gave his wedding tackle a rare rattle."

More Italians moved towards them, the police stood

and watched with complete indifference.

Pincher quickly assessed the situation. Already outnumbered and with the arrival of many more Italians he decided a tactical retreat to the nearest bar was called for.

"Right, lads, in the bar," he shouted. "The bastards have got reinforcements."

"Reckon we should stand and fight." Shiner glared at the Italians. "They ain't got the balls to take us on."

With reluctance the big sailor, still taunting the Italians, backed into the bar. A nervous barman picked with diligence at his nose. Six sailors from *Dunkirk* sat drinking. They waved a greeting.

"Hi ya, mates, glad to see yer." A seated sailor grinned. He was short and stocky and looked the worse for drink, under one eye an ugly bruise.

"What the fuck's going on?" Alby snorted. "Them friggin' eye-ties just had a go at us."

"We had a sort out with them earlier, mate, we gave them a right touse up. Thought the ruck was over when this friggin' mob of them came at us. We dived in here, the rest of the lads legged it to the Trevi Fountains."

Alby shrugged his shoulders. "Ain't over yet, mate, we still have a secret weapon."

Alby nodded towards Shiner who in between large gulps of Chianti pranced about shadow boxing.

"Big bastard ,ain't he?"

"Yeah," agreed Alby. "But half-pissed, him and the two Jocks will be a handful for them friggin' eye-ties."

"Did fancy something to eat," moaned Jeff.

"We'll get something," Spike answered.

"Not with bogy-man over there picking his hooter, look at him having a right root around. Hey yer dirty fucker," shouted Jeff. "Leave yer bugle alone."

"Si, signor," he replied and resumed picking.

"Well, shall we have another round and decide what our next move is?"

"Yeah, good idea," said Shiner. "One thing's certain, I ain't staying here all night, eye-ties or not. Peanuts have a gander outside, see what the score is?"

Peanuts tentatively opened the door; he closed it quickly and pulled a face. "They're still there, mate, most over the other side of road, three or four just outside the door."

Pincher downed his drink. "We stay together, don't run, we walk slowly down the road keep close to the buildings that way they can only come at us from the front, drink up lads."

Shiner gave Pincher an evil grin.

"I'll go first, mate; catch them bastards near the door."

Shiner burst through the door like a raging bull, he was upon the Italians in an instant, and they stood transfixed. A sickening thud as he head-butted the nearest one who collapsed. Snarling he turned and lashed out at another, his big fist smashed into a surprised face; he staggered a few tottering paces and fell. The remaining two Italians stunned by the vicious attack fled.

Slowly they edged their way along the street towards the Trevi Fountains. Sullen crowds of Italians kept abreast of them on the opposite side of the road. With screams of rage they launched themselves across the road as white uniformed sailors poured out from adjacent bars to help their shipmates.

"Stay close together, lads." Pincher screamed as they were engulfed by the furious Italians.

Help came swiftly as sailors from *Dunkirk* and *Trafalgar* hurled themselves into the fray. The Italians reeled under the onslaught. The fighting was short and brutal. They had little stomach for the street brawling which the sailors excelled at, and they broke away and fled leaving several of their number lying in the street.

A burly bearded sailor shouted, "Three cheers for the fighting 7th Destroyer Squadron, hip hip horray."

Loud cheers rang out. The name was to stick, and they would become known as the 'Fighting Seventh.'

Shiner grinned broadly as he raised his hand in triumph, his uniform dishevelled, with blood running down his face from a cut over his eye.

Spike sat on the pavement holding his head, his white uniform stained with blood.

Pincher gently placed a hand on his shoulder. "Yer all right, mate?"

Spike nodded, "Bit groggy, didn't see that bastard until he whacked me with a lump of wood."

"Hold still." Pincher carefully parted his blood soaked hair. "Got a nasty gash, mate, get yer cleaned up soon, sure yer feel all right?"

"Yeah, gis a hand up."

Spike somewhat unsteady on his feet grimaced in pain, he managed a wry grin.

Now at the Trevi Fountain the sailors washed and cleaned up as best they could. Most had minor cuts and bruises.

Darkness was upon them, the bright lights of the bars beckoned them, and soon the serious business of drinking would begin. The night was to pass with no further problems.

With just a short time before the last train to Civitavecchia, sailors milled around outside the bars, many drunk, trying in vain to get their bearings.

The spectacular fountains shot streams of water high in the air, spotlights made the falling water shimmer and shine like jewels. A drenched sailor staggered through the fountain waist high in water, drinking from a bottle of wine.

Jeff looked at his watch. "Only twenty minutes before the train leaves, are we all here?"

"Yeah, bar for Shiner, he's getting a last drink."

"Go get him Alby, while I grab a couple of taxis."

Pincher stood impatiently by the taxi as the big sailor hurried from the bar.

"Come on Shiner, for fucks sake move yerself."

"Keep yer hair on, mate, we got bags of time."

Shiner eased his bulk into the back seat. "Shove up Peanuts and you Spike, I ain't got no room."

On reflection, Pincher thought to himself, it hadn't been a bad run ashore. Plenty to drink and eat, although merry none of them were drunk. True, they looked a bit worse for wear, a fact that the First Lieutenant wouldn't fail to notice.

Civitavecchia station was deserted. Minutes later the platform was alive with sailors, many drunk. Italian police stood near the station exit watching.

"Well here we are, let's get back, could be a right ole ruck here soon."

Shiner rubbed his hands. "Yer could well be right, Pincher; let's stay and see how it goes."

"Ain't yer had enough for one night? Come on, let's go."

"Good night officers," Shiner said sarcastically as he passed the policemen.

Outside the station more police were arriving in vans.

"Bastards," muttered Shiner. "They're looking for trouble."

"Yeah, you're right," agreed Lofty. "But they're gonna have their hands full with that lot."

"Which way, Peanuts?"

"Straight down turn right and the jetty is at the end of the road."

Slowly they walked towards the jetty. Police vans sped past, sirens blaring, lights flashing.

Shiner kicked at a can in frustration. "We should be there with our mates," he complained.

Jutland was bathed in light, two armed sailors stood at the bottom of her gangway.

Muffer grinned as they approached the gangway. "Don't think we should let you clowns on board, we have strict orders to keep undesirables away. Ain't we Dusty?" he addressed the other guard.

"Go shag yerself, Muffer," Jeff held two fingers up.

"What's gone on, mate?" asked Dusty. "Just had some fat, high-up copper on board, shouting and screaming at the First Lieutenant. You lot look like yer been in a ruck."

"What are you having down there, a mothers meeting?"

Petty Officer Wilson stood at the top of the gangway, with arms folded.

"Let's be having you ladies, come and get your cards."

"One moment, Petty Officer." The First Lieutenant appeared through a doorway, his face twitched like he had an affliction. "I would like a word with these ratings. I have just had a visit from the local Chief of Police," he spluttered. "And most embarrassing it was too, were you ratings involved in the brawling at the railway station?" he demanded.

"No Sir, not us, Sir." Shiner snapped to attention.

"You certainly look like you've been brawling, Wright."

"Yes Sir, it was earlier at the Piazza Novona."

Petty Officer Wilson turned away to hide the smile of

amusement on his face.

The First Lieutenant stared hard at Shiner. He trembled with rage.

"Dammit man," he shouted. "Can't any of you go ashore without causing trouble?"

"Wasn't our fault, Sir."

"Shut up, Wright, it's never your fault."

"It wasn't, Sir," Shiner persisted.

Desperately the First Lieutenant tried to think of a charge he could put them on, with extreme reluctance he dismissed such thoughts. The Captain's stinging remarks still irked him. With a last critical glare at the sailors, he turned to the Petty Officer.

"Carry on, Petty Officer."

"Aye aye, Sir."

Returning the Petty Officer's salute, he disappeared through the doorway.

Chapter 9

Back to Chatham

"Pass the teapot, Jock."

Stormy poured himself a strong mug of tea.

Breakfast was well under way; the talk centred on the previous night's run ashore.

Stormy was impatient to relate the confrontation between the police and the crews of the destroyers at the station.

"Come on then, get on with it Stormy and cut the bullshit out."

"All right, Shiner, gis a chance." Stormy was revelling in the attention. "It all started," he said, "when these eye-tie cops tried to drag a lad from the *Trafalgar* into a paddy wagon. The lads went berserk, charged the eye-ties, right ole punch-up it was."

"Don't sound much of a ruck to me," scoffed Shiner, "not like ours at Piazza Novona. Look around, Stormy, we're all walking wounded, poor old Spike near got his friggin' head knocked off."

The Tannoy clicked as it came on, followed by the shrill bos'n's pipe.

"Attention, Attention, the Captain will address the ship's company."

"Good morning, this is the Captain speaking. I have received a message from a rather irate Chief of Police, apparently a serious disturbance occurred at the railway station last night, and a number of police officers were injured. He claims the assault on his officers was unprovoked, further incidents have come to my notice, of brawling in Rome, this time involving locals, some of them were admitted to hospital. Much to my dismay we have been requested politely but firmly to terminate our visit. The whole squadron will proceed to sea at 13:00 hours. I have been in communication with the Commander in Chief Mediterranean and now await orders. That is all."

"That's bloody choice," moaned Nobby. "Me friggin' run ashore is up the creek."

"Just as well, Nobby, the natives ain't friendly, mate. Yer got one consolation."

"Yeah, what?" interrupted Nobby.

"Yer got money left, us paupers are broke, lend us a quid?"

"Bloody sauce, get stuffed."

"Hands to muster work ship, hands to muster work ship. Gunners party to muster 'B' gun-deck."

Pincher gulped his tea down. "Who's cooks of mess."

"Me an' Stormy," Nobby replied.

"Right you two, stand fast, good clean up lads, the rest of you girls, time for work."

"Put them fags out. Leading Seaman Martin, is everyone mustered?"

"Yes, Petty Officer, bar for Hook and Clarke, cooks of mess."

Petty Officer Wilson called them to attention as Lieutenant Anderson approached 'B' gun-deck. "Thank you, Petty Officer, stand the men at ease."

"Gunners party stand at ease."

"First I would like to congratulate you all, rather belatedly, I must apologise for that, for your excellent performance at Suez, well done. I will leave it to you, Petty Officer, to secure all guns for sea. Could you put the canvas covers on P1 and S1?"

"Yes, Sir, will do."

"Thank you, Petty Officer, any questions?"

"Are we going back to Malta, Sir?"

"Your guess, Jackson, is as good as mine; the Captain will make an announcement later."

With the departure of the officer, the Petty Officer detailed the men to various tasks.

"Pringle, director, have a tidy up, Wright, Bancock and Lacey P1 and S1, the rest of you on muzzle covers. Look busy and keep out of the way."

Lofty grunted as he dragged the heavy canvas cover from the locker. Between them they manhandled it over the mounting. "Somehow I don't reckon Malta is our next port of call."

"Just hope yer right, mate," Shiner grinned, "don't think I could put up with Jock mooning over that Velda."

"You three, get on with your work."

Looking up towards the bridge the three sailors saw the First Lieutenant glaring down at them.

"Did you hear me? I said get on with your work."

"We heard yer, you big ugly wanker," Shiner muttered.

"What was that, Wright, what did you say?" he demanded.

"Nothing, Sir, just said to Able-seaman Lacey, we'd better get on."

"That's right, Sir, that's what he said."

For a long minute the officer scowled down at them, his face contorted in anger, and then abruptly he was gone.

"Shiner, yer don't half push yer luck, mate. He heard yer."

"I don't give a frig, he's a wanker." Shiner pursed his lips and frowned. "Yer know what, before this trip's over

130

I'm gonna have that bastard?" The words were spoken as a matter of fact with no hint of bravado.

"Steady on, mate, yer poke him and it's two years in the stockade."

"Only if I get caught," said Shiner. "Come on, let's get to the mess for stand-easy."

Alby was first down the ladder into the mess. "Where's me tea? Who's cooks of mess?"

"Me," said Nobby. "Me an Stormy."

"Well, where's me rosy lee? Stand-easy will be over soon."

"Ain't our fault Alb, that friggin' First Lieutenant has been poncing about down here giving us hassle. Stormy was about to make the tea, he had us washing the portholes, the bastard was in a right strop."

"Ain't surprising, Shiner upset him, didn't yer mate?" Shiner clenched his big fist and shook it. "Like to do more than that to him."

"Here comes my man." Jeff grabbed a mug as Stormy clattered down the ladder.

"Sorry lads, bit late. Nobby tell yer about that clown of a First Lieutenant! Saw Peanuts just now, he said we're off to Cyprus."

"Yes don't want to take no notice of him, Stormy; the little fucker makes it up as he goes."

"Don't know, mate, he said he saw a signal."

The sound of the bos'n's pipe vibrated through the Tannoy.

"Attention, Attention, the Captain will address the ship's company."

"Thank you, this is the Captain speaking, a short while ago I received a signal from Commander in Chief Mediterranean. The squadron will not now be required to escort the French battleship back to her home port. That task has now been allotted to a squadron of D class destroyers. Consequently, with no role to fill, the Commander in Chief in his wisdom has decided that we should return to Chatham via Gibraltar where we take on fuel. Hands will go to dinner at 11:15, special sea-duty will close-up at 12:45. That is all. Thank you."

"Told yers, didn't I," said Spike. "That Peanuts is a lying little bastard."

"So now we know, it's home lads home." Pincher grinned.

"Don't make a lot of difference to me," said Shiner indifferently, "ain't got nowhere special to go. How about you, Jock?"

"Nae, gonna stay doon London."

"Where yer gonna stay?" Lofty asked.

"Seaman's Mission I reckon, mate, nowhere else to kip."

"Tell yer what, I flop out at me sisters, she lives in Croydon. She's got plenty of room, when we get to Chatham I'll give her a bell, she might put you two up. What about the other Jock, is he still writing to that bit in Eastbourne?"

"Yeah he's at it now, hey scribes, yer gonna miss the last post."

"Awa an' frig yersels." He continued writing without looking up.

"Out pipes, out pipes.

"Hands to carry on work.

"Standby to take down awnings.

"Mail will leave for shore in 15 minutes."

"Petty Officer Wilson spoke from the top of the ladder. "Make sure you lash the covers secure lads, bit of a blow coming according to Lieutenant Norton, force 8. When the other gun cover is on get out of the way in 'B' gun turret, or else Petty Officer Stannard will rope you in for taking down awnings."

"Will do, Petty Officer."

Just aft of them the funnel shuddered as the boilers flashed up. White whiffs of smoke gently spiralled upwards with intermittent belches of angry-looking black smoke.

"Won't be long now, mates," said Alby looking up at the funnel. "Hope it don't blow up too rough."

"Too right," nodded Shiner. "That Bay of Biscay can be a right bleeder, came through it once on the *Solebay* with the *Eagle*, yer know what? That friggin' great aircraft carrier kept disappearing in the troughs of waves, unbelievable."

"Cooks to the galley, cooks to the galley."

"Up spirits, leading hands of mess to collect rum."

"Ah that's more like it." Shiner smacked his lips in anticipation. "Come on, could do with me tot."

Pincher glanced up as footsteps sounded on the stair of the mess. He measured the first tot out as Shiner entered the mess. "Don't waste no time, do yer?" He took sippers and handed Shiner his tot.

Shiner studied his tot for a brief moment. "Cheers," he said and gulped down half. "Cor, that's better," he sighed.

Within a short time, rum had been issued to those entitled. Dinner under way; conversation centred on home leave.

"What yer gonna do, Jock?" Spike addressed Jock Gordon. "Are yer off to Eastbourne, mate?"

"Course he is, the big tulip, half a dozen letters an' he's in love, ain't that right, Jock?"

"Awa ye go an get knotted, bloody Sassenach."

"Now now, Jock, don't be like that." Shiner grinned.

"Weren't your fault, mate, it's down to that stupid

stoker who wrote to that agony aunt. 'Lonely sailor needs pen friend.' The idiot had a sack full of mail. For gulpers anyone could have a pen friend."

"Hey, Shiner, yer remember when Dinke wrote to that agony aunt?"

"Yeah, stupid woman. Dinke wrote and said when my boyfriend kisses me good night I feel something hard in his pocket, is he a cosh boy? She only printed it in a magazine."

"Duty-watch the First of Port to muster, muster starboard side amidships hoist gangway."

"Bloody Tannoy, switch it off, ain't finished me dinner yet." Spike stood up, yer ready, Jeff, Alby?"

"Special sea-duty men to muster in 5 minutes.

"Hands to muster for leaving harbour in 10 minutes."

Captain Warrington leaned over the bridge wing watching the Shore Party waiting to cast off from the bollards.

"Good afternoon, Sir." Lieutenant Norton came to attention.

"Good afternoon, Lieutenant, I take it you have had conformation from *Trafalgar* of our course to Gibraltar?"

"Yes, Sir, due west through the Straits of Bonifacio, then a degree or so south of west on to Gibraltar, I have it marked on the charts Sir."

"Excellent, Lieutenant, what is the weather forecast?"

"That, Sir, is not too good. There is a deepening depression moving across from Spain into the western Med towards Algeria; if my calculations are correct we should be in that area tomorrow afternoon."

"What force winds can we expect?"

"Eight, perhaps nine as we proceed further west. The forecast for the Bay of Biscay for the next few days is rather ominous."

"Damned stretch of sea. Bloody awful," he exclaimed.

"Yes, Sir." Lieutenant Norton nodded in agreement. "Anyhow, Lieutenant, how did your shore leave go?"

"Very well Sir, Lieutenant Anderson and I did the tourist round. It was most enjoyable."

"Good, I understand the First Lieutenant did have plans to go ashore this afternoon, I hear he's a little vexed."

"Yes Sir, I would put it a little stronger than that."

"No doubt, Lieutenant, no doubt," his eyes twinkled in amusement, "as they say, the best laid plans."

"Sir, *Trafalgar* has slipped, she's under way."

"Very good."

"Attention to port."

"Special sea-duty men close up."

Captain Warrington stood to attention and saluted to port as *Trafalgar* glided past, seconds later the bo's'n's pipe piped the carry on.

"Bridge, this is wheelhouse."

"Wheelhouse, Bridge."

"Quartermaster and telegraph men closed up, Sir."

"Very well, thank you, pipe hands to stations for leaving harbour."

"Aye aye, Sir."

Captain Warrington raised his megaphone. "Fo'c's'le, slacken off head rope and spring, Lieutenant Norton ring the quarterdeck, tell them to let go aft."

"Aye aye, Sir."

"Let go forward."

"Wheelhouse, port engine slow ahead, starboard engine slow astern."

"Very well, Sir."

Peanuts hurried onto the bridge. "Signal from *Trafalgar,* Sir."

"Thank you, signal-man, what is the message?" Captain Warrington carried on looking through his binoculars.

"From *Trafalgar*, squadron to proceed line ahead speed 18 knots, any reply, Sir?"

"No, just affirmative."

"Wheelhouse, both engines full ahead, revolutions one two zero, steer on *Trafalgar's* stern."

"Aye aye, Sir."

"Both engines full ahead, Sir, revolutions one two zero now on, Sir."

"Very well. Quartermaster, pipe special sea-duty men to fall out, duty sea-watch to muster."

Petty Officer Stannard called the afternoon duty sea-watch to attention.

"All mustered and correct, Sir."

The First Lieutenant cast a critical eye over the mustered men. "See that all boats are firmly lashed and detail men to relieve special sea-duty men."

"Aye aye, Sir."

"Wright, Jackson and Gordon, wheelhouse. O'Brady, Seaton, bridge look-outs. Warner, bridge messenger, the rest of you sea-boat crew."

"Right, Petty Officer, I am off to the bridge, Lieutenant Norton is Officer of the Watch."

Captain Warrington yawned loudly, stretched himself vigorously and got down from the captain's chair; he paced backwards and forwards across the bridge still stretching. "Didn't sleep at all well last night," he addressed Lieutenant Norton, "Had that damned Chief of Police shouting and waving his arms about till nearly one in the morning, bloody imbecile, quite incapable of holding a civilised conversation. Well, enough of my troubles, have you had lunch yet?"

"Yes, I had it early, Sir."

"Capital, I haven't had mine yet, I shall be in my cabin if there are any problems. Oh, there you are Number One; I am just about to have my lunch."

"Yes, Sir, upper-deck secured for sea."

"Thank you, Number One. Bridge messenger, could you chase up the chief steward and inform him I will take lunch in my sea-cabin."

"Yes, Sir." Ordinary Seaman O'Brady came to attention then hurried off.

Lieutenant Commander Jenks-Powell strutted around the bridge. He eyed the captain's chair; the temptation to seat himself in it was great. He contented himself with the thought that he was the senior officer on the bridge of the destroyer. He deeply resented the fact that he had been passed by for promotion on several occasions. The *Apollo* incident had been a severe setback and had left him with contempt for lower-deck ratings. His thoughts were interrupted by Lieutenant Norton.

"Would you like some coffee, Sir?"

"Yes, thank you, Lieutenant."

"Nice to be going home, Sir. Be back in Chatham in five days."

"Yes, Lieutenant, back to the rain."

Looking astern the First Lieutenant noticed the wake snaking from side to side. Angrily he shouted down the voice-pipe. "Helmsman, watch your course."

Shiner cursed as he swung the wheel to starboard.

"Following sea, Sir," he shouted up the voi "difficult to maintain straight course."

"Sounds like the First Lieutenant," said Jacko.

"Yeah, who else? Tell yer what Jacko, I've done me stint on the wheel mate, you can have a bash."

"Bridge, wheelhouse."

"Bridge."

"Permission for Able-seaman Jackson to take the wheel, Sir."

"Who is helmsman at the moment?"

"Able-seaman Wright, Sir."

"Permission denied, Wright; you could do with the practice."

"With respect, Sir, *Trafalgar* is also yawing."

"Permission denied, Wright."

Shiner stared at Jacko in disbelief. "He's a right bastard ain't he? Hey, Jock, keep yer eye open, the skips should be back soon."

"Aye, will do, mate."

Jock peered through the tiny window.

Lieutenant Norton had heard the helm's request to be relieved on the wheel. As Officer of the Watch he was technically in charge in the absence of the captain. The fact that the First Lieutenant out-ranked him prevented him from intervening. He knew full well he should have the courage of his convictions and countermand the order. He was spared the struggle with his conscience as the captain walked on to the bridge.

"Shiner, yer man is on tha bridge dae ye ken," Jock said, "He's nae far from the voice pipe."

Shiner grinned.

"Bridge, this is wheel-house."

"Wheel-house, bridge."

"Permission for Able-seaman Jackson to take the wheel, Sir."

"Yes, helmsman, carry on."

138

"Thank you, Sir." Shiner shouted loudly into the voice pipe.

Lieutenant Norton watched the First Lieutenant's reaction, quite clearly they both had heard Shiner's request. The officer rocked back and forth on his heels then turned and looked out to sea.

Time passed quickly as sea-watches came and went. The squadron had now been at sea eighteen hours. Morning watchmen sprawled and dozed in the port passage way. Pincher looked at his watch and yawned loudly. "Seven o'clock," he said. "Morning watch, hate it," moaned Pincher.

"Yeah, four in the morning; what a time to start," said Muffer. "Never mind, mate, another hour and we'll be off watch, time we had a cuppa, ain't it?"

Pincher nodded. "Hey, Nobby, make some tea, mate."

For the past two hours the destroyer had been running into steadily deteriorating weather. The gentle rolling had given way to the occasional heavy roll to port or starboard. These were now becoming more frequent.

Nobby lurched from side to side as he made his way along the passage way with the tea.

"Well done, Nobby, Muffer give the ole cups a rinse, mate."

Pincher lined the mugs up and poured, saying, "Who's gonna take the lads in the wheelhouse and lookouts their tea?"

"How about you?" He looked at Ordinary-seaman Marsh.

"I feel sick." The young sailor put his hands to his mouth.

"Don't yer throw up here, get yerself to the heads."

"Dusty, run the teas up, mate."

Moments later the young sailor dashed to the toilets, the sound of retching followed immediately.

"Call the hands, call the hands.

"Wakey, wakey rise and shine.

"Cooks of mess to the galley."

Whistling cheerfully, Petty Officer Wilson strode down the passage way. "Good morning, lads," he said amicably, "good morning, Leading-seaman Martin."

"Morning, Petty Officer."

"Best get the ladies up," he grinned, and then seconds later his voice was heard from the seamen's mess.

"Come on my lucky, lucky lads, let's be having you out of those wanking pits. Let's hear them feet hit the deck. Now who's the fucking comedian who put, do not disturb on the door, what do you lot think you are, newly weds?

"I shall return in five minutes, any ladies still turned in will have a honeymoon with the First Lieutenant."

The Petty Officer walked up the passage from the seamen's mess grinning broadly.

Alby stumbled half asleep to the washroom, towel draped round his neck; he was duty cook of mess with Shiner. Wash basin full of water, he liberally splashed water over his face.

"There yer are," Shiner said.

"Yeah, mate, take me towel back down the mess," Alby said drying his face. "I'll nip up the galley and get brekkers."

"Will do, mate, then I'll make the tea, you'd better tell cookie to put seven brekkers aside for the lads on morning-watch."

Pincher looked at his watch. "Won't be long now Dusty, another half hour and it'll be brekkers. How was Marsh when yer had a leak?"

"Couldn't see much of 'im mate, on his knees an' head down the pan."

"Poor bastard," said Pincher.

"He's all right, he's got company. Seaton and O'Brady are in the next two pans, them three look like they're praying to Mecca."

"Attention, attention. Hands are advised the starboard weather decks are out of bounds.

"Weather conditions are expected to deteriorate.

"Forenoon watch to muster in the port passageway, hands will not be required to work ship."

"Lovely job." Dusty rubbed his hands in glee. "Brekkers, then up with me wank sack and get me head down. Tell yer what, mate, if yer want a crap, you'd better get one quick before each pan has a resident Ordinary-seaman."

Captain Warrington pulled the brim of his hat down as sheets of spray swept the bridge. He watched as *Trafalgar* ahead of them wallowed in the heavy seas.

"Damned foul weather, Sir." Lieutenant Allen managed a wry grin.

"Yes, Lieutenant, supposed to get worse before it improves."

Huge white capped waves washed over the starboard weather-decks. The destroyer rolled violently to port, submerging her port decks.

Lieutenant Allen watched in awe at the seas coming in from the beam. Spin-drift blew, in long white streaks along the waves.

"Bit scary, is it not, Sir? Makes one feel very insignificant."

"Indeed it does, Lieutenant."

Below decks in the seamen's mess, hammocks swung in unison near touching the deck-head, lockers bolted together and secured to the deck groaned and creaked under the strain. Portholes normally above the waterline dipped under water, the sea bubbled and frothed around them in a kaleidoscope of colour, the immense sea pressure exerted externally forced droplets of sea water past the rubber seals which ran down the bulkheads of the mess. Cases stored on the topmost lockers littered the decks. Through all this movement and noise, sailors had slept soundly in their hammocks. Many of the younger sailors, unused to such adverse conditions, hovered within a few paces of the toilets; the passageway where the toilets were situated reeked of vomit causing even seasoned sailors to gag as they hurried past. Towards midday the weather had begun to moderate considerably.

Yesterday's storms were forgotten as the destroyers slowly edged their way into Gibraltar harbour. The rock towered an impressive 1,398 feet above the sea and sheltered a fine harbour enclosed by breakwaters. It had been a British colony since being captured in 1704. Gibraltar was of great strategic importance as it was the gateway to the Med.

Now refuelled, the destroyers, with *Trafalgar* in the lead, increased speed as they passed through the Straits of Gibraltar into the Atlantic Ocean, 150 miles due west they would turn northwards to follow the coast of Portugal on their starboard side, briefly flirting with the north western coast of Spain before crossing the Bay of Biscay. The next landfall would be France before turning east into the English Channel.

At twenty knots, the destroyers steamed through the

now calm seas. Excitement mounted among the younger sailors, their first ship now returning to their families with, no doubt, widely exaggerated tales of action. Amid all this exuberance, Shiner sat and brooded.

"What's up, me ole mate?"

"Just pissed off, Spike, look at that lot." Shiner gestured with his hand towards the young sailors. "Yer think that lot had won a war single handed."

"Don't be like that, Shiner, yer remember when we came back from Korea?"

"Too right I do, all eighteen months of it, froze me friggin' nuts off."

Spike nodded. "Don't seem like three years ago does it, mate? Anyhow, cheer up you'll be on leave soon."

"Cheer up, yer must be joking, that First Lieutenant had another go at me. 'Wright,' he says. 'This passageway is a disgrace, get it swept up.' 'Ain't on duty,' says I. 'That's an order,' he said. He's a big turd. Anyhow, got some dhobing to do."

Towel round his waist, Shiner, dhobi bucket in hand entered the washroom. The lights flickered off then on; once again they flickered this time they remained off. Shiner cursed. As he stood near the doorway, footsteps sounded in the darkened passageway. Shiner stared intently down the passageway trying to accustom his eyes to the dark.

"Damn, damn these bloody lights."

Shiner immediately recognised the hated First Lieutenant's voice. He froze. A rush of adrenalin swept over him as the footsteps came closer, and the vague figure of the officer appeared silhouetted in the darkness before him. Shiner's fist shot out like a piston. With a jarring force it connected.

With a groan of pain and surprise the officer

collapsed.

Shiner descended the steps to the mess two at a time, grabbing the hammock bars he swung into his hammock.

"Thought yer was going to wash yer skids, mate?" said Spike.

"Was, the lights went out, better get me head down. I've got the middle watch."

Jeff woke with a start from his doze. "What's the time Dusty?"

"Twenty to midnight."

"Better shake the middle watchmen."

Dusty gently shook Shiners hammock. "Come on, mate, time to get up."

"Fuck off Dusty, go get knotted."

"Yer awake then, give Alby, Seaton and O'Brady a tug."

"Okay, Dusty, who's officer of watch for the middle?"

"First Lieutenant, I think."

"Cheers, Dusty."

Petty Officer Wilson saluted Lieutenant Anderson.

"Middle watchmen closed up, Sir."

"Very well, Petty Officer."

"Excuse me, Sir, I thought the First Lieutenant was Officer of Watch?"

"He was, but he seems to have had a most unfortunate accident, apparently the lights failed in the port passageway. He remembers nothing until coming to, lying on the deck. The general conception among the officers is somebody hit him. Between you and me, Petty Officer, the Captain, although taking a very dim view of this assault, found it amusing. He was, of course, most sympathetic to the First Lieutenant."

"Of course, Sir." The Petty Officer grinned.

"On a much more serious note, Petty Officer, no

144

names no pack drill, there is a member of our gunner's party that is quite capable of committing an offence of this magnitude. That being so, if found out, he surely must realise the consequence of his action."

"Yes, Sir, I am sure he does."

Coming down the bridge ladder Petty Officer Wilson made his way across to the passageway where the middle-watch not closed up sat playing cards or reading.

"Listen up; I will leave Able-seaman Wright in charge till I come back. Able-seaman Wright, a word in your shell-like." The Petty Officer walked to the end of the passageway.

Shiner followed. "Yes, Petty Officer?"

"You can forget the 'Petty Officer', Shiner; this is man to man, some fucker whacked the First Lieutenant, was it you?"

"No, not me." Shiner eyed the Petty Officer grinning.

"No, I didn't think it would be. According to Lieutenant Anderson he didn't see anything, so you were bloody lucky, just keep your head down. When we get into Chatham tomorrow afternoon you will be on leave the next day, now frig off and read your book."

Clouds scurried across the sky threatening rain as *Jutland* turned into the River Medway. A brisk wind lifted and flapped the collars of the sailors as they lined the upper decks. Two tugs escorted them towards the jetty, now gently nudging them into position. Heaving lines snaked out towards the jetty to be grabbed by dockyard workers. The lines were hauled shore-wards with the berthing wires attached.

Captain Warrington spoke into the voice-pipe.

"Wheelhouse, stop both engines.

"Pipe duty-watch out gangway.

"Out fenders."

Petty Officer Wilson raised his hand. "Avast heaving."

Alby slammed the capstan into stop.

"Slack off on the capstan, secure head rope to the cleats. You two," he bellowed at Seaton and O'Brady. "get those bloody fenders over the side."

Shiner had an uneasy feeling someone was watching him. He paused as he wound the surplus head-rope back on the reel and glanced up.

Lieutenant Commander Jenks-Powell stood intently watching him. Shiner turned away, grinning. The First Lieutenant's eye was closed and swollen. Above the eye, a large strip of plaster.

Chapter 10

Home leave

"Attention, attention, all ratings who are entitled to extended leave will be in the first leave party. Names have been posted on the ships notice board, leave will commence at midday."

"Hey, Lofty, have yer rung yer sister yet, mate?"

"Yeah, only just got through."

"What she say?"

"Yeah, as long as we behave."

"Nice one, mate."

Ordinary seaman O'Brady stormed into the mess; angrily he hurled his hat on the deck. "Bollocks to it, second leave and only two weeks, most of you friggers have got eight and first leave."

"Calm down, yer saucy sprog, us friggers had just come back from abroad or gunnery school when we got shipped to *Jutland* with no leave."

"Attention, ratings due first leave will be paid in fifteen minutes, muster outside Paymasters Office."

"Where's me hat?" beamed Shiner. "Gonna be first in the queue, eight weeks loot, sixty four quid. Look out smoke here I come."

Pincher grinned broadly and shook his head as Shiner disappeared up the stairway. "Yer know, Spike, two weeks of boozing, a few bunk ups and that big lump will be back on board skint."

"Attention, attention, up spirits leading hands of mess

to collect rum. Two naval buses will leave from the jetty at 12:15 hours to transport ratings to Chatham station."

"That's service for yer. Who said the navy don't look after yer."

"You'll be after promotion next, Spike," quipped Lofty.

"Sorry to interrupt you two girls," Shiner said. "Have yer been to the sickbay Lofty, to pick up the French letters? You don't want to fancy a tremble and catch a nap hand."

"Yeah, picked us up eight packets each."

"Eight packets, you think I'm a friggin' rabbit? Ah good of Pincher here comes the rum."

"First leave party to muster on the jetty."

Pincher measured his own tot and drank it down. "Stormy, take over rum bos'n mate, only second leave to come."

"Course I will, be glad to see the back of you lot. Can't move for cases."

"Bye, lads," Pincher called as he moved to the stairway.

"Get yourselves sorted out into two ranks; have your station cards ready, Wright, Lacey which rank are you two in front or rear?" Chief Petty Officer Brown barked.

"Front chief," replied Alby.

"Well, take your time, as I collect each man's station card, he will then proceed to board the bus, enjoy your leave."

Impatiently the sailors waited as the bus filled.

"Come on, driver, stop reading that friggin' paper let's go."

Looking up from his paper, the driver impassively looked at Jeff and ignored him.

"Didn't yer hear, mate? he said 'let's go,' and yer can

stop at the Dog and Bone, I fancy a pint," said Shiner.

Putting his paper down, the driver nonchalantly lit a cigarette and blew the smoke towards Shiner. "Yeah, I heard. I don't take orders from you lot, and I ain't stopping at no pub."

"You're a real ray of sunshine, ain't you? How'd yer like a punch in the head, yer miserable bastard," snarled Shiner.

A tap on the windscreen startled the driver; he looked up to see Chief Petty Officer Brown beckon him away. With a final glare at Shiner, the driver started the bus and drove towards the barracks, and minutes later he was in the high street heading for the station. He passed the Dog and Bone.

"Didn't want a drink there anyway," grinned Shiner. "Get one at the Ferryman next to the station."

"Thank you, driver!" Shiner said sarcastically. "I shall recommend you to my friends." He stepped from the bus turned and said, "You big wanker."

Lofty lit a cigarette. "Jock, yer fancy a pint?"

"Aye, wud go doon a treat."

"Come on, Shiner; so long, lads, see yer later."

Lofty walked into the bar. It was empty. A smiling barman greeted them with enthusiasm. "Hi ya, lads, just got in, ain't yer?"

"Yesterday, mate."

"You're one of the first back. Bloody towns dead, even the tarts are looking for jobs. What's it to be,beer or scrumpy?"

"Scrumpy, can yer top them with lemonade?"

"Will do, six shillings, mate."

Lofty looked at his watch as they started their third pint. "Better make this our last one; don't want to arrive at me sister's pissed and late."

"Train leaves in ten minutes," said the barman as he walked over to collect their empty glasses. "Have a good leave."

"Cheers, mate."

One hour later the train came to a halt at London Bridge. The three sailors made their way to the exit. Walking to the nearest taxi, Lofty peered through the half open cab window. The cabbie was deeply engrossed in the racing page of his paper, he looked up. "'ello, me ole china, where'd yer want to go?"

"Croydon, mate, Lyndhurst Street."

"Op in, boys."

Slowly the taxi weaved its way through the chaos of central London traffic. Once clear of the city the traffic gradually thinned as they joined the main road to Croydon.

"Driver, just past the lights take a left, Lyndhurst is first on right, number nineteen," said Lofty.

"Here yer are, lads, that'll be three quid."

"Cheers, mate, come on you two, meet me sister."

Lofty rapped sharply on the door, it was opened by an attractive woman, in her early thirties.

"Hey sis, how are yer?"

"Robert!" she cried with obvious delight. "Come in, come in all of you, don't stand out there, come in."

"Sis, this is Shiner and that's Jock."

"Pleased to meet you both, call me Babs, would you like a wash? Robert will show you to your room; you don't mind sharing do you?"

"Course they don't, sis, come on, I'll show you to your room."

Jock tossed his hat on one of the single beds. "Yea ken Lofty, yir sister's a right bonnie lassie."

"Yeah, she is," agreed Shiner. "Is she married,

150

Lofty?"

"Yeah mate, her old man's a marine; he's probably still in the Med."

"Everything all right?" Babs called up the stairs.

"Fine, sis."

"Well, don't be too long; I have made some sandwiches and tea."

Shiner reached for his second sandwich. "These are great Babs, how much for our keep?"

Babs looked embarrassed. "I hadn't thought about payment," she stammered.

"Aye, yer canna hae us here fur nothing."

"Come on ,sis, we don't mind paying our way."

"Give me enough for your food; one pound ten shillings should be plenty."

"Reckon two quid a week each would be fair," said Shiner. "And still cheap."

Nights of drinking and brief encounters with the opposite sex were taking a heavy toll on their resources. Now two weeks into their leave, they sat drinking at the local pub.

"That's my leave fucked," moaned Shiner. "Seven quid left, seven friggin' quid."

"Ain't much better off," said Lofty. "Under nine, how are yer holding, Jock?"

"Dinna ask mate, doon twa five quid."

"Get another round in, Lofty, pass us that magazine, Jock."

Shiner looked despondent as he casually flicked through the pages. Suddenly he stopped. "Listen up, there's an advert in here; sounds good. 'Personnel required immediately to service 20mm and 40mm weapons, £300 per week, duration of employment 14 days.' What yer think?"

"Probably a right load of bollocks," Lofty said with a sceptical air.

"Dunno, mate, gonna give 'em a buzz. Got nothin' to lose."

Shiner walked over to the public telephone, soon he was engrossed in conversation, and after much nodding of his head he replaced the receiver.

"Seems to be above board, I spoke to a Mr Kumbo, apparently they need personnel to instruct and service anti-aircraft guns round this airport in Katanga."

"Katanga, where the fuck is that?" Lofty asked.

"Africa," grinned Shiner. "Africa, mate."

"Yer out of yer mind, Shiner."

"Soon see, Kumbo is sending a car for us, at least we can talk to him."

Lofty shook his head in disbelief. "Yer friggin' mad, Shiner."

A dapper black man dressed in a grey chauffeur's uniform smiled a greeting as he entered the bar. "Mr Wright, I have instructions from Mr Kumbo to convey you to his office."

"That's me, James; lead on."

"I don't believe this," muttered Lofty as he stood up.

A large black limousine awaited them. The chauffeur rushed forward to open doors for them.

Twenty minutes later the limousine purred to a halt outside a tall plush office building.

"Please if you would follow me." The chauffeur led them along an opulent white marbled corridor. He stopped, adjusted his tie, and gently knocked on the large oak door. A deep voice beckoned them enter.

"Sir, Mr Wright and his associates."

"Ah, gentlemen please do sit. Would you like a drink?"

"Yeah, wouldn't mind a whisky," said Shiner.

"Three whiskys." Mr Kumbo gestured with his hand, the chauffeur moved quickly to comply.

Behind his large desk Mr Kumbo drummed on the top with broad fingers. His large heavy spectacles gave his face an owl like appearance; he was grossly overweight but dressed immaculately.

"Now to business, gentlemen. I understand you are all conversant with the weapons we spoke about, Mr Wright?"

"Yeah that's right, we just finished a course on 'em," confirmed Shiner.

"Excellent, you seem to be just the men we desperately need."

"Awa yer go, we hae nae said we wud go."

Mr Kumbo looked at Jock then turned to Shiner.

"What he said, mate, is we ain't heard yer proposition yet."

"Of course, Mr Wright. I have been authorised by my government to engage suitable personnel, £300 per week for the two weeks you would be required. You would fly to Katanga and then on to Bolobo airport where a Colonel Kossanto is in command."

"When could we expect to be paid?" asked Lofty.

"On completion of your contract; Colonel Kossanto would pay you."

"Yer say it's only for two weeks?"

"That is correct."

"When would we leave?"

"Tomorrow afternoon from Heathrow at four o'clock. You would be required to dress in civilian attire; my driver would pick you up."

"We ain't got no civvies, only uniforms," Lofty said.

"You will be advanced £50 to buy clothes."

"Could we discuss this, Mr Kumbo?"

"Yes by all means."

Lofty looked at Shiner. "Well, what shall we do?"

"I vote we go, how about you, Jock?"

"Aye, count me in."

"Me too," nodded Lofty.

"Well, gentlemen what is your decision?"

"Yeah, what time will yer driver pick us up?"

"One o'clock sharp from the public house. I forgot to mention, on your arrival at Bolobo you will be housed in adequate accommodation. All your comforts will be tended to. Please do not forget your passports, here is your £50. Thank you, gentlemen, my driver will take you back."

Shiner slammed the limousine door. "Thanks, mate, see yer tomorrow."

"Yes, Sir," the chauffeur nodded politely.

"Rum turn up ain't it? The ole finances have improved dramatically." Shiner waved the notes gleefully. "Liked that bit when Kumbo said your comforts will be tended to. Yer know what that means, don't yer? It means minge will be laid on. Come on, let's get some nosh, then find some seedy club."

"Better save some loot for our clobber," said Lofty.

"Sorted. We'll nip down the Army & Navy surplus shop, get us some of that smart yank army gear. Think we're friggin' officers won't they? Lieutenant Wright, got a nice ring to it, ain't it?" laughed Shiner.

"Babs, what the hell do I tell her? Can't say I'm off to friggin' Africa. She'll think I need me head felt."

"Leave her a note saying, see yer in a couple of weeks."

Chapter 11

Katanga

"Passengers flying to Katanga please report to the departure lounge now."

"Ere we go. What departure lounge we leave from?"

"Ten mate," Lofty grinned at Jock. "Yer know Jock, that yank army gear suits yer. Yer look right smart."

"Awa an frig yersel, yer long streak."

"Ain't too many flying," observed Shiner glancing around the lounge. "Hey up, they're boarding."

The slim stewardess greeted them cordially as they entered the plane. "This way if you please." She escorted them to the first class seats. "Drinks will be served as soon as we are airborne."

"Bit of all right, ain't it?" beamed Shiner. "The old red carpet treatment, I can put up with this."

With engines gaining power the jet taxied down the runway. Now at full power the plane lifted off.

"You can unfasten your seat belts now," the stewardess smiled. "What can I get you to drink?"

"Whisky darling, a bottle and three glasses," Shiner joked.

"Of course, Sir, right away." She turned and hurried away, minutes later she returned with a bottle of whisky and three glasses on a tray.

"I was only joking, luv," Shiner smiled.

"You, Sir, are a guest of the Katanga Government, I have been instructed to treat you as such."

"Unbelievable." Shiner shook his head. "Might as

155

well have a few beers to chase the whisky down."

Drinking steadily the three sailors were halfway through the second bottle of whisky. Their mood was mellow and convivial.

"Just think, me ole mates, in two weeks time we could have 600 quid in our pockets." Shiner rubbed his hands in glee.

"Seems far too friggin' good to be true, a year's loot for two weeks' work."

"Fuck me sideways, Lofty, you heard what that Kumbo said, strip down the 20mm and 40mm guns, instruct the dopey fuckers to use and maintain them, collect our loot, back home and finish our leave. Yer don't hear Jock complaining."

Lofty nodded towards Jock. "Yer right, mate, he's fast asleep and that's what I'm gonna do, get me head down."

Banking steeply the aircraft began its descent, it slid lower tentatively at first, then with a rush, its flaps lowered, and it touched down on the runway with its engines screaming in reverse thrust, slowing quickly it taxied down the runway to turn into the first exit. Lofty struggled with his mixed emotions as he watched Shiner open another can of beer; he gulped greedily and belched loudly. What the hell was he doing sitting on an aircraft in the middle of Africa? He was beginning to feel very apprehensive. Further thoughts were interrupted as the stewardess smiled her way towards them. "Gentlemen, we are about to disembark, I hope you had an enjoyable flight. If you would follow me."

Descending the gangway they noted armed soldiers standing around languidly. A short obese officer lounged against a large car. On seeing them he with an effort waddled towards them; he flashed them a dazzling white toothed smile and nodded. "Welcome, welcome!" he gushed.

"You must be the technicians, my name is Major Caungula; I am at your disposal. I have booked you into a hotel; you must be tired after your long flight."

"Too right, mate," yawned Shiner. "I'm knackered."

"So sorry gentlemen, come, my car will take you to your hotel. We fly to Bolobo at eight o'clock sharp in the morning."

"Dinna leave much time tae sleep."

"Yeah, Jock, the sooner we get our heads down the better."

Morning came all too soon. Lofty woke with a curse as the telephone rang on his bedside table. "Yeah," he said abruptly.

"Good morning, Sir," a quiet voice answered. "It's seven o'clock, breakfast will be served downstairs in twenty minutes."

"Thank you." Lofty stretched, yawned loudly and swung his legs out of bed; he stood up half asleep and stumbled into the shower. The tepid water washed over him. Now revitalised, he towelled himself down with enthusiasm. Pulling on his trousers he walked over to the window and pulled aside the heavy curtains. The hot early morning African sun streamed through the net curtained windows; now dressed he made his way down the stairway to be met by a woman clad in a white apron.

"Good morning, Sir. This way to the breakfast room."

Seated at a large table sat Jock and Shiner.

Shiner looked up briefly in between fork-full of bacon as Lofty seated himself. "Morning, mate."

A waiter hovered close by, attentive and eager for his order. "Coffee, eggs and bacon," he ordered.

Lofty consumed his ample breakfast with relish;

washed down with hot strong coffee. "That's better." Lofty reached for his cigarettes. He looked at his watch.

"That little fat smiler should be here soon."

"Yer right, Lofty. Talk of the devil."

As if on cue Major Caungula ponderously laboured his way towards them, a huge smile etched on his black face.

"Good morning, my friends, I trust you slept well. I see you have eaten, good. If you are ready my car is waiting."

They sped through the sprawling urban district towards the airport. The contrast between the rich and poor was all too evident. Large colonial type houses with neat well tended gardens and lawns. At the other end of the spectrum, the dirt and squalor of the shanty towns with corrugated iron leaky roofed huts with small patches of vegetables grown for mere subsistence. Skirting the main entrance the car turned down a bumpy side road leading on to the runway. The road was barred by an army check point with armed soldiers stood in the roadway. Major Caungula, his window down, let out a torrent of obscenities which galvanised the hapless soldiers into action as they rushed to lift the barricade.

On the runway an old DC3 Dakota, stood with engines running, the plane was in desert camouflage; its engines smoked and stuttered.

"Bloody hell." Shiner studied the plane. "Does a fucking parachute come with that friggin' crate?"

"You make joke?" Major Caungula smiled at Shiner.

"No I don't joke, chief, that thing is a heap of rubbish," Shiner said adamantly.

Major Caungula looked up at the big sailor who towered above him. Somewhat perplexed, he answered,

"The plane very reliable; I am flying with you."

Inside the plane, conditions were spartan with wooden bench seats, the floor was littered with rubbish, and the whole interior reeked of oil.

Lumbering down the runway, its engines at full power, the Dakota climbed effortlessly into the sky.

"How long before we land at Bolobo, Major?"

"In about two hours."

Lofty nodded and resumed his study of the parched and barren scrubland below.

The ancient Dakota circled Bolobo airport. With a bone jarring jolt the Dakota touched down and taxied down the uneven runway. As if some giant torch had been switched on, sunlight cascaded in to illuminate the dark interior of the plane as the door was wrenched open.

Blinking in the strong African sun the three sailors, with caution, made their way down the dilapidated monstrosity which passed as steps.

Watching the proceedings, a tall, thin officer with insignia proclaiming his rank as colonel, his chest was bedecked with rows of ribbons. He clicked his fingers as they approached him.

"Yer must be, Colonel Kossanto?" Lofty extended his hand.

"I am, indeed," came the reply. The colonel made no attempt to grasp Lofty's outstretched hand. "And you," he said impassively, "must be the technicians?"

Anger flashed in Lofty's eyes as he returned his hand to his side. "We are," he said curtly.

"How soon can you begin work?" Colonel Kossanto said brusquely. "Major Coungula will sort out your accommodation."

"Hang about, chief, before we start work let's get settled about our wages, how are we to be paid and when?" Shiner demanded.

Taken aback by Shiner's direct approach Colonel Kossanto stared at Shiner. Finally he said, "You will be paid on completion of your work 600 Pounds sterling."

"Any chance of a sub, mate?" Shiner asked with a grin.

"You will require no money, the manager of your hotel will be authorised to provide all your needs. Now back to the matter in hand. Sergeant Mbulamuti and two corporals will assist. You will instruct them on maintenance and use of the weapons. Sergeant Mbulamuti speaks excellent English so will translate. I am late for an appointment; the sergeant should be here soon."

Jock watched as the Colonel departed. "Dinna like that bastard, yea canna trust him."

A cloud of dust heralded the arrival of Sergeant Mbulamuti and the two corporals. The battered pick-up screeched to a halt, coal black was the face that appeared from the passenger's window. A floppy bush hat covered its head.

"Hi ya, boss, da Colonel told me to pick ya up," the Sergeant grinned broadly.

"Take it we're in the back?" Shiner pulled the first pin of the tail-gate. With the tail-gate down, Shiner pushed aside one of three Sten-guns laying in the pick up. About to vault into the pick-up, he noticed magazines in place in the weapons, cranking back the bolt of the nearest one a live 9mm cartridge was extended from the chamber.

"For fuck's sake you two, these stens are fully loaded with one up the spout."

"Something wrong, boss?" Sergeant Mbulamuti joined the three sailors.

"Wrong? Midnight, your gonna get yer black arse shot off with these, or, worse still, ours." Shiner cleared the remaining stens. "They function by spring and recoil, if yer bang the stock on the ground the friggin' thing will fire."

"No understand, boss, what is Midnight?"

"Just a name for you, mate, can't pronounce yours." Sergeant Mbulamuti slapped Shiner on the back, smiling he said, "Ah, now I understand."

Driving down the runway they passed four Dakotas. Armed soldiers were evident in profusion as they headed for the perimeter. Sandbags encompassed the heavy 20mm machinegun, the barrel and cocking lever was tinged with rust, thick grease covered the breech. Empty magazines were stacked up against the sandbags. Numerous boxes of shells lay around, some open. Forty yards away on a mobile carriage the 40mm was dug into the soft sand.

Jock frowned, "Yer ken these guns are set up fur a ground attack."

"Yer right, Jock, them sandbags are arranged to give a clear field of fire to the front."

Shiner rubbed his chin thoughtfully, "Midnight, what's going on, what's these guns for?"

Sergeant Mbulamuti looked nervous.

"Come on, Midnight, what the fuck is going on?" Shiner repeated.

His eyes rolled in terror. "Simba, boss, they come soon."

"Who the fuck are the Simba?" Lofty demanded.

"Lion men very bad, many of them, they kill everybody."

"Nae wonder all you soldier boys are here."

"Yeah, Jock. Where's that fucking Colonel, I'll strangle the bastard." Shiner strode over to the pick-up; he opened the driver's door. "Out of it, you two."

With a screech of tyres he roared off. The pick-up

161

skidded to a halt as Shiner spotted Major Caungula leaving the main airport building. Reaching into the back of the truck, Shiner grabbed the nearest Sten-gun. The magazine clicked as he pushed it home, he released the bolt retaining pin, and the bolt flew forward picking up a cartridge from the magazine. "Major, hang about, I want a word with you."

"Yes, what can I do for you?" he said pleasantly.

"Where's that Colonel?" growled Shiner. "And don't give me any bullshit."

Visibly shaken the Major lost his composure as the muzzle of the sub-machine gun swung towards him. "He's in the lounge having a drink with friends."

Shiner sneered, "Very cosy."

Relief showed on the Major's face as the big sailor turned and stamped off.

Colonel Kossanto sipped his drink delicately as he attentively listened to the elegant woman sitting beside him.

Shiner swore as he kicked the lounge doors open.

"What is the meaning of this intrusion? How dare you enter in this way?"

"Shut up yer arrogant long streak of piss. Just tell me about the Simba."

"Simba!" he retorted. "They are of no consequence to you, a ragtag army of rebels; I have adequate troops here to deal with the situation."

"Troops, yer must be joking," scoffed Shiner. "What I've seen of them they couldn't fight their way out of a friggin' knocking shop."

Colonel Kossanto looked at Shiner with contempt. "Is there anything else?"

"Yeah, you've got our money, ain't yer?"

"Yes, you will be paid as soon as you have completed

your task."

Shiner scowled, "Just checking."

Sergeant Mbulamuti watched intently as Lofty stripped the weapon down. As he handed each part to the Sergeant he explained its function. Nodding with enthusiasm the Sergeant in turn passed the part onto the corporal, who, with diligence scrubbed away at each part in a bucket of paraffin. He beamed in delight as the thick hardened grease dissolved. Drying each part he neatly arranged them on an oily rag.

Sergeant Mbulamuti tugged at Lofty's sleeve. "Da big Shiner, he come back."

"So I see, hi ya, mate, how'd it go?"

"Don't ask, that bastard reckons we ain't got nothin' to worry about. According to him, Midnight fed us a load of bollocks."

"Dunno about that, ole Midnight was bloody terrified of the Simba coming."

"Yeah I noticed, we'll have to get this job wrapped up an' away, how's Jock doing with the 40mm?"

"Not too good, shell guides and block rusted up."

"Better give him an hand."

Shiner leaned against the mounting and lit a cigarette. "Problems, Jock?"

"See fur yersel, mate. Canna move tha bastard. Block back rusted right up, gonna gid tha cocking lever a wee tap wi me hammer."

"Not too hard, Jock, are there any spares?"

"Aye, box full. It's bloody hot, mate, canna we gat nae beers?"

"Yeah, gonna send Midnight after some."

"Fancy a beer, Lofty?"

"Not half, mate, I'm as dry as a camel's chuff."

"Midnight, me ole mate, nip and get us some beers. Any trouble, see the colonel or Major Coungula."

"Yes, boss," he grinned. "I go now."

"Yer putting this back together already, Lofty?"

"Yeah, new gun, mate, never been fired, once the hard old grease has been cleaned from the working parts and oiled it's fine. When Midnight gets back will show him how to fire it. Load that magazine, mate, while I finish off."

Shiner nodded and picked up an empty magazine. Deftly he pushed shell after shell into the spring loaded magazine. "Full mate, where's that Midnight? I'm getting dehydrated, look at me, bloody soaked," moaned Shiner, as he stood perspiring freely.

Sergeant Mbulanti hurried over and laid the case of beer on the sandbags.

Shiner grunted in satisfaction as he impatiently ripped the box open. "Ere, Midnight, get yer laughing gear round this and you two corporals. Lofty, give Jock a shout."

Lofty reached for his second beer. "What's the situation, Jock?"

"Nae twa bad. Got the block free; extractors are frigged but plenty of spares."

"Good, right Midnight, yer about to start yer training as a gunner and you two corporals."

With apprehension the sergeant approached the gun.

"Now get yerself sat behind it. You okay?"

"Yes, boss, think so, boss."

"Right, sergeant, grab that magazine, you push gently forward, it will click when engaged."

"That's it, well done."

"Is that it, boss?" the sergeant said nervously.

"Yer ain't fired it yet, have yer?"

"No, boss."

"Yer see that lever to yer right."

"Yes, boss."

"Pull it right back."

"Okay, boss."

"Now press that button under the lever."

Sergeant Mbulanti jumped as the bolt flew forward into the fire position.

"Now put yer cheek on the pad and look down the barrel. Yer got that, Midnight?"

"Think so, boss."

"Nearest to you is the rear-sight that little circle. Yer get the foresight in that circle on the target then squeeze the trigger. The gun will continue to fire until you release the trigger. This is the safety catch." Lofty indicated the small lever above the trigger. "Yer push it forward to fire."

Lofty looked across the open scrubland, a small group of stunted acacias about two hundred yards away offered an easy target. "Yer see them?" Lofty pointed. "Fire at them, off safety catch, fire."

The sound of the heavy machine gun reverberated around the airfield, the ground erupted well wide of the acacias.

"Good, boss, yes?"

"No, mate, bloody terrible," grinned Lofty. "Try again, this time keep yer peepers open."

Awkwardly the sergeant squinted with one eye then the other. Empty shell cases momentarily hung in the air before clattering to the ground. Geysers of sand rose near the acacias.

Lofty nodded his approval. "Better, Midnight, better."

"Well done, Sergeant Mbulanti, well done." The colonel clapped quietly, unbeknown to them, he had watched the proceedings.

Colonel Kossanto looked smugly at Shiner. "Seems

my men have mastered the art."

Shaking his head in amusement Shiner said, "Colonel, yer man has two left eyes; he can't aim."

"Perhaps you should give me a demonstration," sneered the colonel.

Gulping down his beer the big sailor ambled over to the gun. "Let's have a go, Midnight; yer Colonel wants me to 'ave a bash."

Shiner slid easily behind the gun. A short burst of fire was followed by a longer one. Dust and sand enveloped the acacias shattering and splintering them skywards.

"Very impressive," conceded the colonel. "Very impressive. I intend to send a squad of men for you to train. Sergeant Mbulanti and the two corporals will assist you. I take it you are as efficient on the 40mm?"

"Yeah, but shouldn't I be helping me mates?" Shiner protested.

"I am sure your associates can manage adequately, but it is imperative my men are trained to use these weapons."

"S'pose so," admitted Shiner with reluctance. "Is it all right if we use the pick-up, Colonel, and where do we get our meals?"

"Midday you can eat at the airport lounge. An evening meal will be provided at your hotel. Sergeant Mbulanti will drive you there and leave the pick-up."

"Cheers, colonel."

Midnight looked at Shiner in admiration. "You number one, boss."

"Yeah, mate, that's me. Get yer two corporals to fill a couple of magazines. Gonna make you number one."

"No, boss, I number two," he grinned with pride.

Jock wiped the perspiration off his face with the back of his hand. He surveyed the now removed bolt.

"Dinna look twa bad. Good clean up an plenty of oil, gie the barrel a sponge out an I'll gat it back together."

Lofty worked the brush back and forth. Sweat ran down his bare chest in rivulets as he gasped from his exertions. He paused for a moment to watch a soldier run out to place a forty gallon drum in front of the 20mm.

Shiner went through the gun drill slowly; Sergeant Mbulanti translated to the reluctant-looking would-be gunners.

"Now who's gonna be first? How about you?" Shiner pointed a stubby finger at a soldier. The soldier spoke excitedly to the sergeant gesticulating wildly.

"What's he say?" growled Shiner.

"He doesn't want to," shrugged the sergeant.

"Doesn't want to, you tell him to get his black arse behind that gun now."

With a sullen glance at Shiner the man positioned himself. "That's better, sunshine. Close yer left eye look through the sights. Good man, now push the safety catch off and squeeze the trigger gently."

Recoiling, the 20mm sent a devastating stream of shells towards the target. Clouds of dust and sand obscured the drum.

"My man," grinned Shiner. "Midnight, tell him to do it again."

Once again the machinegun fired. The drum spun upwards as though grasped by some unseen hand.

Shiner walked over and slapped him on the back. "Take his name, Midnight. Sit him over there on them ammo boxes and give him a beer."

All traces of sullenness had evaporated as the soldier basked in the limelight; he danced a little jig as he claimed his beer.

"Midnight, me ole mate, time to get something to eat.

Where do you eat?"

"Barracks, boss. Food no good, all the time soup and bread."

"Yer could eat with us, mate."

"Boss, da Colonel will tell me to do the big frig off."

Somewhat apprehensively Sergeant Mbulanti followed the three sailors into the lounge; he cast furtive glances towards the seated officers. He sat down next to Shiner looking uncomfortable.

"Yer want a beer?" Lofty addressed Midnight.

"Yes, boss."

A European looking woman came to take their order.

"What can I get you?" she enquired.

"You English?" asked Lofty.

"No, Belgian," she replied. "My husband is working up country on some telephone project."

Shiner looked at the woman. "What's going on here?"

"Simba," she said. "The military closed the airport two weeks ago, banned all civilian flights in and out, sent soldiers to protect us. But we need protection from them, they are a drunken rabble."

"We dinna want twa gat involved wi fighting Simba, how far are tha awa?"

"Not too far. I had better take your order; Colonel Kossanto is watching. He won't like me talking to you."

"Yeah, talk to yer later. What's to eat?"

"African dishes mostly. We have steak with veg and yams."

"Sounds fine, we'll have that and four beers."

"Told yer, didn't I."

"Told me what?" snapped Shiner.

"Easy money, no such thing, mate. I had my misgivings about this venture from the start."

"Nae point noo in gabbing on about it; let's gat tha job

done an awa."

"Yeah, Jock's right, the sooner we get done the better."

"How's yer steak, Midnight?"

"Good, boss, good. Here comes da Colonel."

"Not again," moaned Shiner. "Stand by for some more crap."

"Afternoon, gentlemen, I trust your meal was to your liking. How are you progressing?"

"Not too bad, be testing the 40mm after lunch," replied Lofty.

"Excellent, and how is the training going?"

"Yer got one man a natural gunner. Gonna train him to instruct the others. Me an' the sergeant will move on to the 40mm tomorrow to train more of yer men."

"Excellent! Is there anything you require?"

"Yeah, Colonel, some straight information. How close are these Simba?"

"We have had this conversation earlier, I believe," said the colonel brusquely.

"Yeah, we have," said Shiner. "But yer never tell me fuck all, just give me bullshit."

"About 100 miles west of us," admitted the Colonel.

"Thank you, Colonel, and how many are there?"

"According to the latest reports, about 4,000."

"Yer what?" said Shiner in amazement.

"Your job will be done when and if they decide to come here," the colonel snapped icily.

"Colonel," Lofty interrupted. "Yer need to dig in light machineguns with overlapping fields of fire to protect those heavy weapons."

"Yes, I am well able to prepare for a defence in depth, thank you; perhaps you are unaware that I attended Officers Training School in England."

"One more thing, Colonel, we'd like to go to town tonight, so how about some money. Also, can yer issue us with side arms?"

"Yes, I will see to it."

As the colonel departed Lofty stood up. "Come on, girls, let's get started. Sooner we get stuck in sooner we get finished."

Jock dropped the second clip of shells down the guides and hauled back on the cocking lever.

"All yours, mate."

Lofty nodded as he sighted on a small outcrop of rock 1000 yards away. Four seconds later the eighth empty shell case hit the ground. The sharp cracks of the gun echoed around the airport. Four shell flashes blinked back from the rock.

Throughout the afternoon, gunfire resounded as Shiner with curses and praise cajoled the black soldiers. He strove to teach them the rudimentary skills required. Shiner slumped down on an empty ammunition box. "That's me lot, Midnight. Had enough for today, I'm knackered. Detail a couple of yer boys to clean the gun."

"Yes, boss, then do you want me to take you to hotel?"

"Cheers, mate, I'll be over with Jock and Lofty."

"Look up, Jock, here comes gunnery instructor Wright."

"Fuck off, Lofty, I ain't in the mood. It's bloody hard work getting through to them."

"Can't be that bad, mate."

"Not for you it ain't, bloody frustrating. Been over the drill dozens of times, one man is okay another so-so. The rest are fucking rubbish. Be a right bloody pantomime when we get on the 40mm when they have to work as a team. Come on, let's frig off, get a shower and go to town."

Sergeant Mbulanti waved them a jovial "good-night" as they entered the hotel lobby. Thick carpet covered the floor; large paintings adorned the oak panelled walls.

A fan slowly rotated from the ceiling. The man behind the lobby desk resplendent in a white suit rose from his chair to greet them. He approached them with hand outstretched, and he shook their hands in turn with vigour.

"Welcome, most welcome," he gushed. "I have been expecting you. I am the manager, your rooms are ready. I have something for you behind the desk."

Gingerly he placed three pistols in holsters on the desk top along with boxes of cartridges followed by a sealed envelope.

Shiner yanked a pistol from its holster. "Nice, very nice," nodding his approval. "Only got Yank 9mm Brownings, ain't we. Open the envelope, Lofty, see how much loot we got."

Lofty thumbed through the notes. "150 francs, whatever that is."

"Lot of money," confirmed the manager.

"Good," beamed Shiner. "Let's get our arses in gear and spend some of it, how far is the town, mate?"

"Not far, five minutes walk."

"Yer don't seem very busy, chief?"

"No," agreed the manager. "Since the army closed the airport, everyone they go."

"Why should they be leaving? According to Colonel Kossanto they ain't got nothing to worry about?!"

"My friends, if the Simba get much closer I too shall be leaving. The only people left in Bolobo will be those who have no means of escape. The Katanga army is undisciplined and untrained."

Shiner gave a wry grin. "Yer can say that again, chief, they ain't got a friggin' clue. Anyhow, come on you girls, let's get showered."

Bolobo was a small but flourishing town. The revenue created by the airport was considerable, as was the money generated by the many Belgium workers based in the town who worked on various projects throughout Katanga.

The main street was deserted as the three sailors walked towards the nearest bar. The sound of breaking glass made them turn abruptly. Drunken soldiers staggered from a bar further up the street laughing loudly and brandishing weapons.

Lofty shook his head as he watched them. "Bloody load of wankers," he said contemptuously. "Let's get the fuck out of their way."

Bursts of automatic gunfire sounded from the street as they sat down and ordered beer. The barman looked agitated as he frequently glanced towards the door.

"Nice to see you again," the woman smiled from behind the bar.

"Yer the lady from the airport, ain't yer? You work here as well?"

"Just help out, my father-in-law runs the bar."

With a crash the bar door flew open. The doorway was filled with a huge black soldier. He scowled threateningly as he walked to the bar, followed by an entourage of grinning companions. He waved a Sten-gun.

"Beer now," he ordered.

"Get out," the woman shouted defiantly.

"Yae heard the lassie." The 9mm Browning in Jock's hand pointed unwaveringly at the man's chest. "Put yir weapons doon on tha table an' fuck off."

"Move yer black arse," snarled Shiner. "Do yer

understand?"

Nodding meekly the soldier placed his Sten-gun on the table.

"An' the rest of you."

Obediently, the disgruntled soldiers complied under the watchful gaze of Jock; they looked sheepish as they shuffled about with downcast eyes.

"Right ladies, don't let us keep yer. I'll get my sergeant to pick yer toys up tomorrow."

Relief showed on the woman's face as the last soldier departed. "Thank you, let me buy you a beer."

"No need luv, we've got the colonel's money to spend," said Lofty. "Do yer get much trouble from them soldier boys?"

"Nothing but trouble since they arrived, drunken and abusive with little money. If you refuse to serve them they help themselves."

"What about the officers, why don't you complain to them?"

She laughed, "That's a joke, they are worse than the soldiers, much worse." She added, "When do you think you will be leaving?"

"In about four days."

"Do you think you could arrange for my father-in-law and me to leave with you?"

"Shiner's yer man, he's well in with the colonel, he's yer ole mate, ain't he, Shiner?"

Shiner looked at Lofty. "No," he grunted. "He ain't no mate of mine, but I'll ask him."

Chapter 12

Betrayal

Colonel Kossanto studied the list of names before him, he nodded his head and glanced up.

"I have underlined the men I recommend as gunners Colonel, the rest are loaders."

"You have done well," the colonel said with a smile. "All of the weapons are now fully operational, I take it."

"Yeah, Colonel, all in tip top order. When do we get a flight out?"

"Tomorrow morning at ten."

"And payment?"

"You will be paid before you board."

"Fair enough, Colonel, just one more thing can we take out this Belgian woman and her father-in-law when we leave?"

"Yes, I see no reason why not."

"Thank you, colonel."

Grinning Shiner entered the bar. "All sorted, mates, we leave in the morning, with you and your father-in-law," Shiner addressed the Belgian woman.

"Good, the sooner the better," she replied. "I was telling your friends a man was in for a drink early this afternoon. He said the Simba are on the move heading this way. I feel awful about leaving the other Belgian woman and children behind."

"Don't worry, I'm sure the colonel will evacuate them."

"Dinna ken about you's twa, but I'm gonna hae an early night."

"Sounds good to me," Lofty said. "I'm bushed."

"Well, let's go." Shiner stood up. "By the way the plane leaves at 10 o'clock, see yer at the lounge."

"I'll be there," the woman replied. "Thanks."

Lofty rose early, showered, dressed and made his way down the stairs to the breakfast room. He was somewhat surprised to find the table not laid, no waitress greeted him. He shrugged, sat down and lit a cigarette. Minutes later he stubbed it out and walked into the lobby and rang the bell. He turned at the sound of footsteps.

"Oh, it's you, Shiner."

"Who'd yer think it was, mate? Where's brekkers?"

"Nobody about."

"Nobody about, that's fucking choice ain't it? Get Jock an' we'll ride over to the airport for some nosh; I'll get the pick-up started."

Jock and Lofty heard Shiner curse loudly.

Shiner waved his arms in the air in despair. "Fucking pick-up has been nicked. It's that bastard of a manager, he's legged it with the pick-up."

"What does it matter, mate. We're out of here soon anyhow, let's walk."

Walking down the street towards the airport Lofty had a sense of foreboding, the eerie silence and absence of people compounded the feeling.

"Bloody quiet, ain't it?" frowned Shiner. "I don't like it, something's wrong."

No soldiers guarded the airport, the place was desolate.

"What the fucks going on?" growled Shiner.

"Yer ken the bastards pulled oot. Nae aircraft on the

runway."

Two open-backed trucks moved at speed down the runway towards them. A heavy machine gun was mounted and manned on both vehicles. With caution the trucks neared, both machine guns covered the three friends.

"Awa an' fuck yersels," Jock shouted.

At the sound of Jock's broad accent both guns swung sky-ward. A grinning soldier with sergeant's stripes on his arm stepped out of the passenger side of the leading truck. "Yer a long way from home, Jock, what are you boys doing here?"

"Looking for that bastard, Colonel Kessanto. He owes us money an' he's fucked off. If ever I get my hands on his neck I'll strangle the skinny fucker," Shiner said vehemently.

"You will have to wait until I have finished with him," the sergeant said grimly. "We were supposed to reinforce his troops to hold Bolobo and the airport."

"Hold Bolobo," snorted Shiner. "Sarge, the only thing I'm likely to hold is me dick, us lads are off."

"Off?" laughed the sergeant. "Where yer going? Four hundred miles of open country before the next town."

"Think I'll just get legless," groaned Shiner.

"You lads would be better off coming with us. The rest of the boys are digging in on the hill just outside of town."

"Do we have a choice?" asked Lofty.

"Yer don't," said the sergeant. "By the way, my name is Johnson; Major Lindle is the Officer in Command."

"Not of us he ain't," retorted Shiner. "We've finished our job here; maybe yer major can pay us what that bastard colonel owes us, the wanker."

"You'll have to talk to the major, mount up let's go."

Grinning, the mercenary extended a hand to help them

as they clambered aboard the truck.

"Thought you three were bleeding yanks," he said cheerfully. "Welcome to the party."

"Didn't want an invitation," said Shiner as the truck lurched forward and sped down the runway. Minutes later they turned off the road and bumped their way across open ground towards the hill. Parked at the base of the hill were five three ton Bedford army lorries. Soldiers laboured and sweated as they toiled to prepare defensive positions.

Small and slightly built, the Officer approached them as they dismounted from the truck; his crumpled uniform was soaked in sweat.

"Well, Sergeant, any sign of the colonel and his men?"

"Afraid not, Sir, the bastards have gone."

"Thank you, Sergeant. You chaps, I take it have been servicing the airport weapons."

"Yeah, that's right Major, how'd yer know?"

"I had the dubious pleasure of speaking to Kossanto on the radio yesterday; you three will be a great asset as I intend to move the airport weapons here."

"Hang about Major, we ain't been paid yet for the work we've done. That bastard Kossanto shafted us, yer ain't gonna do the same, mate, we want paying."

Major Lindle said nothing as he scrutinised Shiner.

"Well, Major," Shiner demanded.

"While I am sympathetic," he replied. "to your predicament, I can do nothing about your prior arrangements regarding pay. As for the present, I will see what I can do."

"Hardly an answer, is it, Major? It's not a yes or no."

"Nevertheless, it's the best I can do at this moment. Right now I have more pressing problems, damn it man the Simba are right behind us." He snapped, "Sergeant

Johnson."

"Yes, Sir."

"Detail Corporal Marsh and a squad of men to start transporting the 20mm's from the airport. How is the ammunition situation?"

"Plenty for the 20's," said Lofty. "Not a lot for the 40's."

"Do you think it's worth hauling the big 40mm's here?"

"Yeah, Major, they have the range, and are effective against ground targets."

"Could we tow them with the Bedfords?"

"No problem."

Two teams of four mercenaries cursed and struggled their way to the crest of the hill with the first two 20mm guns. Others followed with boxes of ammunition.

Shiner watched with indifference.

"Soldier boys are busy, ain't they?" he commented.

"Aye, dinna yae think we should gie them a hand?"

"You can, Jock, I ain't till the Major say I'm on the payroll. Here comes that sergeant. Wonder what he wants?"

"Enjoying your holiday lads?" The sergeant said with a hint of sarcasm. "The Major would like a word with you."

"Would he now? Well I don't particularly want to talk to him unless it's about pay."

"Pay lad!" Sergeant Johnson frowned at Shiner. "Tomorrow, pay will be the last thing on your mind, staying alive will be your main concern. Come on, lads, find the nice Major, see what he wants."

Major Lindle briefly glanced up as he supervised the siting of the second pair of 20mm guns.

"Yer wanted to see us, Major?"

"Yes, I thought I had better put you in the picture. We are expected to engage the Simba sometime tomorrow. You are experienced on the 40mm; I would be obliged if you could man three of these weapons. Amongst my men I have enough ex Royal Marines to crew the fourth gun and act as your loaders."

"Fucking charming," Shiner moaned. "What other job have yer got us lined up for?",.

"I would like you each to take charge of a 20mm as soon as the ammunition for the 40mm's has been expended."

"I don't believe this," said Shiner. "Stuck on a poxy hill with a load of pongos."

Chapter 14

Simba

Sergeant Johnson stood watching as an endless convoy of trucks and vehicles approached the wooded area in front of their position. The Simba had arrived.

"Come on, lads, come on, don't you worry about them; you've seen them before. Now get that ammunition to the 20mm." He watched grimly as the mercenaries manhandled the heavy boxes to the guns.

"Range 1,200 yards," Shiner shouted. Major Lindle nodded.

"Stand to, load and engage."

Jock pressed the fire button, the 40mm recoiled. The first shot of the brutal battle for Bolobo had begun. Sweating profusely, the mercenaries passed clip after clip of shells hand to hand to feed the guns as they each poured a devastating fire into the advancing convoy. Burning lorries littered the open ground beyond the cover of the woodland as the 40mm's took their toll. Above the sharp reports of the guns, the distinctive thump of a mortar. Mortar shells burst nearby as the Simba lobbed projectiles over the trees.

One of the 40mm shifted targets in a futile attempt to destroy the mortars. Shell flashes raked the woodland. Lofty stared in disbelief; he screamed at the nearest mercenary. "Tell them fuckers to leave the mortars."

Smoke and dust from the mortars enveloped the hill, oily black smoke spiralled skywards from the burning vehicles.

One by one the 40mm's ceased firing as they ran out of ammunition.

Lofty eased himself out of the cramped gun-layers position. Standing up he pulled a face as he stretched and groaned about his back. Picking up a canteen of water he gulped at it greedily. Thirst satisfied he poured the rest over his head. He stood there with water running down his face. He held his hand straight out in front of him. "Bloody hell, have stopped shaking, gis a fag, Shiner."

"Not so many now," grinned Shiner.

"Fall in, you three." Sergeant Johnson addressed the three sailors. "The major wants to talk to all of us."

"Not us, Sarge, we don't come under your orders."

"Aye, we're on our way, Sarge."

Shiner spat on the ground, swore loudly but followed with reluctance.

Major Lindle, an ex paratrooper and a man of no pretence called for silence.

"Right chaps, I wish I could start with do you want the good news first or the bad, the fact is it's all bad. As you well know the government troops have pulled out. We will get no assistance from them, we have a choice pull out and leave the women and children to the Simba or stay and fight. You have seen what the Simba does to its prisoners. The Simba took a mauling today but their forces still number about 4,000. The Belgian nationals in Bolobo are to supply us with food and water. We are faced with a dilemma, that is if the Simba decide to send some of their forces around us to attack the town, we must be ready to move quickly with a third of our force to protect them. That would, of course, leave us hard pressed to defend this position. Very much is going to depend on the six 20mm machine guns. That is about all I have to say, are there any questions?"

"Yeah, I have one," all eyes turned to Shiner.

"Who's paying me an' me mates? That skinny colonel has fucked off with our money."

"Not again," the major sighed in despair. "This is not the time nor the place to discuss money. Sergeant Johnson, a word with you, if you please. Good luck, chaps. Get something to eat and get some rest."

"Good luck," moaned Shiner. "I reckon we need a miracle not luck."

The smell of food cooking wafted over the hill. A short, fat, greasy-looking cook stirred the large pots of bubbling soup; he ladled out a large spoonful, tasted it and smacked his lips in satisfaction. "Lovely," he complimented himself.

"Come and get it," he shouted in his high pitched voice.

It was to be their last hot meal on the hill. Small groups of men made their way to the field kitchen; they sat by their trenches and gun positions eating and talking quietly amongst themselves. Daylight was fading fast, soon it would be dark, and in the morning they could expect the first big assault. Beyond the woodland the sound of chanting rose and fell like waves on the ocean.

Long would be the night. It would be a time for reflection. How many of them would be here this time tomorrow? The very lives of all in Bolobo were in their hands.

Veterans of many battles with the Simba, they had staunchly defended village after village before retreating before massive odds. Half their number had fallen. The force now numbered 104 of the original 200. This was to be the ultimate battle with no retreat.

Lofty pulled a face in disgust as he tipped his

remaining soup away.

"Bloody garbage, ain't it? Yer know what I could do with? A beer."

"Aye, wud go doon a treat," agreed Jock. "Was talking tae one of tha soldier boys, he reckons tha Simba are steamed up on drugs when they attack."

"Dunno bout that, Jock. It's them witch doctors to blame waving them old bones about. Drives the dopey fuckers into a frenzy. Shiner patted the barrel of the 20mm machine gun. "This will bring them back to reality."

Sleep for the defenders of Bolobo had been fitful. Many had hardly slept at all, and they rose bleary-eyed, dirty and unshaven. Matches flared as cigarettes were lit. The sun appeared on the horizon, a panorama of red and gold. The heavy ground mist quickly burnt off as the sun rapidly climbed into the sky. Strong tea was being ferried around to the gun pits and trenches.

Low chanting could be heard beyond the wood. The chanting increased to a roar. Vehicles could be heard revving up.

"Hi ya, mates." Lofty winked at his two loaders who were busy loading the 20mm magazines.

"Me name's, Lofty."

"Pleased to meet yer, mucker. Call me Doggy, this 'ere is Spike."

"Lads, don't try and hurry the reloading of the magazines, nice and steady get it right first time."

"Will do, Lofty," grinned Doggy.

"What the fuck are they waiting for?" Lofty said impatiently.

"Won't be long, mate. They like a bit of a chant to get worked up," Spike said without looking up as he pushed 20mm cartridges into the magazine.

Major Lindle watched intently through his binoculars as lorries and armoured cars made their way from both sides of the wood to form up in front of them.

"Sergeant, I don't like it," the major spoke without taking his eyes from his binoculars.

"It's all right Sir, they're good lads. They will cope."

"Damn it, Sergeant, if only we had some more ammunition for the 40mm's. Tell the men to stand to."

"Will do, Sir."

Sergeant Johnson saluted and strode down the hill. He stopped midway down.

"Could I have your attention," he bellowed. "The 20mm will engage at 600 yards. Concentrate your fire on the vehicles. Bren guns hold your fire until they reach 100 yards. Pick your targets; there will be no falling back. You stay where you are; good luck."

His orders were greeted by metallic clicks as bolts went forward to ready weapons.

Shiner on the lower part of the hill manned his 20mm machine gun. He was protected on both his flanks by Bren gunners as were all the 20mm's. This allowed the heavy machine guns to concentrate on mass targets leaving the Bren guns to deal with small break-throughs. The Bren gunners were nicknamed, Guardian Angels. Just how this would stand up to mass attacks was still to be tested.

Mortar shells burst on their positions. The earth was flung upwards as if by huge shovels. The attack had begun.

Sun glinted and flashed on machetes as the Simba, chanting loudly, advanced.

Jock was the first to open fire. The leading truck shuddered from the impact of the heavy 20mm shells as they tore it apart. Smoke poured from the truck, seconds later the five other machine guns opened fire.

Vehicle after vehicle came to a grinding halt. Impervious to casualties the Simba advanced on foot to be met by heavy rifle and Bren gun-fire. Rapidly, the Simba advanced on the flank. Already the Simba had overrun the protecting Bren-guns. The lowest 20mm was in danger of being overwhelmed by an irresistible force of numbers.

Shiner waved frantically as he indicated he was going to support them. His 20mm slewed round. Devastating fire swept the Simba as they continued their suicidal onslaught. Unable to depress their machinegun low enough to meet the attack the three mercenaries grabbed Sten guns and faced the Simba. The unstoppable flood of Simba engulfed them; machetes rose and fell as the Simba cut them to pieces.

Shiner watched in horror as his loader replaced the empty magazine. Hardly was he aware of Sergeant Johnson leading a platoon of men to clear the Simba from the lower slopes of the hill. Sten guns blazing, they threw back the Simba. Brutal hand to hand combat was quickly over. No quarter was asked and none was given, there would be no prisoners in this battle. Now in full retreat the Simba withdrew.

"Yer bastards," Shiner snarled as he savagely re-cocked his gun, he laughed insanely as he sent long bursts of fire at the retreating Simba.

"Cease fire, cease fire!" Major Lindle's order fell on deaf ears as Shiner emptied his magazine.

Shiner stood up and glared towards the Officer.

"Yer can't tell me what to do unless I'm on the payroll. Another thing, Major, I ain't going to man this gun next time. Get yer soldier boys down here."

Jock grinned at Lofty. "Dinna think Shiner likes tha major, mate. Come tae think about it, wha does he like?"

Burying the dead mercenaries proved to be a traumatic experience. Their hacked and mutilated bodies were carefully laid in shallow graves. In death they were laid with the Simba, arms draped over one another like brothers, now at peace, freed from the bitter fighting to come. This would be left to the living.

Major Lindle, solemn faced, read a passage from the Bible over them. A volley rang out from the mustered firing party.

Tears ran down the cheeks of some of the hardened mercenaries as their comrades were laid to rest.

"Go easy on the Major, mate." Lofty's face was serious. "We're all on the same side; he's not a bad bloke."

Shiner winked. "Didn't mean it. Just came out."

"Yer an evil bastard," grinned Jock. "But I'm glad yer on my side. Say sorry to the Major."

"Go frig yerself," retorted Shiner. "What I said to the Major about not staying down here, I meant. I'm going to pull back higher up the hill."

Mercenaries began the grim task of clearing the Simba dead from the positions they had taken briefly at such a terrible cost.

The open ground in front of the hill was a graveyard of still smoking lorries. Simba dead were everywhere, but on the next attack the Simba would have the cover of the wrecked vehicles.

Major Lindle joined them. He looked at Shiner, and to his surprise the sailor grinned but said nothing.

Major Lindle felt uneasy. Fully he expected an outburst from Shiner, but none was forthcoming.

"I intend," he said, "to move both 20mm's higher up the hill."

"That's good news, Major. Call me Shiner."

Major Lindle looked puzzled. Nodding curtly he turned and strode up the hill.

Already the Major's men dug franticly at the hard unyielding ground to prepare the gun-pits to receive the two machineguns. The hot African sun beat down, sweat poured from them as they laboured. From this new position they would be less vulnerable and have a commanding field of fire.

Lofty nodded his approval as he surveyed the sites.

"Beats me why the Major didn't site them here in the first place."

"About time you sailor boys done some work, ain't it?"

The voice belonged to a tall, thin, mercenary with a strong London accent as they struggled to manhandle the heavy guns up the hill.

"Not us, mate," replied Lofty. "Bad back, excused duties."

"An' we ain't been paid. Anyhow, we're on leave," said Shiner. "Reckon we ought to have a run ashore in Bolobo."

"No way, mate. I don't think the Major would approve."

Shiner looked at the cockney. "Well, he ain't coming."

Battered and old, the lorry made its way the few hundred yards from Bolobo to the base of the hill. Steam rose in a cloud from the radiator. The driver, a young Belgian, jumped down from the cab and lifted the bonnet of the lorry. Fresh bread, fruit and water along with several cases of beer were stacked in the back.

Major Lindle greeted the young Belgian. "How are things in town?" he asked.

In perfect English came the reply. "Not too bad, Major. All the locals have left, the Belgian women and children are barricaded up in the school, and they are being protected by about a dozen Belgian men. We are short of arms and ammunition, can you spare any weapons?"

"Yes, a couple of Brens and a few Sten guns. My men will instruct your people in their use."

"Thank you, Major. One more thing, Major, we had a brief visit from the Simba just after they attacked you. They looted a few shops, got drunk and rode out."

"Damn it, damn it." The Major shook his head. "This is what I have been afraid of. I have already detailed a third of my force to move into Bolobo to protect the women and children if the situation demands it. Please keep hidden and not to engage the Simba unless absolutely necessary. I will send a squad of my chaps back with you."

Sergeant Johnson came to attention and saluted.

"Permission to distribute beer to the men, Sir?"

"Yes, carry on, Sergeant, oh one more thing Sergeant, could you detail 15 men to escort this chap back to Bolobo?"

"Would you like me to go with them, Sir?"

"No I can't spare you. Corporal Marsh can take charge, include the three naval personnel in the 15."

"Begging your pardon, Sir. Do you think that wise, that Shiner won't take orders from Marsh."

"Please, Sergeant, don't question my orders; just carry them out."

"Very well, Sir, as you wish." The Sergeant turned and left.

Shiner gulped down the last drop of his beer.

"One friggin' can of beer," he whined tossing the empty can away in disgust. "Wish I was back in Chatham."

"Hey, you three, report to Corporal Marsh."

"Who said?" demanded Lofty.

"Sergeant Johnson," came the reply.

"Well fog off back and tell the Sergeant to get knotted," said Shiner. "What's it about, anyway?"

"Dunno, mate. Something about going into Bolobo."

Shiner's eyes lit up, his attitude changed. "Tell the nice Corporal we're on our way."

Corporal Marsh was a tough ex-Royal Marine. Having been attached to the navy he would have much in common with the sailors.

Mustered on the summit of the hill they could see Bolobo a short distance away.

Now unloaded, the battered old lorry was ready to make the return journey back to town.

Chapter 14

Bolobo

Corporal Marsh greeted them cordially.

"Welcome aboard, grab some webbing and spare Sten magazines, we don't expect to meet any Simba, but who knows."

"Right, lads, check yer weapons and make yer way to the transport." The three-ton Bedford's engine burst into life as they climbed aboard.

Behind the wheel of his lorry, the young Belgian cursed as he struggled to start the engine. Turning, it spluttered, fired, started, then stopped. Again he turned the engine over, this time it roared into life as he revved up. With a rending of gears he lurched forward. Bumping across the rough ground they joined the road and cautiously made their way into the outskirts of Bolobo.

Lights flashing, the Bedford overtook the Belgian and came to a halt in front of him.

Corporal Marsh jumped down from the passenger side of the Bedford; he pushed a magazine into his Sten gun.

"Right, lads, fall in. Driver park in that side street; we will deploy and proceed on foot. Where are yer heading, mate?"

"Back to the school," replied the Belgian.

"Okay, see yer there later."

Corporal Marsh split his force in two. They advanced along the main street on both sides of the road. Shops had been looted; goods were strewn over the pavements. The grey uniformed mercenaries moved quietly and efficiently. Two dead bodies lay in grotesque distortion outside a looted goldsmith's shop. Well dressed, they had been dead for some time, looting government troops could have been the cause of their demise.

Shiner and Jock disappeared into a liquor store, they came out empty handed.

"Greedy bastards," scowled Shiner. "They took everything."

Corporal Marsh raised his Sten gun high above his head signalling them to stop. Ahead of them was the airport. Orders to advance were passed man to man.

Fanning out in skirmish order at a fast crouching run they crossed the runway. Bursting into the departure building, they were confronted by a mass of looted goods. Piled high were cases of beer, wines, spirits and thousands of cigarettes.

Lofty shouldered his Sten gun. "Cor, we've hit the jackpot," he exclaimed.

Jock ripped open a case of whisky, looked lovingly at the bottle, smacked his lips and unscrewed the cap. Closing his eyes, he took a long swig.

Shiner stood for a second trying to take in the sight before him. Pleasure showed on his face. Now, bottle in hand, he gulped greedily. The soldiers made for the beer.

Corporal Marsh now faced a dilemma: should he allow his men a few beers or should he stop it now?

Lofty opened his beer and tossed one to the corporal.

"Just a friendly word, Corp. I should move out of here soon, them two are mates of mine, but full of booze them bastards will take on the Simba on their own. Worse still, anybody else."

Corporal Marsh nodded. "Listen up," he shouted. "We are going to locate the school and assess the situation.

Take a few beers with you; we will come back for booze."

"Me an' Jock will stay here on guard Corp, pick us up later."

Shiner looked at Jock. "Won't we, mate?"

"Aye, you lassies go play soldiers on yer own."

Corporal Marsh made as if to go towards the two sailors. Lofty put a hand on his shoulder to restrain him.

"Come on, Shiner, I'm going with the corporal."

Anger flashed in Shiner's eyes. He looked long at his friend, grinned, nodded his head and said, "Okay, mate, but we're coming back."

Once outside, the glare of the bright sunlight hurt their eyes. They moved quickly towards the main street. The sign read 'school' as they turned left. The sound of an approaching vehicle sent them racing for cover into gardens and behind neat hedges.

Turning into the street, the open-backed lorry slowly made its way towards them. It stopped; heavily armed Simba disembarked, many of them drunk. Firing their weapons indiscriminately as they systematically looted house after house as they moved ever closer.

Corporal Marsh swore.

"Fuck it, how many are there, Spike? I counted nine."

"Made them ten, Corporal."

"Right, let them come closer, make sure we get them all."

Two Simba walked up the garden path towards the front of the house. Crouched against the hedge the mercenary fired.

Automatic fire erupted from the gardens. Taken by surprise, the Simba fell under the heavy fire. Three Simba untouched by the hail of bullets returned fire from across the road.

Mounted on the lorry-cab the Bren gun opened fire; bullets tore through the hedges which offered little protection as the mercenaries hugged the ground. A man screamed in pain as he was hit.

Pinned down, Lofty tried desperately to return fire. "Get that fucking Bren," he shouted.

Corporal Marsh looked over to where Mitch was. "What yer reckon, Mitch?"

"Reckon we should try for the Bren before it cuts us all to pieces."

"Yeah, take two men with you, try and work yer way through the gardens. Get them bastards, Mitch."

"Right, Corp, will do. Pete, Jimbo, with me. Let's go."

Slowly the three soldiers inched their way forward through the hedges. The chatter of the Bren stopped as Mitch peered carefully over the low hedge. Ahead of him he could see the Bren, he watched as the loader quickly changed the magazine.

Once again the Bren fired.

"About fifty yards away," Mitch said softly. "We need to get close to make sure."

Mitch looked at the two young men; both had served with the Paras, full of pride and eager to risk all in one mad hectic charge. They had fought their way across the Congo together.

"Mitch it looks like shit or bust. Shall we go as they change the magazines?"

Mitch nodded.

Jimbo looked at his mate.

Pete grinned. "Say when, mate."

Shaking hands the three wished each other luck. Together they rose from cover as the Bren ceased firing. Barely had they covered ten yards when the Bren resumed its deadly fire.

Jimbo, hit, staggered forward firing as he dropped to his knees and fell face down.

Mitch swore and gritted his teeth as he fired. As if in slow motion, he watched as the Bren gunner was thrown backward as the heavy 9mm bullets hit him. The loader lay draped on the cab.

Mitch gasped for breath as he reloaded and vaulted onto the rear of the lorry.

"No, no!!" Tears welled in his eyes; Pete lay motionless a few yards away.

Fighting back tears, Mitch savagely kicked the dead loader off the cab. Grabbing the Bren he opened fire on the two surviving Simba.

"Cease fire, cease fire, Mitch." The two Simba stood up hands held high. Squinting down the sights the heat haze from the hot barrel distorted the Simba. They seemed to dance and sway.

Mitch calmly pulled the trigger.

Gently Mitch turned the young ex-Para over, his face in death still bore a grim look of determination, and he carried him over to where his comrade lay. Tears streaming down his face; he came to attention and saluted them.

Quietly he said to himself, "In the quiet times I will think of you both, you are not dead; you have just passed to another room, by and by in a brief moment in time we will meet again."

"Sorry, Mitch."

"Not your fault, Corporal, let's get the fuck out of here."

"Mitch, I'll get the lads to take Pete and Jimbo back. Also Sinclair: he caught one. He's dead, we have four wounded as well, bastard Bren."

"Right, clear the Simba dead out of sight. One of you take the truck back to base. We press on to the school."

Shouts of joyous welcome greeted them as they moved into the school grounds. Doors burst open as a tide of cheering women and children engulfed them.

Dirty, dishevelled, unshaven, the mercenaries were overwhelmed. Women flung their arms around them to embrace them. Initial excitement over, the women talked in groups, coffee was brought out, and food was being prepared.

"Nice to see you again, Corporal." Hand outstretched the young Belgian warmly shook hands.

"And you, some welcome."

"Yes, they think you are part of a larger force who are going to take them out."

"Poor bastards, we'll be lucky to get out of here alive ourselves."

"Heard all the firing, what happened, Corporal?"

"Ran into a bunch of Simba. Three men dead, four wounded, we got them all so they won't be reporting back."

"Sorry we couldn't help, thought it best we stayed hidden. What the hell is going to happen to us, Corporal? What chance have we got if they move into here in force?"

Concern was etched on his face. Full well he knew what fate awaited them if the Simba took the school. With the realisation that they were not to be evacuated an air of despondency overcame them, their future was very dubious.

"Corp, reckon yer should have a word with them to reassure them," Mitch said. "They have been asking if we are staying to protect them."

"Christ, Mitch, what can I say?"

"Dunno, mate, just tell them something."

"Like what? The truth, eighty five of us on a friggin' hill and four thousand of them."

Inside the school hall, the floor was bedecked with blankets and bedding. Canned food was in abundance. Power was supplied by a generator; the gentle throb of the diesel engine could be plainly heard. To over 40 women and children this was home. The men had a classroom as living quarters.

Corporal Marsh climbed onto a table; he looked at his apprehensive gathering.

"Ladies," he began, he stopped looked at the young Belgian driver. "Could you translate for me, please?"

With a nod he affirmed.

"We will not be able to take you out, but plans have been made to send help to you if needed. I will have a word with Major Lindle when I return, but I cannot make any promises. All I can say is we intend to hold the high ground outside Bolobo."

Excitedly, the dark haired woman in her native tongue addressed the Corporal. In her arms she held a young baby, at her side a child of about three. Fear showed in her eyes. Tears rolled down her cheeks as she sobbed uncontrollably.

"Corporal, she wants to know why you are leaving them?"

Corporal Marsh averted his gaze away from the sobbing woman; he could find no words to comfort her. Unable to contain his emotions he stepped down from the table and briskly walked out of the hall.

Outside, he fumbled in his pocket for his cigarettes. Lighting one, he inhaled deeply.

Private Drummond, Doggy to his friends, finished

reassembling the Bren gun which was mounted on the flat roof of the school. Under his expert instruction the Belgian men now had a working knowledge of the weapon. Picking up an empty magazine with practised ease he pushed cartridges into it.

"Now it takes 28 rounds. When full you place the magazine thus, push down. It will snap home. Let the bolt go forward, you are now ready to fire. You do of course have to push the safety catch off. Try it with an empty magazine. To unload, just press this button and lift off."

Doggy watched as they went through the drill.

"How's it going, Doggy?"

"Not too bad, Corp, think they've got it."

"Good, get yerself down here. We're pulling out."

Robust laughter could be heard as the Bedford made its way towards the hill; it came to a lurching halt.

Major Lindle watched as the men, somewhat unsteady on their feet, piled off the lorry.

Shiner's loud voice could be heard above the laughter.

"Think I'll desert."

"Good fucking riddance," someone shouted.

Major Lindle fumed as he watched. "Corporal Marsh," he snapped. "These men are drunk."

"No Sir, I don't think so, not yet."

"Don't be so bloody insolent, Corporal, where did this beer and whisky come from?"

"From the airport, Major."

"The Major's face contorted in rage. "You men get to your posts."

Mitch drank slowly. Can empty, he tossed it at the Major's feet and burped loudly.

"Chuck us another can, Doggy. Cheers, mate, and this one, Major, is for Jimbo and Pete. Major, if yer don't like it go fuck yerself."

"Naughty, naughty, Mitch, don't talk to the Major like that."

Shiner grinned at the Major as if to challenge him to reply.

Sergeant Johnson hurried towards them. "Sir, the Simba are on the move, bloody hoards of them."

Bending down, the sergeant removed a bottle of whisky from the case; he was a man with a taste for a dram.

"With your permission, Sir." He took a gulp and pursed his lips. "May I suggest we give some of this to the lads, Sir."

Chapter 15

No Retreat

Lofty lit a cigarette; he opened a can of beer and took a gulp. The bolt of the 20mm slid forward with a solid thump as the weapon loaded.

"Well, Doggy, it looks like this is it."

Doggy was Lofty's loader. So engrossed was he in loading shells into the magazine he failed to hear.

Spasmodic fire came from the burnt-out trucks as the Simba used them for cover. Bullets hissed overhead, dust kicked up around their positions.

"Hold your fire," Major Lindle bellowed as a Bren opened up on the Simba.

Well prepared and dug in, the mercenaries waited. The Simba would have to cross open ground before moving up the hill.

Lofty smiled to himself as he watched both Jock and Shiner swig away at their whisky.

Half-drunk, Shiner was at his most dangerous, but he was glad to have him on his flank. Just below him, Jock; between each 20mm, the weapon pits with Bren guns.

"Come on, yer bastards come to uncle Shiner!" Shiner was impatient.

Mitch had this feeling of impending doom. Since the death of his two friends he had brooded and thought a lot. He had been in the army since leaving school. What made a soldier, he pondered, was the born soldier a myth? Was it that some just tolerated it better than others? He had left the army and came to Africa as a mercenary. This caper, the whole thing couldn't be any madder, and all of them must be stark staring mad. Why couldn't he be like Shiner, who didn't give a fuck for anything or anybody? God knows what will become of these men when this is all over. Shut them up like mad dogs, I reckon.

"Stand to, stand to."

Mitch hardly heard the shouted command as he watched the Simba came forward in massed ranks over the open ground. Wild-eyed, they advanced, chanting loudly at a run.

"Open fire, open fire."

Bren guns chattering mingled with the heavy reports of the 20mm machineguns.

Mitch fired burst after burst at the Simba. How could they advance into such withering fire. They must be drugged for they had this air of invincibility about them. Up the hill they swept like an unstoppable tide. Within a few yards of the weapon pits the attack faltered, then broke as the Simba retreated.

Simba dead, lay as if strewn by some prodigious wind. Beside the lower weapon pit, a mercenary lay dead. His blond hair bare to the sun, one leg straight, the other drawn up as though he had died climbing. His hands clutched the sand. Another lay, arms bent, fingers neatly curled.

Major Lindle surveyed the corpse strewn battlefield, and he stretched his lips until his face was like a mask. Screwed up his eyes as though against some blinding light, he slowly shook his head.

"What a waste," he said. "What a bloody waste."

"Stand down, lads, well done." Sergeant Johnson shouted as he moved from position to position taking details of casualties; the Major would need to know.

Seated on empty ammunition boxes the three sailors and their loader discussed the action.

"Close run thing, weren't it?"

"Yer right there, Doggy." Shiner pulled a face. "This big Simba near got me. Didn't see the fucker, he just appeared with this big machete. Christ I thought it was me lot, me whole life flashed before me."

"Must have been horrible, mate?" Lofty tried to look serious. "Having yer life flash before yer, I mean."

"Ever the comedian, ain't yer, Lofty? Weren't funny, mate, if it weren't for the corporal I wouldn't be here. He nailed him with a Bren."

"Now, now, what's this?" Sergeant Johnson strode up. "A mother's meeting? Come on, no time for idle chat. You loaders get some more ammunition to these guns. One of you sailor boys take a decco at that middle 20mm, bloody thing keeps jamming."

"Aye, will do." Jock got to his feet. "Sounds like the extractors."

"Hope not," commented the Sergeant. "We left all the spares at the airport. Lofty, Shiner, can you check the other guns?"

Shiner nodded in agreement. Full well he realised the Simba onslaught had only been stopped by the firepower of the 20mm's. They would remain a crucial factor.

"Sarge, how many men did we lose?" Lofty waited for a reply.

"Five, four wounded, two badly by mortar. Watkins lost a leg. Don't think he'll make it, pity. Damn good soldier."

"Come on, Sarge, do yer think any of us are gonna get off this poxy hill alive?"

Sergeant Johnson looked at Shiner who had asked the question. How could he begin to understand the big sailor?

The man looked indifferent to the situation.

"Well, Sarge?!" Shiner asked again.

"Hard to say, lad, reckon we have a 50-50 chance of holding them."

"One thing's certain," grinned Shiner.

"What's that?"

"Definitely the worst fucking leave I've ever had; be glad when it's finished. Sarge, do yer reckon this is a good time to see the Major about me getting paid?"

Sergeant Johnson walked away shaking his head and smiling to himself.

Midday: the sun climbed high in the sky, the heat was oppressive; no shade was to be found. Men stripped to the waist sat close to their weapons. Of the Simba, not a sign; they had vanished as if into thin air.

Soup was being ladled from the dixie into mess-cans as food and coffee was brought round to the men.

Major Lindle was deep in conversation with Sergeant Johnson and Corporal Marsh.

"One 20mm up the creek, Major. Broken extractor won't clear the empty cartridges from the chamber."

"Could be a lot worse, Sergeant, I take it the other guns are okay?"

"Yes, Sir, they're fine."

"How is the ammunition situation, Corporal?"

"Plenty for the 20mm's and Brens, Sir, but a bit short of 9mm for the Stens."

"I see, Corporal, tell the men to go easy on the 9mm. Can you arrange to remove the damaged 20mm and replace it with two Brens?"

"Yes, Major, I'll see to it now."

"Damn the Simba, Sergeant, why don't they attack? This waiting is getting the men down; it's been four bloody hours since they came."

"Perhaps they are having a little think, Sir, this is the first time we have stood our ground to fight them. Anyhow Major, we are ready."

"Thank you, Sergeant."

"Oh, by the way, Sir, one of the lads picked up a news programme on his radio. Seems like the rest of the world knows what is going on here. He said something about the Belgium Government is asking questions, some talk about them intervening."

"Asking questions," the Major exploded. "Bloody ludicrous, this is their country, it's up to them to protect their own nationals," he fumed.

"Yes, Major. Another thing, Sir, Private Watkins died a short while ago."

"Thank you, Sergeant; that will be all."

Sergeant Johnson came to attention, saluted and briskly walked away. He passed the neat mounds of earth where his comrades lay. Sadly, he mentally counted, coming up with twelve. No neat cemetery for them, no war graves commission employing a host of workers to see to it in perpetuity that their resting place would not offend the eye of any beholder. No headstones to mark their graves, but their sacrifice would never be forgotten

Doggy drank the rest of his soup and pulled a face. "Well I don't think I'll have seconds."

"Yeah, bloody horrible."

"Is there any beer left?"

"Naah, Jock scoffed the last one."

"What the fuck happened to all that beer we brought back from the airport?" scowled Shiner.

"The Major had it taken to the field kitchen for that fat chef to look after," said Lofty. "No wonder the fat git always looks pissed."

Doggy looked at Shiner. He knew full well with a few chosen words he could provoke the big sailor into getting a case of beer, he thought for a moment.

"That's it then," he began. "If the Major says we can't have any beer until he says so…"

"Fuck the Major," said Shiner as he rose to his feet. Swearing loudly, he stamped off in the direction of the field kitchen.

"Nice one, Doggy," grinned Jock.

Shiner approached the field kitchen. In the shade of his portable kitchen the chef reclined on a box. In one hand a cigarette in the other a beer.

"Where's the beer?" snarled Shiner.

"No beer without the Major's permission," replied the cook as he took a swig at his can.

"Fuck the Major. Get out of my way, you fat maggot."

"You touch that beer and I'll do you, so fuck off."

Shiner spat in contempt. "You!" he laughed. "Yer couldn't pull the feathers off a sick chicken."

Looking at the big sailor he decided discretion would be the better part of valour.

With a triumphant look on his face, Shiner returned with a case of beer under each arm.

"As I was saying," beamed Shiner. "Fuck the Major."

Major Lindle's face contorted in rage as the whining cook related every detail of Shiner's raid on the beer.

"I told him, Sir, no beer without yer orders; he called me a maggot and said 'Fuck the Major.'"

The Major looked at the chef. He had only contempt for this fat, greasy, little man. Trying hard to suppress his feelings he dismissed him.

He slunk off with a smirk on his face, his mission to find Sergeant Johnson as requested by the Major.

"Got yer message, Sir, you wanted to see me?"

"Ye,s Sergeant, I want that Shiner put under bloody arrest."

"Arrest, Sir. May I ask why?"

"He has complete disregard for orders, stole beer from the cook-house. We must have discipline, Sergeant, or we become a rabble."

"Yes, Sir, I understand. But I think, Sir, you should let me deal with this."

"Why, Sergeant; why?"

"Where could we put him? We would need men to guard him. Also, I would need a man to replace him on the 20mm. Sir, for all his shortcomings he is an excellent gunner."

"Sergeant, much against my better judgement I will leave it in your hands, but I want this sorted."

"Sorted it will be, Sir."

Doggy waved a greeting as Corporal Marsh, accompanied by Mitch, came towards them.

Shiner rose grinning. "Thanks, Corp, I owe yer one, mate, have a beer."

"Don't mind if I do, where'd yer get this from?"

"My dear Corporal, that is a naval secret."

Mitch sat down; he nodded to Private Hudson, Shiner's loader. "How'd yer get on with that old bastard?" he said with good humour.

Private Hudson glanced at Shiner and burst out laughing.

"What's funny?"

"Yer know that big Simba that near got Shiner, the poor bastard fell half in our gun-pit, his loin cloth was open, he had this big todger hanging there, do yer know what he said? 'Fucking hell his mum must have hung a big rock on that.'"

Above the laughter, Shiner looked indifferent to it all,

his only comment was, "The biggest trouser snake yer ever saw, more like a python."

"Corp, what are the Simba up to?"

Corporal Marsh shrugged his shoulders. "Been some movement, the Major has got two guns closed up. Near forgot, Shiner, the Sergeant wants a word with you."

"What for?"

"Dunno, mate, but he said he would be at the field kitchen."

Sergeant Johnson opened a can of beer. He took a swig and remained seated as Shiner walked up.

"Yer wanted to see me, Sarge?"

"Yes, sit yourself down, lad. Time we had a little chat. Help yourself to a beer. We must get one thing straight," the Sergeant paused.

"What's that?" said a puzzled Shiner.

"That is Major Lindle is the Officer in Command."

Shiner shook his head. "Not of me, he ain't."

"Now, now, Shiner, don't let me and you fall out lad. You don't have to like the man, just give him a little respect. I was in Korea with the Major; he won a Military Medal, he is a good officer."

A grin appeared on the big sailor's face, he liked the Sergeant. The men he treated fairly, and never did he shout at them or bully them. It would be a mistake to underestimate him; underneath he was a tough soldier.

Shiner's eyes lit up. "If I'm under the Major's command, then it stands to reason I must be on the payroll." Shiner smiled broadly. "Fair enough, Sarge."

"Right, lad, get back to your mates, won't be long before we have guests."

Movement had been spotted among the wrecked vehicles. The Simba were back. A Bren gun chattered as men rushed to their positions. Heavy small arms fire came from the cover of the wrecked vehicles. Bullets whined overhead dust kicked up around the gun-pits.

Lofty briefly glanced to his right and below him; both Jock and Shiner were ready.

"Stand by lads. Pick your targets, open fire."

Lofty watched fascinated as empty 20mm shell cases hung momentarily in the air to drop with a metallic clink from Jock's gun.

Exulted,he left; this was certitude to kill or be killed.

Echoes lashed across the hill as the tempo of fire increased. In battle, the courage and endurance of human endeavour, when the limits have been reached, there is always one who can surpass those limits and drive them on.

Mitch licked his dry lips. He snuggled more closely to the butt of his Bren-gun, and seconds later the Simba came into his sights.

Into a curtain of fire the Simba advanced. Interlocking tracer formed an impenetrable wall. Time, after time, the Simba hurled themselves against the hill to be thrown back with catastrophic losses.

Doggy yelped in pain as he lost his footing, slipping on empty shell cases he fell heavily against the hot barrel of the machinegun.

"Only three full mags left," he shouted to Lofty as he replaced the empty magazine. "Can't load 'em fast enough, mate."

Major Lindle walked calmly from position to position as if on a Sunday stroll. He called encouragement to his men ignoring the bullets that hissed around him.

The tumult of gunfire eased, then silence. A short burst of fire from the Simba was answered perfunctory by a Bren-gun. Of the Simba, no sign as they withdrew.

Men appeared as they cautiously clambered out of trenches and weapon-pits. No small arms fire greeted them, and loaders busied themselves re-loading empty magazines.

Doggy swore vehemently as he scooped handfuls of empty shell cases out of the gun-pit. "Cor, look at me bleeding shoulder," he whined. "Look at that burn, I should go sick."

Lofty ignored Doggy as he carried on cleaning his gun.

"How yer doing, mate?" Shiner stood looking down into the gun-pit.

Lofty let the bolt of the gun slide forward. With a final wipe of the oily cloth he looked up. "Gis yer hand, mate."

Taking Shiner's outstretched hand he hauled himself out of the gun-pit.

"Jock alright?"

"Yeah, he's fine."

Shiner sniffed and wrinkled his nose in disgust. "What's that smell? What a bloody stink."

"Doggy's bleeding feet. They're rotten, he's cornered the body odour market."

"Can't help it," protested Doggy with a pained look on his face. "Some people say it's healthy."

"Well, it ain't doing my health any good," said Lofty.

"Listen up, lads," the sergeant bellowed. "The Major would like a word."

"Thank you, Sergeant. Can everyone hear me? Good.

"About 300 Simba have moved to our rear. My guess is they are going to launch an all out attack simultaneously on two sides. It will be difficult for them to take the rear ground as it is much steeper, also they have a lot of open ground to cover. Our problem is it will mean splitting our fire-power; the two highest 20mm are sited to meet such an attack. It is imperative to break up any attack quickly. I would like two of the naval gunners to man these guns; Sergeant could you detail extra loaders and get plenty of ammunition up to them?"

"Yes, Sir, will do."

"Another thing, Sergeant, I want four Bren-gun crews to support them. Also as many men as you can spare to protect the 20mm. Carry on, Sergeant, thank you."

Lofty looked at Shiner. "Which two of us, mate?"

"Get Jock, we'll toss for it. First two heads to go."

Jock spun first, the coin came down tails.

"Got a head," grunted Shiner. "What yer get, Lofty?"

"Same as you mate, a head."

"Dinna want to go up there anyhows." Jock shook hands with his two friends. "See yea both later take care of yersels. Come on Vice-Whore."

Jock nodded to his loader who had the ridiculous name of Harold Grice Moore. The men invented variations of it like, Mice Graw, Twice Poor. He took no notice, he had heard it all before.

Lofty eased himself behind the gun. "Gis a fag, Doggy, cheers, mate."

Full magazines were stacked in a row; two extra loaders were busy loading more magazines.

Doggy pushed a magazine into his Sten and laid it within easy reach on top of the weapon-pit ready.

500 yards away the Simba massed. Private Hudson stared open mouthed. "Bloody hell, hundreds of the fuckers!"

"Won't be so many soon," Shiner muttered to himself.

Lofty smiled, his thoughts fleeting back to Malta. Shiner and Jock both drunk, staggered out of a bar to be accosted by a young Midshipman straight from Officer Training School. He demanded they salute him.

Comedy ensued. Jock wriggled like an embarrassed virgin. He dug Shiner in the ribs. "Go on, Shiner, gie tha nice boy a salute, go on."

Shiner hung his head and gurgled, "No, no, I am so shy, you give him one."

"Oh, I couldn't really," Jock said writhing in mock bashfulness, a crowd had gathered to enjoy this travesty of mock femininity.

Blushing like a girl himself; the Midshipman beat a hasty retreat.

There was a curious numbness in Lofty's mind, he neither dreaded or anticipated the impending action. He was coming to terms with the possibility of death.

Chanting, the Simba moved forward on both sides of the hill.

Lofty pushed the safety catch off. Both heavy machineguns opened fire at 400 yards. The first of the fire struck the Simba.

Men flung their arms skyward quivering and taut as though gripped by some sudden ecstasy. They fell as if corn before a sickle. Men following behind tripped over their fallen comrades. Now well in range of the Bren guns which chattered incessantly. On this front the machinegun was the master.

Massive was the attack launched on the other side of the hill. Unrelenting and with grim determination, disregarding casualties they pushed up the hill. As the threat on Lofty's front diminished he glanced behind him and became immediately aware of the seriousness of the situation. Swinging the gun round he fired long bursts into the closing Simba.

Major Lindle calmly replaced the empty Sten gun magazine. The whole hill was thick with fire. Crouching as he moved through a haze of smoke, the major continuously moved from position to position, shouting, encouraging, and swearing.

Two of the 20mm machineguns no longer fired. Loaders grabbed Sten guns to engage the Simba at close quarters. In front of them Bren guns had been overrun. The survivors backed up the hill firing as they retreated.

A pitiless hail of fire swept down from the hill as Shiner and the Bren guns turned their fire on the Simba. It was to be decisive.

Under fire a man either surrenders to fear or becomes a burden to his comrades, or he cultivates the ability to withdraw himself from his surroundings. The frightened man only wants to escape from his ordeal. In his fear, he does not shrink from death but embraces it as a welcome end to his terror.

Face glossed with sweat of terror, the cook wild-eyed stared unblinkingly ahead. Suddenly, he clawed frenziedly at the sides of the trench and scrambled out waving a dirty white cloth. "I surrender," he screamed. "I surrender." Hands upraised he ran towards the Simba into a hail of fire from the hill crest.

Under heavy fire the Simba faltered then withdrew. Behind them on the fire ravaged hill, their dead lay, too numerous to count. In front of the Bren gun pits where fearsome hand to hand fighting had taken place white soldiers lay with the Simba. The stench of death and blood was overpowering.

"Cease fire, cease fire."

Major Lindle's voice rose above the din of battle. Exultation and a burning feeling swept up inside him, a savage pride possessed him. These men, what men they were. They had fought the Simba to a standstill despite overwhelming odds with feats of gallantry far too many to be chronicled.

Lofty stood up and moved away from his gun, he shook his head. "What the fuck am I doing here?" he asked Doggy.

"Dunno, mate, you tell me."

"Doggy, I don't know myself mate."

"Wonder how the lads fared?" Doggy asked thoughtfully. "They broke through one section; a lot of Simba dead are behind the first trenches."

Shiner hurried towards Lofty, he looked apprehensive. "Got a bad feeling, mate. I think Jock could have bought it."

"Come off it, Shiner, the old bastards too mean to get himself killed, let's go see him."

Jock's 20mm gun barrel was pointing skyward, Simba dead were everywhere, of Jock no sign.

Sergeant Johnson came towards them, he looked grimfaced.

"Shiner, Lofty, I am so sorry, lads."

"Bloody knew it, the poor bastard's dead, ain't he?"

"Yes, Shiner, afraid so."

"Where is he, Sarge?"

"Still in the gun-pit."

"Leave him, me an' Lofty will take care of him."

Jock lay on his back his face turned sideways; eyes closed, the lids smooth and peaceful with deep ascetic folds in the cheeks. Blood stained the front of his shirt. Private Grice Moore lay beside him still grasping an empty Sten gun.

Shiner's shoulders began to shake uncontrollably as tears streamed down his face. "Yer stupid scotch bastard why did yer go an' get yerself killed?" he sobbed.

Casualties for the defenders were high. Eighteen dead, eleven injured, now only 38 fit men faced the Simba.

Ammunition was running low.

Time had no meaning for the defenders as they sat around gun-pits waiting. It had been three hours since the last Simba attack. It seemed an eternity. Weary from fighting there was no elation at repulsing the Simba. Tired men in filthy uniforms deafened by gunfire but with a determination to hold this hill at all costs.

Major Lindle, with Sergeant Johnson, walked from position to position with words of encouragement for his men. Outwardly confident and resolute he moved cheerfully among the men. The conflict was beginning to get to him; to the men he showed nothing of this.

"How's it going, Corporal Marsh?"

"Not too bad, Sir. Any chance of some beer?"

"Yes, I had forgot, detail two men to distribute it."

"Yes, Major, thank you."

"Sergeant, how are our injured?"

"Not too good, Sir. We have very little medical supplies, Doc is doing the best he can."

"What a bloody shambles this is, Sergeant, how many of our casualties can still fight?"

"Seven, Sir; I have already detailed their positions."

"Thank you, Sergeant."

Shiner expertly dismantled the 20mm, carefully cleaning each part, deftly he reassembled the weapon.

Mitch watched in admiration. "Yer know yer way round them there guns, mate."

"Hi ya, Mitch, seen Lofty?"

"Yeah, he's checking Evans' 20mm. Sorry about Jock, mate."

Shiner, eyes closed, was immured in an anguish of memories. "Gonna miss the old bastard, me an him were mates a long time. We had some right laughs. Now he's gone, them fucking Simba are gonna pay."

Mitch gently put a hand on Shiner's shoulder. "I know, mate. Jimbo, Pete now Jock and a lot of other good lads."

"Yeah, I know Mitch, but it don't make it any easier. What's the latest on the Belgian's intervening?"

"Ain't heard nuttin', mate, the batteries on Midge's radio are knackered."

"Hey, you two," Corporal Marsh yelled. "We're gonna move the lower pair of 20mms up here, give the lads a hand will yer?"

"Yeah, mate," Mitch replied.

"Be the last friggin' move," Shiner said, "nowhere else to go, we're out of real estate."

Doggy lurched and stumbled under the weight of the heavy boxes of 20mm shells as he trekked up the hill.

"Pick your feet up, lad." Sergeant Johnson grinned as he strode past Doggy carrying two boxes of shells.

"It's me legs, Sarge, they're too short," whined Doggy.

"Well, lad, you can go brew some tea for your mates after you have taken that ammo up."

The remaining four serviceable 20mm guns were now dug in on the crest of the hill. Boxes of ammunition were stacked beside them.

Major Lindle nodded his thanks as Doggy handed him a mug of tea.

"Thank you, Drummond, how are you?"

"Fair to middling, Sir. Be much better when I get off this bleeding hill."

"Won't we all. How is the water and food situation?"

"Plenty of canned beans; not much of anything else, Sir."

"And the water?"

"Enough for half a dozen brew-ups Sir; still got several cases of beer."

"Nice mug of tea, Drummond."

"Thank you, Sir."

"We need a cook, Drummond, how would you like to take over?"

"Me, Sir, I ain't no chef."

"Come on, Drummond, what culinary expertise do you require to heat beans?"

Chapter 16

Relief

"'Ere,' mate, what they up to now?"

Private Hudson looked anxious as small groups of Simba darted between wrecked vehicles.

"Mitch, nip an' fetch the Major, let him have a decco."

Major Lindle looked puzzled as he watched. "Can't see any point in that, can you, Sergeant?"

"No, Sir, perhaps they just want to keep us on our toes or draw our fire."

"You could be right, Sergeant. Keep two Brens closed up, tell the remainder of the men to get what rest they can."

"What's for supper, chef?" called 'Topsy' Turner with a grin.

Doggy stopped opening the can of beans and glared at Topsy. "Go shag yerself, yer Geordie git."

"Now, now, don't lose yer rag, mate."

"I ain't." He emptied the can of beans into the large pot, then reached for a can of beer. With a flourish he opened the can and drank with relish.

"Cor, gis a beer, Doggy."

"Fuck off, Turner yer piss taker. Chef's perks."

Doggy cursed loudly as, beer flying, he dived for cover as heavy fire swept the hill from the cover of the wrecked vehicles.

"Here we go again, Sir," Sergeant Johnson said quietly.

"Tell the men, Sergeant, not to return fire unless they try to advance up the hill. Detail six of your best marksmen to act as snipers."

"Yer back again then, Doggy?"

"Yeah, Lofty, being chef out there ain't no good. Still yer loader, mate."

"Fucking hell, Doggy, them bleeding feet of yours, they don't get any better."

"It's me socks; can't help it."

Mitch slowly and deliberately pushed a clip of cartridges into the Mauser 7.63mm rifle. Carefully, he scanned the wrecked vehicles through the telescopic sight. He stopped abruptly and watched as two Simba fired automatic weapons from inside a burnt out bus. The cross-wires of the sights centred on one of the Simba. The high velocity bullet tore half his head off as he was hurled backwards; the demise of the Simba went unnoticed as the other Simba continued firing. Mitch quickly worked the bolt to re-load, once again he fired.

Groups of screaming Simba rushed from cover intent on occupying the lower trenches. They were met by a withering catastrophic hail of fire, and the human tide was thrown back, bloody and broken.

Major Lindle watched as the Simba again burst from cover in a renewed frenzied attack. Like apparitions they moved forward. With sudden brutality, the heavy machine guns opened fire. The scene of carnage before him was scarcely imaginable. The remorseless barrage abated as the surviving Simba sought cover; intermittent bursts of Bren gun fire followed, then an eerie silence. Only the pitiful cries of the dying and wounded could now be heard.

Lofty lit a cigarette as he leant against the side of his trench; he felt an overwhelming feeling of nausea as he stared at the Simba dead.

"Bloody hell, Doggy, why the fuck don't they pack it in?"

"Don't know about that, mate, but we're running out of ammo, only three boxes of 20mm left."

"Right, Doggy, you'd better chase up the Sarge. See if yer can rustle up some Sten ammo."

"Will do, mate."

Doggy turned to go, and then stopped and listened intently.

"Ere mate, ain't that an aircraft?"

Lofty shielded his eyes against the sun and looked towards the sound. "Yer right, Doggy, there it is, looks like a single engine old prop fighter."

Lofty swung the 20mm around. "Stand by, Doggy, just in case."

Sergeant Johnson, binoculars trained on the aircraft spoke without interrupting his study.

"Looks like a Typhoon, Sir."

"Can you make out any markings on it, Sergeant?"

"Not at the moment, Sir. Wait a minute, I think it's Belgian, yes it is."

"You sure, Sergeant?"

"Yes, Sir, it's Belgian."

Major Lindle shouted loudly.

"20mm stand to, aircraft closing from the west; do not engage unless fired on."

Clearly from his cockpit the pilot could be seen waving as he came in low. Banking sharply away he made a lower pass. Once again he waved as he swooped low towards the Simba. White smoke billowed from his wings as he strafed the Simba's positions.

Cheering men stood as the Typhoon resumed its attack with rockets. Wispy trails of smoke followed the rockets down as with unerring accuracy the projectiles burst among the Simba.

Major Lindle looked relieved. He felt as if some heavy weight had been lifted from him.

"Nice for the men to have something to cheer about, Sergeant, it looks very much like we are at last going to have some overdue help."

"Yes, Sir," agreed Sergeant Johnson.

Wave after wave of Typhoon's screamed overhead as they pounded the Simba.

Shiner slapped his loader on his back and vaulted out of his trench. He laughed dementedly as he urged the pilots on to greater efforts.

"Go on ,yer birdie boys give the bastards some stick."

Retreating in confusion, the Simba stampeded back towards the woodland. The earth shook as a choking fog of whirling dust obscured the Simba, lit up by flashes of glimmering lights as rockets exploded among them.

Doggy, grinning at Lofty, gestured towards Shiner.

"Yer mates in good voice, ain't he?"

"Yeah, makes a change, don't it?"

Doggy offered Lofty a cigarette; lighting his, he inhaled deeply. He looked thoughtful. "Yer know, mate," he said. "It looks like we could get back to Blighty after all. Had me doubts. Cor, what I'd give to be having a pint in me local."

"Yeah, me too, Doggy, only problem is me an' Shiner should have been back on board ship over a week ago."

Smoke spiralled skywards from beyond the woods as the Typhoon broke off their attacks.

"Seems like a good opportunity for the men to have a

brew and some hot food, Sergeant."

"Yes, Sir, will get Drummond to organise it. What happens now regarding the men if the Belgians take over?"

"Sergeant, I want them out of here as soon as possible. Our contract with the Katanga government is finished. An explanation as to why that bastard Kossato pulled out and left us in the shit. Also, I am most anxious to confirm payments have been made into our bank accounts after what happened to the naval personnel."

"Speaking of them, Major, I think they should be paid the same as us, not forgetting Jock's next of kin."

"Yes, Sergeant, I intend to have a word with our employers just as soon as we reach the capital."

"Just hope that Kossanto ain't about, Major, hate to think what Shiner would do to him."

"That, Sergeant, I would like to see," he grinned.

"Yer don't have to bleeding eat 'em," Doggy said curtly as Shiner pulled a face as Doggy unceremoniously slopped the beans into Shiner's mess tin.

"Ain't got no friggin' option, have I?" moaned Shiner. "I'm bloody famished. Yer wait, when I get off this poxy hill I'm gonna get me a big steak."

"We ain't off yet, mate," Mitch stated matter of factly.

"Come on, Mitch, stands to reason the Belgians will send troops."

"Yeah, when? One big push an' them Simba will be over us like a rash, plus we're near out of ammo."

"Don't be so fucking morbid, Mitch, me an' Lofty are absent without leave. We have to go back to that First Lieutenant. Just see him now rubbing his hands in glee, the bastard."

"How's the food, lads?"

"Yer can't have had any yet, Sergeant, or yer wouldn't be asking," growled Topsy.

"Never mind, lad, with a bit of luck we'll be out of here soon, then yer can have big eats, Corporal Marsh."

"Yes, Sergeant."

"It will be dark in an hour or so, detail two gun-crews to close-up and rotate them hourly throughout the night just to be prudent."

"Will do, Sergeant."

Sergeant Johnson looked at Shiner for a moment. "A word with you, lad." The sergeant turned, beckoned to Shiner and walked a few paces.

Shiner rose and followed.

"Yeah, Sergeant, what have I done wrong now?"

"Nothing, lad, nothing. Just thought I would let you know the Major is going to have a word with the powers that be about you getting paid, also a lump sum for Jock's next of kin."

"Cheers, Sergeant, I appreciate it especially for old Jock."

Mitch struggled to keep his eyes open. His watch had been uneventful. The sound of footsteps galvanised him into action, instinctively he swung round Sten gun ready.

"Steady on, Mitch, it's me, mate, Doggy," he said urgently.

"Fuck you, Doggy, yer gonna get yer head shot off you bloody idiot, why ain't yer asleep?"

"Can't sleep, mate. Everything okay?"

"Yeah, all quiet."

"Might as well get a brew on, it'll be light soon."

In the eastern sky, the first tinges of red and yellow spread slowly across the horizon to herald the dawn. Mitch grinned to himself as he lit a cigarette; he watched as Doggy filled the tea urn and lit the primus. Men stirred from sleep, limbs aching from an uncomfortable night spent cramped in trenches. Already Doggy was cheerfully handing out mugs of tea.

"'Ere yer are, Shiner me old mate, a nice cup of rosy lee."

Shiner stretched and groaned. "Fucking hell, I feel like I've been shagged by an elephant; me friggin' back it's done in." He pulled a face.

"This will put yer right." Doggy handed him a brimming steaming mug of tea.

"Cheers, Doggy, just the job."

"Good morning, Sir."

"Good morning, Sergeant, I trust you didn't sleep well?"

"No, Sir, getting too old to sleep rough."

"Won't be for much longer, bit of luck we could be away soon."

"Need to be, Major, we're running out of water."

"Any sign of the Simba?"

"Very quiet, Sir. Turner reported hearing them during the night, since then nothing."

"Good, keep two guns closed up just in case."

"Very well, Sir."

Midday came and passed. The sun climbed to its zenith. The entire landscape shimmered in the heat. Men strove in vain to find shade. The stench of the dead was overpowering. Swarms of flies plagued the mercenaries. Wheeling, hooded vultures circled overhead before dropping to join their companions in a seething mass of squawking as they fed on the dead.

Mitch cursed as he swatted angrily at the flies that buzzed around him incessantly. It was a futile effort.

"Fucking flies, they're as big as bleeding vultures," he

moaned.

"Yeah, Mitch," Topsy growled. "I feel like a poxy turd, I'm pissed off with this. I'm outta here soon, Simba or no friggin' Simba."

Sergeant Johnson looked long and hard at Private Turner, and finally he said, "Patience, lad, patience; don't be stupid, we all go together, won't be long now."

"Yeah, when?"

"Don't know, lad, shouldn't be long. The Belgians know the situation."

"Aircraft, aircraft." Corporal Marsh waved excitedly, all eyes turned towards the incoming aircraft.

"Ain't fighters, are they?" stated Doggy.

They watched in delight as the empty sky filled with tiny black figures. Parachutes opened and slowly drifted downwards. More planes arrived to disgorge their human cargo. Wheeling away, the planes slowly circled. The Belgians had arrived in force.

"About bloody time," said Major Lindle.

"Yes, Sir," agreed the Sergeant. "But at least they're here."

"Not in time to help the men we lost," the Major said with a shake of his head.

Lofty shouldered his Sten gun. "Chuck us a couple of magazines Doggy, looks like we'll be off soon, mate. Gonna have a word with Shiner."

"Ere yer are, hang on a mo, I'm with you."

Shiner waved a greeting and smiled broadly.

"Hi ya, Lofty, Doggy, look like the Paras have secured the airport, their planes have just landed."

"Yeah, Major, are we pulling out?"

"Give the Belgians time to get themselves consolidated." Even as he spoke the sounds of heavy and sustained automatic fire resounded from the woodland area.

"With respect, Sir, by the sound of it I should say the Paras are sorting the Simba out."

"Yes, Sergeant, you could well be correct. Disable the 20mms, on completion we march into Bolobo as a disciplined unit."

"What about our dead?" Shiner's voice quavered, sadness showed in his eyes.

"Sorry, Shiner," the Major said quietly. "I will inform the British Embassy where they are."

"Bloody lovely, Scots git, he was me mate," the big sailor said bitterly. His bitterness was enhanced by the ineptitude of the Belgian Military to intervene sooner caused by the ditherings of the politicians. It was made worse by the knowledge that these failings would be swept under the carpet along with their dead.

In step they marched towards Bolobo; burdened with weapons, filthy, unkempt and bearded. Walking wounded bringing up the rear, more seriously injured being carried on makeshift stretchers.

Cheering paratroopers rushed forward to embrace them warmly and shake their hands. Medics moved quickly to tend the injured.

"I am Lieutenant Charles Katz." The young officer came to attention and saluted, he extended his hand towards Major Lindle.

Major Lindle grasped the offered hand in a firm handshake.

"Damned glad to make your acquaintance, Lieutenant, I am Major Lindle."

"Yes, Sir, I know who you are."

"Oh, how come?" said a puzzled Major Lindle.

"Newspapers in England and Belgium are full of your

exploits; you and your men are celebrities, Sir."

"Bloody reporters, Lieutenant, they're a pain in the arse; surprised they didn't fly in with you."

"Not for the want of trying, Major, believe me; they will be waiting for you in the capital."

"No doubt, Lieutenant, no doubt."

"By the way Major, off the record, we are under orders to evacuate you and your men from the area as soon as possible. Your government has been in contact with ours. You my friend, seem to be an embarrassment to them with all the news coverage you are receiving."

"Sooner the better," grinned Major Lindle.

"Could you and your men please wait here, Major. Transport is on its way to take you to the airport. I must also request your men leave their weapons here."

"Dammit, Lieutenant, you're in a hurry to get shot of us."

"Sorry, Major, orders from Brigadier Herman."

Lieutenant Katz waved them on their way as the two open backed army lorries moved off. Nearing the airport, several armoured vehicles sped past them. Paratroopers well dug in, manned the machine guns guarding the airport.

"Looks like the Paras have everything well in hand," observed Doggy.

"Right, yer horrible lot, off," shouted Sergeant Johnson as they stopped outside the terminal. Paratroopers beckoned them towards the open doors and into the main lounge. Joyful shouts greeted them as the women of Bolobo rushed to greet them, arms outstretched they embraced them.

Tears streaming down her face, the woman clung to Shiner. "So glad you're safe," she sobbed. "When we arrived at the airport it was deserted, we went back to the bar and hid in the cellar. We heard all the firing it was horrible."

"Never mind, you're okay now."

She smiled, turned and hugged Lofty. "Your friend?!" concern etched her face. "Where is he?"

Shiner slowly shook his head. "He didn't make it," he replied.

"Oh no, I am so sorry."

Shiner was relieved to see Brigadier Herman enter the lounge. He could not come to terms with the death of his friend; he felt an overwhelming sense of remorse and guilt. The Brigadier's entrance was a welcome distraction from his thoughts.

Brigadier Herman glanced briefly around the lounge before stepping gingerly up onto a chair. He waved a hand for silence.

"Ladies and gentlemen, could I please have your attention, thank you. Ladies, you are now at liberty to return home. Arrangements have been made for your husbands to join you tomorrow. The Simba are no longer a threat. My men are in the process of eliminating the few pockets of resistance remaining. To Major Lindle and his men, my deep gratitude and admiration for their resolute and brave stand against odds too great to contemplate. Also, my sincere regrets for the loss of your fallen comrades who paid the ultimate price for defending Bolobo. I assure you gentlemen they will not be forgotten. Right, enough from me, it only remains to say facilities are on hand for you men to bathe. A hot meal and a change of clothes will be provided. Thank you, that is all."

Brigadier Herman followed by an entourage of lesser officers made his way over to Major Lindle, he smiled pleasantly.

"So pleased to meet you, Major."

"Likewise, Sir."

"My only regret that it wasn't sooner."

"Never the less, Sir, a timely arrival."

"Bloody politicians, Major, we were well aware Colonel Kossanto had abandoned you, but until the politicians had spent days debating on what action to take, we couldn't come to your assistance."

"Yes, I understand, Sir."

"It seems, Major, the British ambassador is most anxious to have a word with you."

"I've no doubt, Sir."

"Yes, Major, I am afraid it's a sign of the times, anti colonial feelings are epidemic. Your government frowns on its nationals fighting in Africa. Well, Major, I will leave you to get cleaned up; we will talk again before you leave. Oh, I forgot to mention a plane should be arriving within the next two hours to transport you and your men back to the capital."

"Thank you, Sir, we will be ready."

The spirits of the mercenaries were high. Showered and now dressed in Belgian combat fatigues they were indistinguishable from their Belgian counterparts. Meal finished, they sat drinking beer.

Doggy winked at Lofty. "Yer know what, mate? The old plates smell like violets now."

"In yer dreams," Lofty grinned.

Mitch downed his beer and snapped open another can.

"Right, yer bastards," he shouted, "let's have some hush; I reckon we should drink a toast to our absent friends." He raised his can. "To absent friends," he said sombrely.

"To absent friends," they chorused in unison.

"Yer alright, mate?" Lofty placed a consoling hand on

Shiner's shoulder.

"No, Lofty, I ain't, mate; it's my fault Jock bought it. If that skinny bastard Kossanto is in the capital ..." Shiner grimly patted his side.

"Don't be a fucking idiot, Shiner. Gis it 'ere mate, we're in the shit enough as it is."

Lofty, grim faced, held out his hand, "Gis it 'ere," he repeated adamantly.

Shiner, tears in his eyes reluctantly handed over the Browning automatic pistol.

Lieutenant Katz entered the lounge followed by a burly Sergeant.

"Gentlemen," he began, "your plane has arrived, if you could please follow my sergeant, it is time to embark."

Lieutenant Katz stood by the doorway; he came to attention and saluted as each man passed on their way to the runway. Lofty hung back. "A little memento for you, Lieutenant." He handed the officer the Browning.

Lieutenant Katz mumbled his thanks as he took the offered pistol.

"You're welcome, Lieutenant. Careful, it's loaded."

Major Lindle stood at the bottom of the gangway with Sergeant Johnson; Brigadier Herman was engrossed in conversation with the two men.

"Ere I don't believe it, mates," Topsy grinned broadly. "They've only got a bleeding guard of honour out for us, ain't they? Cor, stone the friggin' crows."

Even as he spoke the Sergeant of the Guard called the Guard to attention.

With a final word, Brigadier Herman shook hands with both the Major and Sergeant as the guard presented arms. Brigadier Herman stepped back and came to attention and saluted as the two men made their way up the gangway. Each of the mercenaries snapped to attention and returned the Brigadier's salute before ascending the gangway. Now on board the door closed with a dull thud.

"Cor, what a turn up for the books," said Doggy as he settled down in his seat. "A guard of honour for old Doggy, and a Brigadier chopping me off a salute. Yer wait till the lads in me local find out. Should be worth a few jars." He smiled at the thought.

"Fasten your seat belts, please." The order came over the Tannoy as the aircraft taxied down the runway. "Gentlemen, welcome aboard, our flight time is approximately 1½ hours. You are flying courtesy of the Belgian Air Force. Enjoy your flight, thank you."

"We will," Midge said. "The sooner we land the sooner we get home, eh, lads."

"All right for you lot, Midge. Me an' Shiner are the only ones not looking forward to it."

"Come on, Lofty, yer only overdue leave."

"Doggy, the navy will throw the book at us after this caper."

Major Lindle stood up. "Could I have your attention for a few moments? I don't know how to begin to thank you. Needless for me to say no officer could ever have better men under his command. You have done everything asked of you, indeed much more. When I accepted this contract our role was to be a deterrent to the Simba and to assist the Katanga army to become an effective force. Sadly, with officers like Colonel Kossanto, this was not to be. I spoke at length with the Brigadier before our departure, he was under the impression the Belgian government was considering some form of recognition for your defence of Bolobo."

"Yer mean they're gonna give us a gong, Major?"

"Your guess, Turner, is as good as mine, I don't

know. To get back to what I was saying. We will be landing shortly; a plane has been chartered to fly us back to the UK. That is all, once again my thanks. Shiner, Lofty a word with you before we land."

Major Lindle seated himself in the empty seat opposite the two sailors.

"Yer wanted a word with us, Major?"

"Yes, Lofty, I need a contact address for both of you."

"Royal Naval Prison, Portsmouth," quipped Shiner with a wry grin.

"Take no notice of him, Major, I'll give yer me sister's address."

"Thank you, I think it only fair to warn you the authorities are aware of your participation at Bolobo."

"Just how the fuck did they find out?" snarled Shiner.

"Well," Major Lindle said. "It seems Kossanto informed the British Ambassador of your contract at the airport. Then covered his arse by saying after he'd paid you, you absconded and joined us. The ambassador requested that the Brigadier send you back under escort to the capital, he, of course, refused."

"That Kossanto, he's a right lying bastard!" Lofty shook his head in disbelief.

"Yes, I know." The Major agreed. "Unfortunately, it wouldn't come as no big surprise to see the Naval Police awaiting you."

Shiner shrugged his shoulders. "What will be, will be," he said matter of factly.

"I could put a word in for you, but to be honest, I somehow think it would be of no avail."

"It wouldn't, Major, but thanks all the same."

Losing height rapidly the plane began its descent. Shiner unbuckled his seat belt and stood up as the plane came to a standstill. Sunlight flooded through the now opened exit door, momentarily the sun was blocked as a huge policeman stepped into the aircraft, and his uniform was festooned with gold braid and medal ribbons.

"Cor, look at 'im, he's got more tinsel on 'im than a bleeding Christmas tree," grinned Doggy.

He removed his hat and dabbed with diligence at the perspiration that ran down his face with a large white handkerchief. His coal black face erupted into a huge toothy smile.

"Gentlemen," he began, his voice was loud and booming with a cultured English accent. "Welcome, I am the Commissioner of Police. I very much regret your stay with us will be brief. At this very moment your flight is ready to board, my officers will escort you to the departure lounge. On the explicit instructions from your Ambassador you are not to communicate in any way with newspaper reporters. Thank you, gentlemen, for your time. I wish you a pleasant flight home."

Police marched somewhat languidly and out of step in ranks two deep either side of them as they made their way towards the departure lounge. Reporters were roughly pushed aside as they desperately attempted to interview them. Enterprising photographers snapped away enthusiastically from atop parked cars, much to the dismay of the irate owners. Two armed burly policemen pushed open the lounge doors. Inside stood a tall dapper man in a dark suit, he stared at them unsmiling; ominously for Shiner and Lofty beside him stood four Naval Policemen.

"Pompous looking bastard, ain't he?" growled Mitch.

"Yeah," nodded Doggy. "Stand by for a load of bullshit."

"My name is Sir Ralph Stanton," the dark suited man announced. "And I am the British Ambassador."

"Pleased to meet yer, mate," grinned Topsy. "Me

name is Turner but me mates call me Topsy."

Sir Ralph Stanton contemptuously glanced at Topsy then ignored him. "Who is Major Lindle?" His tone was patronising and came over more as a demand than a question.

"I am he," snapped Major Lindle. "And I will thank you to have more respect for me and my men, Stanton."

"Damn you, Major, you're just a bunch of bloody mercenaries."

"Stanton, I have no wish to bandy words with you. I have a list of the men we lost; doubtless you will need it for your records. Will there be anything else?"

"Yes, I believe amongst your company you have three naval deserters?"

"Correction," Major Lindle said icily. "Unfortunately, one of them is beyond any retribution by you, or the navy."

"Yeah, an' he was me mate." Shiner glared first at the Ambassador and then at the Naval Police, his eyes full of menace. "The name's Wright," he snarled. "Yer, here to pick me an' Lofty up, ain't yer?"

Under Shiner's gaze the Regulating Petty Officer looked uncomfortable. "Afraid so, nothing personal just carrying out orders."

"What's the charges?" asked Lofty.

"Absent without leave, also conduct prejudicial to good order and naval discipline," came the reply.

"Yes, yes, all very interesting," interrupted the Ambassador sarcastically. "But could you continue your conversation on the plane?"

"Hey, why don't yer piss off back to yer Embassy, yer big girl's blouse?"

"You impertinent imbecile, how dare you speak to me like that?"

"Easy mate," grinned Doggy. "Why don't yer just fuck off?"

Sir Ralph's face reddened then contorted in rage. Abruptly he turned and briskly strode out of the lounge without a backward glance.

"Gentlemen, your flight to Heathrow is now ready to board." The pretty air hostess smiled pleasantly, "If you would please follow me."

"Just a minute, hang about," growled Topsy. "What yer four bastards gonna do?" He glared through narrowed eyes at the Naval Policemen. "Them's are our two mates, yer ain't arresting them."

"Got no choice, mate, but not until we arrive in the UK, then we have to escort them to Pompy."

"Yeah, well we'll have to see about that, won't we?"

"Topsy, it's all right mate, the sooner me an' Shiner get this sorted the better."

"As I said," the Regulating Petty Officer looked at Topsy. "It's just another job; I don't particularly want to be here."

"Come on, ladies, don't yer want to go home?" Mitch grinned broadly as he turned and walked towards the gangway.

Now well into the flight, men slept sprawled out on the ample number of spare seats. Major Lindle yawned.

"Damn planes, Sergeant, can never sleep on them."

"Nor me, Sir, still it won't be long now before we're back in Blighty."

"Been a right fucking balls up this contract, Sergeant."

"Yer weren't to know, Sir. The lads knew the risks."

"That's as maybe, Sergeant, but we should, with hindsight, have taken the Rhodesia job, protecting the white farmers against the Z.A.P.U. (Zimbabwe African Peoples Union) AND Z.A.N.U. (Zimbabwe African

National Union) along the Mozambique border."

"Trouble is, Sir; we would have been under direct Rhodesian army orders."

"Yes, Sergeant, but we would have patrolled independently as the bulk of the Rhodesian army is fully occupied protecting their borders with Angola and Zambia."

"Well, Major, there's no reason why we can't still take the contract after the lads have had some leave."

"I will be in touch, Sergeant."

"Don't make it too long, Sir. Me old girl gets fed up with me hanging around the house, says I get under her feet."

"Attention, this is the Captain speaking. We will be landing shortly in approximately 15 minutes; our flight has been diverted to Gatwick for security reasons. That is all, thank you."

Airport officials quickly ushered the mercenaries into the arrivals lounge where they were greeted by a high ranking Police Officer. Accompanying him, two uniformed constables.

Major Lindle looked long and hard at the senior police officer before addressing him curtly. "What can we do for you?" he demanded with annoyance.

"You, I take it, Sir, must be Major Lindle?"

"Correct." Major Lindle nodded.

"Major, I have been instructed to collect your passports; if you and your men would deposit them with my two officers, I would be obliged."

"No doubt you would." The Major replied in a voice heavy with sarcasm. "But by whose authority are you acting?"

"Commissioner of Police," came back a muted reply.

"Oh, I see, then perhaps you could be good enough to enlighten us as to what crimes we have committed. These men are British subjects and as such have a perfect legal right to hold a passport. Has the law changed?"

"Don't misunderstand me, Major, it was more of a request than a demand."

"That being the case, request denied," Major Lindle retorted sharply. "If that is all, my chaps would appreciate it if they could be on their way or do you intend to arrest us?"

"Not at all, Major, that was never the intention."

"Good. Right, lads, have a good leave; I will be in touch in a few weeks."

After much hand shaking and emotional farewells the lounge was now empty save for the Major, Shiner, Lofty and their escort.

Major Lindle grinned as he extended his hand towards Shiner.

Shiner shook his hand warmly. "Sorry, Major, for being such a pain in the arse at times, but for an officer yer ain't too bad a bloke."

Major Lindle held Shiner's gaze his eyes twinkled in amusement. "Yes, I must confess you were a bit trying. Good luck to you, Lofty." He clasped Lofty's hand in a firm handshake.

"Thank you, Major."

"Well, I must be off, you take good care of them Petty Officer."

"Will do, Major."

The officer turned to go changed his mind then turned back to face the two sailors. "I will make sure the money due to you will be forwarded to your sister, Lofty. May I just add it has been a privilege to serve with both of you, until the next time."

"Who knows," grinned Lofty. "The next time we meet we could be civilians."

Major Lindle smiled to himself as he strode off, the smile widened as he heard Shiner's indomitable voice.

"Come on, Petty Officer let's get a beer, me mouths as dry as an Arabs jockstrap."

Chapter 17

Court Martial

Portsmouth, one of the three main naval bases known affectionately to sailors as Pompy housed the large blocks of pre-Victorian barracks where sailors awaited drafts. In Portsmouth harbour the home of the navy's gunnery school, the dreaded Whale Island with its uncompromising draconian discipline. This harsh regime produced gun crews unsurpassed by any Navy. The cells were situated in the main barracks attached to the Naval Police quarters. For three days Shiner and Lofty had languished in their enforced accommodation; their kit had been forwarded from *Jutland*.

Shiner morose and aggressive paced his cell like a caged animal. In contrast, Lofty read quietly, his solitude was rudely interrupted by Shiner's frequent outbursts of verbal abuse directed at any Naval Policeman within earshot, and he implied with vehemence that their parentage was unknown to them.

Keys rattled in the cell door as the regulating Petty Officer opened Lofty's door. "Able-seaman Bancock, your Defending Officer would like a word with you in the interview room, your mate is already there."

"Sit down, Bancock." The Lieutenant flourished a hand towards a chair.

"Hi ya, mate," Shiner grinned. "How yer diddling?" Lofty nodded a greeting and sat down.

"Well, chaps, you seem to have got yourselves in a

spot of bother, what?"

"Can't see how," retorted Shiner. "Me an' me mate were on holiday, ain't our fault."

Lieutenant Hunter shot a sideways glance at Shiner as he thumbed his way through a pile of documents on his desk. "According to this," he floated the sheet of paper under Shiner's nose. "You were servicing weapons at a Bolobo airport."

"What lying bastard said that?" growled Shiner.

"British Ambassador of Katanga," came the reply. "It's no good Able-seaman Wright coming up with any cock and bull story, the evidence against you is clear. Who is this Colonel Kessanto? He has submitted a testimony through the British Ambassador which, to say the least, is not helpful."

"Not surprising, Lieutenant," Lofty said. "He was the bastard who shafted us; he left us at the airport."

"I will, of course, endeavour to do my best for both of you, but to be candid with you it will be difficult. Thought your service records might have been some help, but after reading them," he grinned, "it would be a piece of cake being the prosecuting officer."

"That's charming," muttered Shiner.

"It's not all doom and gloom, chaps. I intend to submit to the court that had Colonel Kessanto evacuated you along with his forces you would not have found yourselves in this predicament."

"Yeah, too true," nodded Shiner. "Major Lindle can confirm that Kossanto fucked off and left us."

"Yes, I have read your statements and one of my legal team has managed to obtain an affidavit from the Major."

"Should help!" said Lofty.

"Not if the evidence is ruled inadmissible by the court."

"How likely is that?" inquired Lofty.

"Put it this way, if I was the prosecuting officer I would ask for it to be ruled inadmissible."

"What about Kossanto? The statement he gave is a load of bollocks."

Shiner snarled in disgust, "We're gonna be stitched up, Lieutenant."

"That statement I intend to contest with the utmost vigour."

"Won't do no good, the navy just want to hush this up. When is the Court Martial?"

"Tomorrow morning at 10 o'clock."

"See what I mean? Full steam ahead!"

"Yes," Lieutenant Hunter agreed, "does seem a trifle quick. Incidentally, has your kit been forwarded from *Jutland*?"

"Yeah, yesterday," Lofty confirmed.

"Good, now I must be away to prepare your case, is there any matter you wish to discuss with me?"

"No, don't think so, Lieutenant, how about you, Shiner?"

"No, mate, no questions."

Lieutenant Hunter gathered his papers up and carefully placed them in his briefcase; he stood, then shook hands with them. "See you in court tomorrow."

Lofty woke with a start as the Regulating Petty Officer ran his baton along the bars of his cell.

"Come on, lad, time for a wash and brush up before breakfast, must look ship-shape for your big day."

"Yeah, yer, don't have to remind me, Petty Officer. How's me mate?"

"Don't ask," grinned the Petty Officer.

Breakfast over and now in full uniform the two sailors sat in the guardroom awaiting the appointed time, with them an escort of six Naval Policemen. The Petty Officer in charge looked at his watch. "Right, you two desperadoes, time for us to go." Under escort they marched across the parade ground to the officer's quarters where the dining room had been hastily transformed into a court room.

"What a fucking pantomime," moaned Shiner.

"Quiet in the ranks," barked the Petty Officer.

"Just a load of crap," persisted Shiner.

"Escort and prisoners will come to a halt, escort and prisoners halt," bellowed the Petty Officer.

Two Royal Marines on guard moved swiftly to open the heavy double doors, threw them open and stamped to attention.

"Prisoners, quick march."

Shiner and Lofty marched through the open doors. Before them seated behind a long highly polished dining table, sat four grim faced senior naval officers. Their epaulettes of gold lace gleamed, their chests hung with campaign medals. With a resounding bang the heavy door closed behind them.

"Able-seaman Wright, Able-seaman Bancock, you are both charged with being absent without leave. Furthermore, you are also charged with Conduct Prejudicial to Good Order and Naval Discipline, how do you plead?"

"Not guilty," came the replies.

"Right, stand at ease."

With a click of his heels the Lieutenant came to attention and saluted the Board. "I am Lieutenant Fuller, Council for the Prosecution."

A brief nod towards his counterpart Lieutenant Hunter

240

repeated the procedure, ending with the statement that he was Counsel for the Defence.

"Yes, yes, Lieutenant," the senior officer said impatiently, "now may we get on? Lieutenant Fuller if you would be good enough to proceed."

"Yes, my Lord." Lieutenant Fuller cleared his throat.

"My Lords, I do not intend to waste your time with eloquent drawn out arguments to prove the guilt of the two defendants before you; instead I will present you merely with the facts. The first undeniable fact is both defendants are eleven days overdue leave; also I have a signed statement from a Colonel Kossanto, an officer in the Katanga Army who states the defendants were employed to service weapons at Bolobo airport.

"On being ordered to leave Bolobo, Colonel Kossanto implored the defendants to leave with him and his men. But alas they elected to join a Major Lindle who commanded a force of mercenaries who were advancing on Bolobo. I might add, your Lordships, a third naval rating was involved but sadly lost his life in the subsequent fighting with rebel forces."

"That's a load of bollocks," snarled Shiner.

"Silence in court!" The senior officer of the Board glared at Shiner. "I will not tolerate anymore outbursts; you will have ample time to have your say. Carry on, Lieutenant Fuller."

"Thank you, my Lord, but I think the evidence speaks for itself, therefore, I rest my case." Lieutenant Fuller sat down.

Lieutenant Hunter rose and faced the grim faced judges.

"My Lords it seems this case very much evolves around two conflicting statements, the one I have here from Major Lindle is utterly contemptuous of Colonel

Kossanto."

"My Lords …" Lieutenant Fuller jumped to his feet protesting loudly. "I ask this court to rule as inadmissible any evidence offered by this so called, Major Lindle."

"Sir!" Lieutenant Hunter turned angrily to face the Prosecutor. "I would deem it a courtesy if you would desist from implying any slur on Major Lindle's character, the man served with distinction with the British Army and was awarded a medal for gallantry in Korea, furthermore My Lords, far from ruling Major Lindle's statement inadmissible I think far more credence should be placed upon it. I have a copy for each of you, my Lords, to read at your leisure."

"We will indeed read the statement. Lieutenant Fuller, have you any questions you wish to put to the defendants?"

"Yes, my Lord. Able-seaman Wright, what was your relationship with Major Lindle?"

"How'd yer mean?" Shiner asked puzzled.

"Were you friendly with him?"

"Not particularly," replied Shiner. The big sailor then scowled. "Now I can see what yer getting at, yer trying to say the Major wrote that statement 'cos he was me old mate, well that's crap." He glared at the Prosecutor.

"No further questions, my Lords."

Lieutenant Hunter stood up. "I have no questions, my Lords, but if I might be permitted to say the board has the stark choice of whose statement to accept. The weight of evidence I feel supports the Defence. If Colonel Kossanto had evacuated the defendants they would not be before you now. My Lords, the Defence rests."

"All rise, the court will retire to consider its verdict."

Lofty lit another cigarette and looked at his watch,

now back in the guardroom their escort sat playing cards.

"Bloody pissed off with this waiting about." He looked at his watch again. "Been nearly two hours."

"Patience, lad." The Petty Officer looked up from his cards. "They're probably supping pink gins." He looked back at his cards as the phone rang.

"Guardhouse," he answered. "Yes, Sir," nodding he replaced the receiver. "Right, time to go; they have reached a verdict."

Once again the double doors opened as they marched in and came to attention before the Board.

Rising, the senior naval officer looked long and hard at the two sailors. "The court has deliberated at length on the charges and finds you both guilty on both counts. The sentence of this court is that you both be dismissed from Her Majesty's Navy, services no longer required."

"Told yer them bastards would stitch us up," Shiner gave a sardonic grin. "Come on, mate, lets frig off, we're in Civvy Street now."

Lieutenant Hunter shook his head incredulously. "Sorry about that, chaps, I did my utmost."

"Ain't your fault, Lieutenant, at least we didn't end up in the glass-house."

Walking across the parade ground they turned towards the main gate. "Wonder when the major is going to Rhodesia," grinned Lofty.

Epilogue

Lofty's sister hurried down the stairs and picked up the telephone receiver, a look of apprehension spread across her face.

"Yes, Major I am aware who you are; Bob has been expecting a call from you. If you could wait one moment I'll give him a call, he's still in bed."

"Hey, Bob," she called loudly up the stairs. "Telephone, Major Lindle."

Lofty appeared at the top of the stairs, he groaned softly and held his head.

"Come on, I haven't all day." Babs rebuked him sharply as she handed him the receiver. "Some of us have to work."

"Cheers, sis. Hey, Major good to hear from yer; Shiner, he's fine, bar we had a skin full last night, yeah the Brickmakers Arms know it well, one o'clock, yeah, we'll be there."

Lofty winced as he replaced the receiver. "Any tea mashed, sis?" he inquired hopefully.

"No," she answered abruptly. "I hope you feel as bad as you look."

"Come on, sis, don't be like that."

"How the hell do you expect me to be?" she glared at Lofty. "Since the Major paid you, you and that mate of yours, Shiner, have done nothing but drink. Now I take it you're off to meet him again, him and his bloody mercenaries; you're going to get yourself killed. £600 he paid you. Was it worth it? The navy kicked you out and he got your friend, Jock, killed."

"Damn you, sis, it wasn't the Major's fault."

Tears streamed down her face as she faced her brother.

"Bob, I just haven't got the time to argue with you, I must get to work." She shrugged her coat on. The door banged behind her.

"What's all the noise about, mate?" Shiner yawned at the top of the stairs.

"Nothing, Babs a bit upset, the Major just rang."

"Yeah, what'd he say?"

"Wants a meet."

Major Lindle glanced up as the bar doors swung open. A grinning Shiner walked over to where Major Lindle sat. "Hi ya, Major, nice to see yer again, mine's a pint."

"Likewise," nodded the major. "Where's your mate?"

"Paying the taxi."

"Landlord, two pints if you please."

"Cheers." Lofty sat down. "What's the situation, Major? Yer know we've been chucked out of the navy."

"Yes, so I heard, bloody bad show chaps, what do you intend to do now?"

"Dunno, Major, can't see much future in punching a clock card."

"Yes, not a prospect to look forward to," agreed the Major. "I have had confirmation from the Rhodesian army to recruit sixty men to patrol a hundred miles of Rhodesia's border with Mozambique."

Lofty nodded. "Sounds okay, yer got a place for us Major?"

"That depends; it will mean signing a contract."

"No problem," grunted Shiner.

"I have some reservations," the major looked steadfastly at Shiner. "You would be under my command

and that, Shiner, would mean you would have to comply with orders, not question them. If you cannot accept that it would be pointless signing."

"Fair enough, Major," a grinning Shiner nodded. "Yer the boss."

Major Lindle rubbed his chin thoughtfully, scepticism showed on his face. "As long as you fully understand the implications."

"Yeah, yer coming over loud and clear, Major."

"Well, now we've got that sorted," the Major said. "I need your signatures." He reached down and unsnapped his briefcase. "After you have, of course, read through it."

Lofty glanced casually at the two page document before him and shrugged. "Gis a pen, Major, can't be bothered with all that small print you can tell us the score."

"It would be prudent to read it you know."

"We trust yer, Major." Lofty picked up his pint and gulped it down. "Same again, Shiner, what about you, Major?"

"Small scotch and soda, thank you."

Major Lindle nodded his thanks as he sipped his scotch. "Now, to get back to the matter in hand. Your contract will run for a period of six months, monies due you will be paid monthly into a designated bank account of your choice."

"Yeah, how much?" Shiner looked at the Major with an air of expectancy.

"£3,600 pounds on completion of your contract."

"Bloody hell," whistled Lofty. "Better than working in some poxy factory for ten quid a week with some hairy arsed foreman chasing yer."

"You both need to sign here." The major indicated the bottom of the first page. "As you can see the second page is a Will and Testament."

"Don't think I'll bother," grunted Shiner. "Ain't got nothing to leave and nobody to leave it to."

"If you had taken the trouble to read the small print," the Major said. "You would have been aware that if anything unfortunate was to befall you, your next of kin would receive your full pay."

"Might as well put Babs, yer sister down Lofty; I ain't got no next of kin."

"Up to you, mate. When's the off, Major?"

"We depart from Heathrow midday on Thursday. The Rhodesian's are most anxious for assistance."

"Suits me," Shiner said. "I think yer sister's getting pissed off with me, mate, outstayed me welcome."

"Really," the Major's eyes twinkled in amusement. "Can't for the life of me see why?"

Shiner grinned.

"I think we have covered everything, you have three days to sort out a bank account. Fill in the appropriate section of your contract and post it to the unit's solicitor who will handle all the units' legal and financial aspects."

"Just a pity poor old Jock ain't with us."

"Yes, damned unfortunate, he was a good man."

"Was me mate." Shiner looked uncomfortable. "My mate," he repeated.

Major Lindle placed a consoling hand on Shiner's arm. "It's of no consolation, but I wrote to Jock's parents, expressing my condolences."

"No offence, Major, but I would rather not talk about Jock. What time yer want us at the airport?"

"10 o'clock sharp, report to the Rhodesian Airways' check in. We fly by special charter, no luggage, all your requirements will be catered for when we reach base. We land at Salisbury where the army will transport us to barracks."

"What precisely will be our role Major?"

"Counter-insurgency operations directed against Z.A.N.L.A. (Zimbabwe African National Liberation Army) operating from bases in Mozambique. Most of them have been to training camps in Tanzania, Mozambique and various communist states. Consequently they are armed with AK.47s (Russian Kalashnikov Assault Rifles). Our task will be to patrol our given sectors. The guerrillas have been attacking remote white farms. There has been clashes with security forces but they prefer to hit soft targets. In the north eastern part of Rhodesia, Matabeleland guerrillas fighting under the banner of Z.I.P.R.A. (Zimbabwe Peoples Revolutionary Army) have crossed over the border from Zambia, another group mainly Shona, Z.A.N.U. fighters with the Z.A.N.L.A. have been in increasing numbers moving into Rhodesia across Mozambique's border."

"Bloody hell, Major, yer make it sound like there's a guerrilla behind every bush."

"Hardly," the Major shook his head. "The fact is the sporadic violence is rapidly escalating into a full blown guerrilla war."

"Well," Shiner said. "The sooner we leave the better. Be nice to see the lads again."

Major Lindle rose from his seat and snapped his briefcase shut. "Now don't forget to sort out your bank details and get those contracts in the post, see you both on Thursday 10 o'clock sharp."

"We'll be there, Major."

"See you, Thursday," with a nod the officer turned and walked briskly from the bar.

"Yer fancy another beer, mate?"

"Think I'll pass Shiner, let's find us a bank and get sorted."